OF FEATHERS AND THORNS

KIT VINCENT

This is a work of fiction. All of the characters, organizations, and events portrayed in this novel are either products of the author's imagination or are used fictitiously.

Copyright © 2022 by Kit Vincent

Cover art and design © 2022 by Corey Brickley

All rights reserved.

No part of this book may be reproduced in any form or by any electronic or mechanical means, including information storage and retrieval systems, without written permission from the author, except for the use of brief quotations in a book review.

Library of Congress Cataloging-in-Publication Data is available upon request.

ISBN 978-1-959052-01-2 (paperback)

978-1-959052-00-5 (ebook)

978-1-959052-02-9 (hardcover)

978-1-959052-03-6 (audiobook)

 Created with Vellum

To my feathered friends,
who stuck around despite my thorns

CHAPTER 1
KIEREN

"The Belltower farm is as good as a pile of rubble," the sheriff grumbled, watching me from across the hospital lobby. He was speaking to his deputy, but he made sure I heard every word. He'd made no attempt to keep his disdain subtle since I'd manifested three days ago. And it wasn't just him. Even the nurses dared to check on me only when I pretended to be asleep, and promptly scurried away whenever I made eye contact with them.

The sheriff's deputy folded his arms scornfully. "If the brat had kept to the Belltower lands! Half the trees at Yang's orchard were ripped right out of the ground, not to mention the number he did on the Coopers' ranch."

The sheriff *tsk*ed. "A damn waste, if you ask me. Can't believe one of *them* would turn up in our town."

I shrank into myself a little. Truthfully, I couldn't believe it either. The damage my manifesting had caused to my family's farm and our neighbors'—I'd thought it was all a dream until I'd woken up in the hospital with bruised ribs and a shiny golden letter floating in midair beside my bed. MAGIC SERVICE

SUMMONS, it said in ornate writing. I was so shocked I nearly fell off the cot.

That golden letter was now wrinkled in my hands as I sat on the stiff lobby bench, guarded by the sheriff like some kind of criminal. Like he hadn't known me my entire life. Like I was going to run off and ruin whatever was left of our town just because I could. Of course, I'd never do such a thing.

I didn't even know how it had happened. One moment I'd been talking to my father, and the next, the air had begun to swirl around me, twisting pieces of hay around my boots and rattling the barn walls. I'd blacked out before I knew what had hit me. Why wouldn't anyone believe it had been an accident?

Anyway, I had nowhere to run. Especially now that a senior magician was on his way to collect me so I could officially start my training. That's right: in accordance with the magical law of the United States of America, I was to join the Magic Service immediately and become a magician's apprentice.

Exactly one minute before the promised pickup time, the hospital's front door swung open and a young man walked in, marching confidently toward me. The sheriff and his deputy straightened and glowered at him but didn't dare approach. There was no question: he looked every bit a magician.

He was wearing a double-breasted coat with a high collar, tailored pants, and a pair of knee-high boots, all in shades of midnight blue so deep that in the dim light of the lobby, it looked almost black. His dark, wavy hair was shoulder length, and his eyes were the color of ice, neatly matching the silver thread of a single earring hanging from his left ear. He was quite a sight.

"Kieren Belltower?" he asked, sounding both formal and slightly annoyed.

I was speechless for a moment. I'd heard that many magicians flaunted their extravagant fashion sense, but growing up in rural Virginia, I had only ever encountered one. It was at the county fair the summer I turned nine. The grounds had caught on fire, and a magician had been called to extinguish it. The sheriff had pushed everyone back to a safe distance, so I'd only seen the lady magician from afar and hadn't been able to tell what she looked like aside from the sunflower yellow of her dress billowing around her as she'd battled fire with magic. But this guy here singlehandedly proved all the rumors. Compared to his fancy attire, my own linen shirt and pants with suspenders made me look like a country boy. My straw-colored hair, sun-bleached from a summer spent working in the fields, and the freckles on my tanned cheeks only added to the stark contrast between us.

But what surprised me the most was that the magician couldn't have been much older than me. Nineteen? Twenty years old at most. He must have been highly talented to become a teacher at such a young age.

"So, are you Kieren or what?" he asked again, growing impatient.

"Yes. Sorry!" I blurted, snapping out of my daze. "I just assumed you'd be... older."

The magician's face soured at the suggestion. "My name is Esten," he said tightly. "I am Master Hanska's first apprentice."

My neck reddened with embarrassment. The summons letter hadn't given much detail about my future teacher, only his name—Master Hanska. And now it was obvious that this guy wasn't him, that he was only a fellow apprentice.

Eyeing me icily, Esten continued, "Master sent me to pick you up, as he is currently busy with *important* matters of state." The way he emphasized the word *important* made my mood sink even lower.

Already, my whole town, including my family, wanted to be rid of me after my manifested magic had gone awry. I wasn't sure what kind of welcome to expect from the society of magicians, but now I wondered if perhaps they weren't thrilled to take me in either.

"Sorry," I said again, looking down at my summons.

I felt Esten's judgmental gaze linger on my cheeks for another moment before he declared, "We have to depart now, or we'll be late." With that, he spun on his heel and strutted toward the exit, leaving me to scramble after him as the sheriff hissed "good riddance" at my back.

Our departure from the hospital was followed by a carriage ride, during which Esten chose to stare out the window, devoting all his attention to the passing scenery and completely ignoring me. After twenty minutes, we arrived at an open, grassy field where two dozen men were bustling about, pulling on ropes and trying to secure what looked like—

I gaped. "We're going on a blimp?"

"An airship, actually," Esten corrected smartly.

And for the first time since I'd manifested, I found myself grinning. I had always wanted to ride on a blimp, but I'd only ever seen them in the skies. When they'd first appeared in New York about seven years ago, everyone had thought blimps were a miracle. Not only did they promise to take you above clouds, but you could now travel to the West Coast in less than a day! Despite the steep price, the tickets were sold out for months in advance. But as people's love for sky travel had grown, new routes had been added, eventually connecting smaller towns and more distant corners of the country. They'd even built a stop in my county. Still, blimp rides were expensive, and my family couldn't afford tickets. Not like they dreamed of leaving this place anyway...

Up close, the blimp was even more impressive, its balloon huge and gloriously round with a shiny metal gondola underneath. Its propellers made quite a bit of noise as it clumsily touched down. Esten seemed put off by it. His nose wrinkled in annoyance, but I watched with bubbling fascination as the crew unfolded the metal ladder and invited us aboard.

"So, where are we going exactly?" I asked as we climbed inside.

Esten quickly glanced around, then said reluctantly, "Massachusetts."

Wow. I'd assumed I would be staying at Master Hanska's residence for the duration of my training, but I had no idea where he or any other magician lived. Other than their Service assignments, magicians tended to keep to themselves, and the locations of their homes were kept secret from the general public. So moving to a different state didn't surprise me, but Massachusetts was farther than I'd expected. No wonder we had to take a blimp.

Despite how big the balloon part of the airship was, the gondola, which housed the passenger lounge and the cockpit, was only about twenty feet wide. The lounge, however, was luxurious. There were neat rows of plush armchairs; the walls were upholstered in exquisite purple brocade. A kitchen was tucked away behind the bar counter in the left corner, and a crew member in a suit and bow tie was serving a variety of refreshments. There were two dozen passengers already on board, more than half of them in military uniforms and the others in expensive-looking civilian clothes, merrily chatting over glasses of champagne. I frowned. This was a lot of soldiers for one flight. Did it have something to do with the growing unrest in Europe? According to the newspapers, the government had begun to mobilize troops on the East Coast, although so far the official position was that the U.S. wasn't ready to engage in the conflict lest it escalate things further. I sure hoped we could stay out of the war.

As Esten and I moved down the aisle, the lively conversation that had filled the lounge dropped to a whisper, and most passengers stared at Esten in awed bewilderment.

He paid them no mind. Esten was probably used to such treatment by now. Someday I might have to get used to that, too. Although there was no way I'd ever wear something fancy enough to make people's heads turn.

"May we take the window seats?" I asked as I spotted a set of unoccupied armchairs on the right side.

Esten shrugged. "If you wish. I don't care for these metal things anyway. Magical travel is much more efficient, but it's too dangerous for untrained magicians to try, so here we are."

Ah, that explained Esten's apparent annoyance about having to take the blimp. I didn't consider it a loss. I happily marched to the cushy armchairs and took the one closest to the window. It was the most comfortable piece of furniture I'd ever sat on.

Esten took the other armchair. A flick of a hand and a quiet rustling sound followed, and in an instant, a stack of golden papers appeared in Esten's lap.

My eyes widened—Esten had performed magic right in front of me like it wasn't even a big deal. I badly wanted to ask how he'd managed that and if I was going to learn how to summon things as well, but Esten was already buried in his documents, looking like he was *terribly* busy and had better things to do than to chaperone a newbie like me.

I sighed and instead turned to the window and the patches of land underneath. The airship had taken off and was quickly gaining altitude, making the earth look like a multicolored quilt of farms and towns. Somewhere down there was the farm where I'd spent the first eighteen years of my life. But it was so small now that no matter how closely I looked or how familiar I was with the landscape, I had no idea which little patch of the quilt it was. That hurt in a strange kind of way. I'd had long ago decided that I wasn't going to spend my life on the farm, yet I'd always imagined that I'd at least have a chance to say a proper goodbye to my family before leaving. Maybe I'd even have a send-off party at the local honky-tonk. But neither my parents nor my friends had shown up at the hospital to see me, let alone bid me farewell. One magical accident was all it had taken to completely shatter the only existence I'd ever known.

I leaned my forehead against the window, trying to hide my face as my throat squeezed and the corners of my eyes began to burn. Not like Esten cared to look up from his papers anyway.

It was late at night when we landed in eastern Massachusetts, traded the airship for a car, and took a dirt road through the woods, by which point I was feeling real queasy from all the flying and jostling. My ribs ached, too—my short stay in the hospital hadn't been enough to heal them after my manifesting. I was about to doze off when the car hit the end of the road and jerked me awake. I blinked the sleepiness away and realized we were still in the middle of the pitch-black woods with no signs of life around.

"Is this Master Hanska's residence?" I asked as I followed Esten out of the car. Because magicians were so secretive about their lives, many wild rumors spread about them living in enchanted cabins surrounded by macabre traps that snatched intruders' souls or turned them into frogs. I'd never given those rumors half a thought, but a sneaking suspicion that not all of them were completely untrue was starting to blossom.

"Of course not," Esten huffed. "We're waiting for the driver to leave so we can enter the grounds the short way."

I shivered, staring at the dark web of branches ahead as the car drove off, leaving the moon as our only light source.

Esten fumbled for something in the dark. "Ugh, I haven't done it this way in ages," he complained. Then his boots struck what he was looking for, which turned out to be a flat rock about a foot wide, buried in a pile of last year's leaves. "Ah, there it is. Hop on and take a step forward, will you?" Without further explanation, Esten marched forward and was gone.

"Esten?" I gasped at the empty space where he had just been.

But no reply came, only the eerie quiet of the night. I spun around, peering into the darkness. It was either hop on a rock or be haunted by some dreadful curse probably already lurking nearby.

I promptly did as Esten had said. The world blurred and resolidified around me with dizzying swiftness. The darkness lifted, and I found myself standing at the end of a well-lit, stony path. It was surrounded by a lush garden that was still in full bloom despite it being mid-October.

"W-what on earth?" I said, not quite able to believe my eyes. Had I just done magic?

"Master's shortcut for high-profile non-magical visitors," Esten replied, not bothering to explain further, and beckoned me to keep moving.

That's when I finally noticed the house that the path led to.

It was outright magnificent—three stories high, red brick with white sash windows, a stone-tiled roof, and a pair of ornate white pillars framing the porch. I gaped in awe as I followed Esten past the floppy purple hydrangeas and the enormous bushes of fragrant tea roses.

Once we'd reached the entrance, Esten flicked his hand, and the front door swung open, welcoming us in. The inside was even more stunning. We were greeted by a grand foyer with walls covered in rich, dark wood and an enormous glass chandelier that lit up the moment we entered. A black marble fireplace sat in the center of the room across from a pair of burgundy velvet armchairs that made me want to collapse into them for the rest of the night. To our left was a wide staircase with intricately carved balusters, and large arched doors led to even more rooms on both sides of the foyer. This place was a mansion.

"How many people live here?" I asked in amazement.

"Master, myself, and now you," Esten said, not particularly impressed.

"Only three people?"

Esten's left eyebrow curved quizzically. "People? Yes, just three." He sighed tiredly and unbuttoned the top buttons of his coat, freeing his neck from the stiff collar. His glossy black locks bounced as he did so. "Come on, I'll show you your room."

With that, Esten headed up the staircase, leaving me to wonder uncomfortably what on earth he meant by *only three people*.

Maybe it was because the place was so big and new, but it felt like we wandered through a whole maze before we made it to the room that was to be mine.

"This is it," Esten said, and pushed the wooden door before us open.

As we went in, a pair of wall sconces obediently lit up, illuminating my new bedroom. It was furnished with a huge four-poster bed covered in invitingly fluffy pillows and a cozy quilt. A tall armoire towered against the wall to my right, and a neat writing desk sat underneath the window on the opposite side.

"You can order custom garments once you start receiving a salary for your Service," Esten informed me. "But for now there are some standard-issue clothes in the armoire. There are envelopes on the desk if you want to communicate with someone. Simply jot the recipient's name on the front, and it will find its way. All work correspondence comes in the same manner. Now, if you'll excuse me, I have an early job tomorrow." Esten promptly took off, making it clear that whatever questions I had about my new life would have to wait.

Once he left, the room became very quiet. I stood awkwardly by the door, taking everything in. A faint glow emanated from the stack of envelopes, just like the Service summons I'd received. I was curious to send a letter out to see how it worked . . . only I had no one to write to. No one was waiting to hear from me back home. No one cared if I'd made it to Master Hanska's safely. I had to start my whole life over from scratch. Other than the clothes on my back, I hadn't been allowed to bring any possessions. Such were the rules for all manifested magicians. I was no exception.

I glanced at the armoire—it probably housed some fancy pajamas to change into—but I didn't want those yet. Instead I kicked my boots off and crawled under the heavy blankets in my clothes. If there was a light switch to turn the sconces off the non-magical way, I didn't look for it.

CHAPTER 2
KIEREN

Having grown up on a farm, I was used to waking up before the sun, but Esten's early assignment must have started even earlier than that; when I peeked out of my room in the morning and called for him, no reply came. Master Hanska appeared to be absent as well. Unsure of what to do with myself but feeling the growing emptiness in my stomach, I decided to search for the kitchen.

I wandered through the second-floor hallways for several minutes, gazing at the beautiful emerald-green wallpaper and the many portraits of people I didn't recognize but assumed to be famous magicians. Eventually I found the foyer again. The double doors leading to the big room closest to the staircase were open, and I sneaked a look inside. It turned out to be the most majestic home library. Early-morning sunlight streamed through a pair of arched windows providing a splendid view of the back garden, and the walls were lined with floor-to-ceiling mahogany shelves stacked with books. It wasn't what I was searching for, but I stumbled in anyway, mesmerized. Were all these books about magic? I didn't sense any power coming off them—no mysterious golden glow like the envelopes in my room—but I supposed books didn't need to glow to be magical. I was about to pluck one from the shelf to see what forbidden secrets hid inside when something odd caught my attention.

It was a doll sitting atop the reading desk in the corner of the room, and it seemed to be staring right at me. Intrigued, I approached and picked it up. The doll wore a red fabric cape around its wooden body and had feathers for hair. It had a round white face with painted black eyes and eyebrows, two downward stripes on its cheeks, and a triangular mouth that looked like it was smiling.

How very strange, I thought. The more I looked at it, the more it seemed to smile at me.

Tap, tap, tap! A series of loud knocks came from the main entrance, and I nearly jumped out of my skin. Were we expecting a visitor? Esten had left no instructions about that— or anything, for that matter. Was it safe to answer?

For a moment I stood very still, hoping that whoever or whatever it might be would give up and leave. But that hope was promptly shattered by three more knocks.

I exhaled. "You are being silly, Kieren Belltower," I muttered to myself. I was a magician, and this was my home now. I should at the very least be able to answer the door without being terrified.

"Sorry, I have to go," I said, putting the doll back on the desk, then immediately caught myself—I'd apologized to a *doll*. I shook my head sheepishly and exited the library.

When I opened the front door, a beautiful lady stood on the porch. She appeared to be in her mid-thirties, and just by looking at her style, I could tell she was a magician. She wore a warm toffee-colored dress that reminded me of sweet spices, boots with pointy toes and very pointy heels, and a small hat with a feather that matched the color of her dress perfectly.

"Well, hello, there. Is Hanska in?" she asked with the confidence of someone who knew Master Hanska well.

That left me confounded. What was I to say when I'd never even met him? "Master Hanska is out on state business," I answered, echoing Esten's words from yesterday.

The lady's face fell. "Not back yet, huh?" Then her green eyes narrowed, and she examined me critically. "And who might you be?"

"Oh . . ." I said, once again feeling like I was only a guest in this house. "I'm Master Hanska's new apprentice."

The lady's face instantly illuminated with a most delighted smile. "No wonder you have such a deer-in-the-city-lights look about you! I'm Cynn, senior magician of the Maine branch. Pleased to meet you," she said cordially, and offered her gloved hand.

Maybe it was her straightforward manner of speaking, but there was something warm and disarming about Cynn. I found myself earnestly shaking her hand. When she asked to come in for a proper introduction and a cup of strong tea, I was happy to oblige.

Unlike me, Cynn knew her way to the kitchen. She showed me the pantry filled with deliciously ripe apples, a variety of pumpkins and squashes, and a golden loaf of bread that was somehow still warm, as though it had come out of the oven mere minutes ago. There was also a marvelous icebox, which contained a dozen eggs and a lump of cheese. I grabbed the cheese and apples and quickly assembled the most beautiful tower of a sandwich while Cynn found her favorite bergamot-scented black tea, filled the porcelain teapot with water, and then moved her palm over it. The teapot released a small cloud of steam through the spout. I watched with amazement—Cynn had boiled water with a simple motion of her hand! She offered to make a cup for me, but the tea smelled like strong perfume, so I politely declined.

"Mm, much better," Cynn said after taking a quick sip. I joined her at the small kitchen table. "You must tell me everything now. If Hanska is not here, then how did *you* get here?"

"Esten picked me up," I replied, and took a big bite of my sandwich. It was delicious.

Cynn burst out laughing and nearly spilled her still-steaming cup. "Oh, goodness," she said, trying to stifle her laughter. "You really got *lucky*, didn't you?"

I swallowed a chunk of my sandwich in one gulp, confused.

"Sorry," Cynn said, flicking her hand. "It's just that I've known Esten for a long time, and he can come off as—how should I say it—awfully uptight, if you know what I mean? Must have been a trying experience to be welcomed by him of all people."

I wasn't sure what the polite thing to say was. So far Esten's personality most reminded me of the rosebushes in the front garden. Pretty from a distance, but . . ."He seems a bit *thorny*," I ventured awkwardly, and then, remembering my manners, I added, "But I'm still thankful he came for me."

Cynn's eyebrows rose, and she huffed out another laugh as though enjoying some private joke. Out loud, she said sweetly, "A bit of a late bloomer, aren't you?"

I flushed from head to toe. What was *that* supposed to mean?

"I mean in terms of magic, of course." Cynn smiled again. "You've only recently manifested, right?"

I waited a moment for my voice to come back. "Yes, four days ago."

Cynn hummed nostalgically. "That's so incredibly rare.

Most of us are taken into apprenticeships by age ten. You and your family were probably quite surprised when it happened."

"Yeah . . ." I said, looking down at the uneven dark circle that must have been a branch back when the kitchen table was still a tree in the woods. Nobody had expected me to manifest; I was well out of the age range, and there hadn't been a manifested magician in my area for as long as anyone could remember. "My family wasn't too happy about it," I confessed.

Something flickered in Cynn's eyes at that admission, taking away her playful expression.

"Well, I am *glad* you manifested," she said, sounding somber but also as though she was trying to comfort me. "I truly think this world needs more of us. Especially with all this war talk across the pond and the sludge outbreaks on our own soil. There was just another one in Andover—that's why I came to see Hanska." Cynn sighed heavily. "You've heard of the sludge, right? It should have made its way into the regular newspapers by now."

I nodded. My town was abuzz with rumors about the mysterious phenomenon that had devastated the neighboring Carolinas. Eyewitnesses described it as a dark glob that raged and attacked everything around it like a mad animal, except that it looked like no animal anywhere in the world. Its body was covered in thick muck that instantly poisoned everything it touched, mercilessly rotting the trees and spoiling the land. "What is the sludge exactly?" I asked.

Cynn *tsk*ed, looking to the side. "That's the conundrum, Kieren—nobody knows. After investigating four outbreaks, all we've been able to find out is that it's a type of violent magic, but we still know nothing of its purpose or its origins."

Cynn took a sip of her tea while I processed what she'd said. The fact that even magicians were in the dark about something caused by magic was deeply troubling.

"Well, thank you for the tea," Cynn said finally. "Nothing like a strong brew after a full night of combing the southern coast for shipwreck survivors. Why can't the citizens of Maine hold off with those until daytime, I wonder?"

My heart prickled with sympathy for her. Magicians were often called upon to help during accidents and natural disasters as part of their Service. There was no predicting when such a thing would occur, so magicians' work hours were far from regular.

"Anyway,"—Cynn pushed the chair away and got up—"give my regards to Hanska, and congratulations on manifesting. We welcome you." The confident playfulness had returned to her eyes.

Warmth spread through my chest. Cynn was the first and only person to say something *good* about my becoming a magician. I hadn't known how much I'd needed to hear that.

"Thank you." I smiled in return.

I saw Cynn back to the door and wished her a restful day.

When the door clicked shut, I started back toward the kitchen, then froze. There was a familiar shape on the mantel in the foyer. Another doll sat on it, looking a whole lot like the one I'd encountered in the library. I squinted. Maybe there was more than one in this house and I'd simply been too distracted by Cynn to notice it earlier.

I shrugged and headed back to the kitchen to tidy up.

With nothing else to do, I spent hours wandering around the house, trying to familiarize myself with the layout. To my disappointment, most of the rooms upstairs were locked, and I couldn't find the location of a single light switch. Frustrated, I went back to the foyer and decided to wait for Esten; he was bound to return sometime. There was one log in the hearth, so I managed to get the fire going, curled up in a burgundy velvet armchair, and eventually fell asleep.

By the time Esten finally came back, the log had turned into a pile of faintly smoldering ashes, but the moment he stepped into the house, the grand chandelier obediently flickered to life and woke me up.

"Good evening," I said, groggily wiping my eyes and getting up. The armchair had proven to be much more comfortable than I'd thought.

Esten jumped. In a split second, he raised his arms, which had a faint blue luminescence around them.

My mouth dropped open. Not only could I see it with my own eyes, but for the first time I *felt* the presence of Esten's magic. It was like being pushed underwater by a strong force. Somehow it didn't frighten me, though.

"Holy heavens, it's you!" Esten exclaimed and lowered his arms. With that, the luminescence disappeared, and the invisible water pressure ebbed. Esten looked like he'd completely forgotten about my existence, which was hurtful, to be honest, but I tried to brush it off. He'd probably gotten distracted by his assignment.

Still, it was surprising to see him so alarmed to find someone at the house.

"Sorry," I said awkwardly. "Please don't attack me."

Esten gave me a look as though my suggestion was offensive. "I would never do such a thing," he said, swiftly unbuttoning and removing his jacket. It was covered in dirt, and there were tiny scratches on his neck. "What were you doing in the dark?" he asked.

"Oh," I said bashfully. "I was waiting for you. I wasn't sure where the light switches were, and then it got dark, and I . . ." I trailed off when I noticed Esten giving me a side-eye like there was no hope for me. "Anyway, I just wanted to tell you, a person stopped by today."

Instantly Esten was on guard again, his icy gaze aimed at me. "*Which* person?"

Oof. Maybe it had been a mistake to let Cynn in after all. But how was I supposed to know that? "Cynn," I replied hesitantly.

"Ah." To my relief, Esten's expression relaxed. If there was a list of people not welcome inside the residence, Cynn wasn't on it. "What did she want?"

"She said she wanted to talk to Master Hanska about the sludge outbreak in Andover, but she couldn't get hold of him."

"There's been another one?"

I nodded. "Cynn said so."

"That's only twenty miles from here," Esten muttered, clearly disturbed by the news. "All right, I'll talk to her," he added, deep in thought and ready to abandon me again.

I watched him carry his dirty jacket toward the staircase, puzzled by our whole exchange. Something troubling was happening, something that had Esten feeling on edge inside his own home. Master Hanska was still gone, and Cynn had seemed to imply that he hadn't been here in a while. There was also the question of the sludge. It was becoming painfully obvious that Esten wasn't going to explain anything to me, and I didn't like being left in the dark. One whole day of aimlessly haunting the house had worn me out plenty. I needed answers.

"Esten, when is Master Hanska coming back?" I finally asked. "I mean . . . aren't I supposed to be learning something?"

Esten halted at the bottom of the stairs, caught off guard. "Master will . . . come back whenever he comes back," he said curtly, as though something angered him about my question. I couldn't fathom what was making Esten give me such a cold shoulder; I barely even knew the guy. "Master is on a top-secret mission," Esten continued, scowling at me, "and doesn't owe us any explanations as to his whereabouts. No one is obligated to entertain you. If you're bored, then learn something. The library is at your disposal."

With that, Esten marched upstairs, making it obvious he wasn't going to tell me anything, including the locations of the wretched light switches, if the house even had any.

Well, at least I knew where the library was.

CHAPTER 3
ESTEN

earlier

I crouched behind a row of bushes, observing the busy metal forge from a safe distance as a bell rang, announcing the end of the evening shift. This was it: my chance to get inside. To say I was nervous about breaking in was an understatement. I'd made a strategic decision to wait for nightfall so there would be fewer people around, but even after hours, production didn't stop or slow down. One group of workers simply came to replace another, and I couldn't afford to wait any longer. It had already taken several days to pinpoint this forge as the last place Master Hanska had scouted on his assignment. I had no more leads. Master had always been careful to protect the secrecy of his missions, even from me, if they demanded it. I needed to get inside if I was to find out more.

The tricky part was that I didn't know the layout of the building or what I was searching for exactly. For that reason, transporting myself inside via magic was out of the question. I could accidentally stumble into a room full of people, or worse, end up inside the dome where they melted the ore. So instead I decided to infiltrate the forge during the shift rotation, posing as one of the workers.

I snuck closer and watched several guys leave what seemed to be the changing room, ready to head home. I had but a split second to glimpse the wall of lockers through the open door, but that was enough time. I swiftly summoned the hat and uniform one of the workers had left behind. They landed in a dirty heap on the ground. My skin itched with discomfort. The overalls were covered in soot and grime and were an awful shade of greige. At least they looked the right size. Maybe I could put them on over my clothes so I wouldn't have to touch them directly. I did so, including the smelly hat, and pulled the collar up high, obscuring my lower face as much as possible without looking suspicious. Sadly I'd never had any talent for transfiguration magic, and even in disguise my face was still my own, which meant someone could identify and report me to the Assembly should the mission go south. I couldn't let that happen. Unlike Master Hanska, I wasn't sanctioned to be here.

Clothed in that dreadful uniform, I hurried to the entrance, following a group of stragglers.

Inside, the building was deafeningly loud. The flames cast everything in shades of orange, and waves of sweltering heat escaped from the forge as the liquefied metal was cooled, hammered thin, and pressed into sheets. I separated from the group at the first opportunity, stealing glances at the workers busily carting the finished product to the loading area. But it was impossible to tell the purpose of those metal sheets merely from looking at them. I needed to get to the engineering and design rooms. At least all the clatter and machinery noise provided enough cover for me to slither around the conveyor belt and into the back hallway leading to the upper level, where I suspected those rooms were.

I dashed into a dimly lit corner, tucking myself out of sight as a group of engineers passed me, too preoccupied to notice my presence.

"What they're demanding from us is *insane*," one lamented in a hushed tone. "We need more resources if they want the factory to keep churning out parts at this rate."

"They are running us into the ground," the second engineer said, and the others muttered in agreement tiredly, their boots heavy on the cement floor.

I frowned. What was the reason for the sudden rush in production? Was this connected to what Master Hanska was investigating?

Once the coast was clear, I climbed the metal stairs to the second level and snuck past several smaller rooms, which looked like engineers' offices, until I found a large room with glass walls that provided an unobscured view of the conveyor belt below. I went in.

Half the floor space was taken up by a large oblong table covered in data sheets, graphs, and sketches, but the most important thing was in the very center—a blueprint for an airship. I regarded it with suspicion. The proposed airship was larger than any I'd ever encountered, and it was constructed entirely of metal, making it look like a giant whale wearing armor.

"What do they want it so big for?" I murmured aloud. It didn't look intended for human transport—the gondola was small and seemed to house only the cockpit. It was probably designed to carry things inside the ship's hull, then. But what kinds of things? It would take a lot of fuel to keep this juggernaut afloat, even without cargo.

Hastily I skimmed more papers, searching for clues. Finally

I spotted what looked like a prototype for the airship's fuel tanks, meant to house some kind of combustible gas. Attached was a log of tests titled BLAZING FURY. My nose twitched. "Who on earth would name a fuel something so tacky?" I muttered, when suddenly a voice came from the direction of the entrance.

"Hey! You can't be in here!"

I froze.

One of the engineers was standing tensely at the door.

I kept my head down, trying not to panic. The room had only two exits: the windows, which meant a thirty-foot drop straight onto the conveyor belt, and the door I'd walked in through, which was now completely blocked off by the engineer. My mind reeled. I couldn't let the forge guards catch me here, but I couldn't use magic to escape either—at least not out in the open. I would be in a world of trouble if these people discovered I was a magician engaging in a spying mission not sanctioned by the Assembly. I couldn't let Master Hanska down like that. I had to get out of here.

Given all that, there was only one thing I could do. I had to get my hands dirty. Keeping my head down and not saying a word, I lunged forward, crashing into the guy and knocking him off his feet. Stunned, the engineer landed on his rear, freeing a path through the door. Not wasting a moment, I dashed through the opening and into the hallway.

"Security!" the engineer screamed, scrambling off the floor. "A spy in the design room!"

In seconds, two factory guards armed with batons emerged from around the corner and ran at me.

"Curses," I muttered as I changed direction and swerved into the nearest hallway.

A group of workers were strolling in my direction, chatting. I barreled through them, shoving them out of my way, causing several to fall like dominoes. I did my best not to injure anyone, of course. The guards got tripped up by the commotion as well, and that bought me a few precious seconds.

Swiftly I rounded another corner and skidded to a halt—a dead end. Other than a single door to my left, which turned out to be locked when I yanked on the handle, and a big window at the end of the hallway, there was nothing ahead. I threw a glance over my shoulder—already the guards were catching up to me. I had to think fast. I couldn't use magic to break into the room; that would be too obvious. Besides, it was likely another dead end. But maybe I could use magic in a less conspicuous way, to cushion a fall? There was no other option but to try.

I gritted my teeth and dashed toward the solitary window.

Shards of glass exploded around me as I jumped through it.

Thicken! I commanded, and flicked my fingers. Magic buzzed as the air around me compressed into a shield that stopped most of the pieces from reaching my face and hands. Unfortunately I didn't have the time to be thorough with it; within seconds I had to shift my attention to the fast-approaching ground.

The patch right below the window was unpaved and covered in grooves from the heavy transportation carts. Several shards of glass nicked my neck as I dropped the air shield and flicked my fingers once again, commanding the ground below to soften long enough to absorb the impact from my drop. Argh, Master Hanska was right: I badly needed to practice my control so I could switch between shields more quickly. But when my boots hit the ground, it obediently bowed under me. I curled my body, rolled several rattling feet forward, and sprang to my feet again.

"Lucky bastard!" the guards yelled from the broken

window, but they didn't dare jump after me. Instead, more guards burst out of the building's back door.

Not sparing them another look, I sprinted into the woods surrounding the forge. I ran until the trees obscured me from the guards' view, then stepped into the magic stream and disappeared.

CHAPTER 4
KIEREN

Despite waking up at the crack of dawn, I found the house empty again. My one consolation was that I was becoming more familiar with the layout of the place. This time I easily located the kitchen and the cupboard with a loaf of bread, which was delightfully warm. I also found pears and figs that hadn't been in the pantry yesterday. Considering how fresh the food was, it must have been delivered here by magic. Either that or Esten woke up in the middle of the night and immediately started kneading the dough. I burst out laughing at the thought; I couldn't imagine fastidious Esten getting into something as messy as bread-making. He'd probably get frustrated with the flour flying into his glossy locks and curse the dough until it turned into some kind of deadly poison. I wouldn't want to be the one to taste-test that. No, thanks.

After breakfast, I headed straight for the library, determined not to spend another day literally in the dark. If Esten wouldn't even teach me enough magic to turn the lights on, then there must be something in this place that would help me learn it on my own. The problem was that I had no idea where to start. There were so many books. I counted ten bookcases with a dozen shelves each, stacked all the way up to the ceiling. To get to the top, you had to use a small stepladder that could be rolled along tracks above the shelves.

I started by randomly pulling a handful of books from each bookcase and checking them out.

To my frustration, most of these books turned out to have nothing to do with magic—some were works about physics and chemistry, and some seemed to be collections of historical letters. Nothing remotely resembled the *Introduction to Magic* manual I was hoping for.

I put the books back and took out several more. The second round produced the same results. By the third round, I still hadn't found the magical ABCs, but one book caught my attention nonetheless. It was a collection of essays by the Founders, the group of magicians who had first negotiated the system of Magic Service with the United States government. I curled up on the sofa and flipped through the pages curiously—this wasn't a subject they'd talked about much back in school. In fact, the only thing I knew about the Founders was that they had existed. But I knew nothing of what kind of people they had been, or what had led them to create the Service.

On the first page of the book was a painting of the six of them standing proudly together. I recognized several of them from the portraits in the second-floor hallway. Some hundred and fifty years ago, these six magicians had entered into negotiations with Congress and the newly elected President Harris to grant all magicians in the U.S. special protected status in exchange for their service to the country. That part was common knowledge. What surprised me was that the Founders hadn't initially agreed on the nature of said service. At least one of them, Clarence Toughhold, had insisted that magicians should abandon their civilian status and become a special branch of the U.S. military instead. But during the lengthy negotiations, the other five fervently opposed him. The most substantial criticism had come from Temperance Amala, who had published a pamphlet proclaiming that "using the sacred art of magix for bloodshed will lead both magical and non-magical lives to ruin."

In his own essays, Toughhold openly mocked her for being naïve and lacking foresight regarding what was best for the society of magicians and the future of the country. But in the end, the majority had sided with Temperance. A special nonmilitary branch of government called the Magicians' Assembly had been formed. The Assembly had its own office on Capitol Hill, not far from Congress. It housed the Council, which consisted of the country's strongest magicians, as well as administrative bureaus whose employees were responsible for the daily conduct of magical affairs. All magicians were expected not only to serve the country to the best of their abilities but also to stay neutral in conflict. The only times they were authorized to engage in combat were when other magicians defied the laws of magic established by the Assembly or refused their Service duties.

I frowned—it had never occurred to me that magicians could become deserters. But I guessed if someone broke the rules they'd agreed to follow, they would have to bear the consequences of their actions.

Anyway, despite the Founders' arguments, Toughhold's ideas about forming a magical military hadn't turned out to be useful—there had not been a war on American soil since the Service had been created. It was so successful that within a year of its founding, similar institutions were created by a number of African and Southeast Asian governments, and more world countries followed in their footsteps shortly after. The Service had existed more or less unchanged for a century and a half, bringing peace and an unprecedented level of cooperation between magicians and civil society, which in turn had ushered in the prosperous industrial era.

I rubbed my eyes and shut the book. I had gotten a bit carried away reading. It was now well into the afternoon, and the days were getting shorter. If I didn't start looking for the light switches soon, I would end up haunting the kitchen in complete darkness again. Or I'd have to go to sleep on an empty stomach. As interesting as the Founders' essays were, I'd learned nothing about the practical side of magic from them. Politics were important, of course, but right now I was much more concerned about the light switches.

I became suddenly annoyed with Esten.

"What is his deal?" I said aloud. "He must know nothing in this library will teach me magic. It's like he *hates* that I'm living in his house . . ." But what had I ever done to deserve this attitude? I hadn't asked to be brought here. It was probably some Assembly employee who'd decided to send me to Master Hanska even though I was clearly not wanted. "Master this, Master that," I muttered bitterly. "If Master Hanska is so great, how come he's too busy to even say hello?"

No Hanska fault. Esten a brat, a voice said to my left.

A shiver ran up my spine. Very slowly, I lifted my eyes and found the doll sitting atop the sofa's cushy armrest—the one whose identical twin I'd seen in the foyer yesterday, which I was beginning to suspect was probably not a twin at all. It was facing me with its painted face and black eyes, and it had just talked.

It talked.

It. Talked.

A scream burst out of my mouth as I jumped from the sofa and bolted from the library as fast as I could.

Several minutes later, I collapsed against a wall, panting heavily. I had no idea where I'd run, but by the looks of it, I'd ended up somewhere on the third floor. The sunlight shone dully through a diamond-shaped window at the opposite end of the shadowy hallway.

The situation was dire. It was one thing to see paperwork appear in Esten's lap or the chandelier flicker on and quite another to have a wooden doll speak to you or move about the house like it could *walk*. I shivered. The stuff of nightmares. What was I supposed to do? The sun was going to set in a few hours, and I would be stuck inside a pitch-black house, completely *alone* with it.

As I thought that, I heard a shuffle to my right. Terror zapped my limbs, and I nearly took off again.

You look not as stupid when I watch you, the voice said from beside me. There was a purring quality to it.

I gulped in air. Too late to run now—the doll had caught up with me. What was it going to do to me? Curse me? Spirit me away?

The doll did neither of those things. It continued to chastise me, although it didn't sound particularly angry. It was almost like it was stating a bothersome fact: *Esten a brat and you not entirely stupid, but bad manners.*

"I'm sorry?" I croaked. The doll did have a point. "I didn't... I didn't mean to offend you," I managed to squeak, and then, despite my horror, I slowly inched around to face the doll.

It was a faintly glowing silhouette a mere foot away from my right boot. Either shock was making me see things, or the doll's painted face was leveling me with a very unimpressed stare.

I wracked my brain, trying to figure out what to say. The doll didn't seem to want to harm me—at least not yet. In which case, it was probably good to find out why it had been stalking me.

"Um . . . what, um, is your name?" I asked in an awkward attempt to remedy my earlier rudeness.

Full name too terrifying for you, the doll said flatly, and I couldn't tell if it was being sarcastic or not. *So I allow you call me Oi.*

I swallowed nervously but nodded. "O-okay. Nice to meet you, Oi. I am Kieren."

I know, Oi said matter-of-factly. *New magician don't know magic.*

It was hard not to let my spirits sink at that. Even the doll —who might or might not want to curse me—knew about my embarrassing struggles to learn about magic. "Sorry," I said again.

To my surprise, Oi didn't chide me. The sun slowly continued its descent toward the horizon, but even in the growing shadows of the hallway, I could make out the mischievous expression on the doll's face.

I teach lights if you make deal with me. Oi smirked.

CHAPTER 5
ESTEN

Something was glowing brightly beside me. Sunlight?
"Go away," I grunted, and flicked my wrist, drawing the drapes with my magic. I was exhausted after breaking into the forge last night, and not ready to get out of bed yet.

The annoying glow flickered but didn't disappear. Not sunlight, then. I cracked one eye open. Just as I feared—a golden letter was floating above my bedside table, bearing Probos's seal. Inside was an invitation to meet Probos promptly in his offices. An *invitation*—right. Like I could possibly refuse to see the head of the Council, also known as the top magical official in the country. The thing that bothered me, however, was the timing of the invite . . . right after my unsanctioned excursion to the forge. Had Probos found out already? Had anyone recognized me? No way. It had been dark, and it wasn't like my face was famous among non-magicians. I was only an apprentice. Besides, if Probos knew what I'd done, I would probably be arraigned by the Bureau of Enforcement instead of being politely summoned. So what was this about, then? Did Probos want to talk about Master and his secret assignment?

My stomach knotted at the thought. I'd never been this worried about Master before. I knew it was not my place to doubt him or his abilities. Master was strong, the second-strongest magician in the country; he could defend himself against anyone who dared challenge him. And it wasn't abnormal for him to have assignments he couldn't share with me because of his rank. But this secrecy was starting to get to me. Master Hanska had warned me not to trust anybody while he was on this mission. And lo and behold, a new apprentice had been sent to the house! My skin bristled.

Since I'd come to live with Master fifteen years ago, no one else had been assigned to him as a full-time apprentice. Some magicians had even tried to petition him directly, but Master Hanska had rejected everyone. He'd been gracious about it, of course. But there had only ever been me, whom Master had chosen himself, whom he'd *saved*...

Which begged a question—shouldn't he have approved Kieren, at the very least? Except how could Master have done that when he was busy with his assignment? Something didn't sit right with me about this whole situation.

Grudgingly I got out of bed. I'd spent the better part of the night cleaning my jacket, because the grime and dirt from the forge had managed to get on literally everything. But it was presentable now. I picked out a new pair of pants and a shirt from the armoire, added a silk cravat to hide the scratches on my neck, and then transported myself to Capitol Hill.

Probos's office was inside the Assembly building, located a short walk from Congress and the White House. It housed not only Probos and his many staff but also the assignment task force that determined where magical interference was needed and distributed missions to magicians; a public relations committee to foster good relationships between the non-magical population and magicians; and lastly, the Bureau of Enforcement of Magical Law.

According to protocol, I appeared in the grand vestibule; the rest of the building was protected against direct transport for security reasons. It was a cavernous, hexagonal room with smooth marble walls and a floor lined with plush red carpet. Once cleared by the guard, I crossed to the other side of the vestibule, passing under the ceiling murals that depicted the Founders in all their glory, and ascended the stairs to the second level, where Probos's office was located. His assistant, Cash, greeted me in the waiting room.

"Howdy!" Cash grinned and waved from his desk. When Cash had manifested, he had inexplicably developed a unique magical trait that allowed him to switch his gender and transform his physical body at will. Today Cash appeared to be the male version of himself and was wearing a trim purple suit in a fashion popular in the southwestern states with a thin ribbon bow tie in the same color.

"Good morning." I smiled politely. "Am I allowed in yet?" I flicked my chin toward the closed wooden door to the right of Cash's desk.

Cash shook his head. "Sorry, Esten, Probos's previous meeting has run longer than expected." Then he leaned in and smiled conspiratorially. "Since we've got a moment, do tell—how've you been? I haven't seen you in ages!"

I swallowed; I didn't want to lie to Cash. I considered him a friend.

He was a few years older than me and used to be a regular guest in Master Hanska's home. Even though Master hadn't taken on anyone full-time until now, he occasionally volunteered to give additional training to other magicians' apprentices. Cash and I had trained together often back then. Cash was an incredibly *precise* magician; I respected him for that, and his unique transfiguration abilities were unlike anything I'd ever seen. I wished I had a talent for that. But I couldn't for the life of me figure out why after his apprenticeship Cash had petitioned for a desk job in a politician's office, of all things! I had thought he'd pick something more impactful than bureaucracy.

Suits me just right, he'd said coyly back then, and that was that.

I would be happy to chat with him on any other day, but considering the circumstances, I couldn't let my guard down even in front of Cash.

"You know, keeping busy, learning a lot," I said evasively. "How about yourself?"

Cash sighed, pointing at the pile of magical correspondence on his table. It had grown about four inches taller in the short time since I'd stepped in. "Similarly," Cash said. "These tensions with Europe have us all working overtime to secure *a fast and peaceful resolution.*" The last bit Cash pronounced in the mock tone of a public announcer, one who had to keep his spirits up while reading a carefully worded message of hope while in reality the enemy was already standing on the doorstep.

"And how is it progressing—the fast and peaceful resolution?" I asked carefully, hoping Cash would elaborate.

Cash bit his lip and glanced quickly at Probos's door. He was about to say something when said door blew open and Kavender stormed out of it, his long pewter cloak swirling like a dark cloud behind him. Kavender had never been the most *personable* magician, but this level of discontent was impressive even for him. His heavy boots rattled the wooden floors as he marched past me with barely a scowl in my direction. What had Probos said to him to get under his skin like that?

Cash and I were too stunned to speak until Kavender was out of the room.

Slowly I turned back to Cash, hoping to resume our previous conversation, but already his expression had changed back to one of casual politeness, leaving no visible inkling of what he'd been thinking moments ago. "Probos is ready to see you now," he said with a smile.

I nodded, mentally preparing myself, and walked to the door. Clearly the politician's manners had been rubbing off on Cash.

∼

Probos's office was simple and strategically modest. All the walls were painted a clean, unremarkable shade of white, and the only decoration was an old painting of the Founders in a gold leaf frame. The rest of the wall space was either empty or occupied by bookcases.

Probos was a man in his fifties with golden-brown skin and piercing dark eyes that felt like two abysses full of secrets and therefore were troublesome to stare into for too long. He wore a plain brown suit with no elaborate details, not unlike what regular citizens wore to dress up. I'd always thought that was strategic as well. Probos was the one magician who had to communicate with the non-magical government and whose photographs appeared in newspapers most often.

If Probos and Kavender had had a staunch disagreement mere seconds ago, Probos's face showed nothing of it. He gave a neutral smile and nodded, expecting me to seat myself in one of the chairs in front of his desk. "Good morning, Esten," he said in a warm and sure voice. "I'm glad my invitation found you well."

"Good morning, sir," I replied and sat down, watching Probos closely.

One could never tell what Probos was truly thinking, but from the polite way he greeted me, I gathered that my breaking into the forge was probably not the reason for my summons. It made me breathe a little easier . . . but only a little. I was merely waiting for the other shoe to drop.

"How is Kieren adjusting?" Probos asked, placing his hands in front of him and lacing his fingers together.

I nearly blurted, *Huh?*—I hadn't been expecting this question at all—but I bit my tongue just in time. I took a moment to regain my ability to speak. "He is . . . fine . . . doing fine, sir." Why did Probos even know Kieren's name, let alone care to inquire about his well-being? Kieren was a rookie magician, and Probos was the top magical official in the country. It didn't make sense.

"Good to hear," Probos said pleasantly. "I am quite hopeful that the two of you are getting along well."

In politician speak, this probably meant that Probos wanted me to actively befriend Kieren, which was even more baffling. Was he responsible for Kieren's assignment to Master's house? It was reasonable for Probos to get reports of every newly manifested magician. We were a small percentage of the population, and only a few of us manifested in any given year. Still, his words indicated a higher level of involvement with Kieren's case—and that was in addition to whatever was happening with Master Hanska and his mysterious assignment. I wondered if Master's warning applied to Probos as well. Could I trust him? I didn't know.

I replied dutifully, "I will make my best effort, sir."

"That will be good," Probos said, still smiling, though I

noticed a slight shift in his gaze. What he said next puzzled me even more than his inexplicable interest in Kieren. "In the meantime, I have a special assignment for you, Esten. What do you know about the phenomenon we commonly refer to as the sludge?"

CHAPTER 6
KIEREN

When Esten returned home that night, the house was not pitch black anymore. And it wasn't because I was practically glowing with pride like a lightbulb-studded theater marquee—it was because I had finally learned to turn the lights on.

Oi had told me that magic was already all around me—at least, I thought that's what he'd meant, as he had a peculiar manner of speaking. All I had to do was strongly *wish* for the lights to turn on and then flick my hand, imagining that I was flipping a switch. When I'd tried it, miraculously, every single light in the house had lit up at once. I'd almost been blinded.

I couldn't believe I hadn't tried doing this last night. And Oi—that trickster—had watched me stumble around in the darkness for hours and hadn't said a thing.

After the lesson was over, Oi and I had raided the kitchen. Together we had baked and eaten a splendid mashed potato and parsnip pie—although most of the baking had been done by me and eating done by Oi. He'd asked me to turn away for a moment, and some chewing sounds had followed, and when

I'd been allowed to turn back around, half of the pie had disappeared clean off the plate. For a little doll, Oi surely ate a lot.

After that, I'd helped myself to half of the remaining half, and then Esten had finally shown up in the kitchen.

"Who are you talking to?" Esten frowned instead of greeting me, not bothering to acknowledge my splendid progress with the lights.

I swallowed my disappointment—what else was I expecting from him? Congratulations on learning to turn the lights on?

"I'm talking to Oi." I gestured to the doll sitting lazily on the table, probably still digesting.

Esten's eyebrows rose. "You can *talk* to him?"

I blinked. "Yes. Can't you?"

"N-no," Esten admitted somewhat reluctantly. "Master can, though."

"Oh." *You don't say.* Something like pride burst in my chest again. Could I really do something Esten couldn't?

Oi added unapologetically, *Esten—bad listener.*

My eyes widened, expecting Esten to take offense at that, but I quickly remembered that Esten couldn't hear Oi's comment, and I wasn't about to relay it.

"Anyway," Esten said, "this spirit is Master's guest. He has some business with Master and is free to come and go as he pleases. Master said he wouldn't harm us. Just don't go making deals with him, and don't let him eat champagne glasses—or any house furnishings, for that matter."

"You eat glass?" I asked Oi, astonished. The comment about making deals had come a little too late. I'd already baked the pie for Oi, which was the first half of the deal, but there was still another part that Oi hadn't told me yet.

"Glass!" Esten snorted. "Master already had to get a whole

new set of champagne flutes because that spirit ate them all the day he arrived."

Oi stared at us both, completely unconcerned. *Crunchy*, he purred in explanation. *Oi like.*

"Duly noted," I said, still in awe. "Speaking of food, we left pie for you." I pointed at the remaining piece and the empty plate I'd set for Esten.

Esten narrowed his eyes and glared at the pie with suspicion.

I couldn't believe his reaction. Did he think I was going to poison him? Offended, I was about to withdraw the offer when Esten muttered an unexpected "Okay" and pulled the chair out.

Despite his infuriating behavior, a tiny grin crept up my cheeks. "Want apple cider too? We found a big jug in the icebox. It's delicious!"

"What do you mean, you *found* it?" Esten asked, fastidiously unfolding a napkin on his lap. "I requested it myself this morning. And yes, I'll take some. Thanks."

"Oh." Well, that finally confirmed my theory about how fresh foods appeared in the house.

After I served the cider, Esten waved a hand over his pie, and steam rose from it. He did the same to his cider and proceeded to eat and drink in silence.

I thought he wasn't going to bother to speak again, so I didn't expect the revelation when it came.

"Master is gone," he said, staring at his plate with a few tiny crumbs of pie left on it.

"What? You mean on assignment?"

"Not exactly," Esten said grimly. "I mean, it started as an assignment, but I haven't heard from him in a while."

I straightened up in my seat. Finally things were beginning to make sense—Esten's over-the-top behavior and Cynn talking about Master Hanska like he'd been gone for a long time.

Esten added, sounding grimmer still, "Look, I'm only telling you this because I won't be able to keep it a secret with you around. And also because you really are clueless, and therefore I've concluded that you're probably *not* a spy."

My jaw dropped. I was thoroughly conflicted about whether to be offended by the clueless comment or outraged by the unbelievable suggestion that I'd come here to snoop. Out loud, I said, "A spy? Me? That's ridiculous." Esten gave me a wary look. He did not think it ridiculous at all. "Well, I'm glad you know I'm not," I muttered. "Anyway, do you think something happened to Master Hanska?"

Esten replied slowly, as though deciding how much truth to tell me. "I don't know much. Master had been investigating something—a private assignment he couldn't talk to me about that came *directly* from Probos." My eyes widened at the implication—Probos was the one magician even I knew by name. Esten continued, turning genuinely upset, "Then Master suddenly disappeared without leaving any explanation or directions for me. It's so unlike him. He wouldn't abandon me like that. And a few nights before he vanished, he warned me to be careful and not to trust anyone."

"How long ago was that?" I asked.

"Almost two weeks now."

I inhaled sharply. Esten was right to worry. "Do you know any details about what he was working on?"

"Not really." Esten sighed. "I've been trying to retrace Master's steps this past week, but he was careful not to leave clues, and it seems I've hit a dead end. Things just don't make sense, and I can't ask for help because of what Master said. To top it off, Probos wanted to meet with me, and I don't know if I can trust him either."

My mouth opened in awe. "Probos did what? Did he say anything about Master Hanska?"

"No." Esten shook his head again. "And I don't understand that either. Probos is the kind of person who doesn't use words carelessly. It seemed strange that he didn't bring Master up at all. It *must* have been on purpose. He gave me an assignment, though—to investigate the sludge, of all things."

"Do you think," I ventured, "that it might be connected to Master Hanska's mission somehow?"

Esten mulled this over for a second. "I'm not sure. As untimely and strange as the sludge problem is, I think Master's investigation had something to do with airship manufacturing. Even at the Assembly, they seem mostly concerned about the escalating tensions with Europe instead of the sludge."

Come to think of it, Cynn had sounded more anxious about the war too when she'd stopped by. "Are we going to war?" I asked.

"I wouldn't think so. But the government might," Esten replied. He must have registered the confusion on my face because he offered an explanation. "We magicians still believe in neutrality. Even though this issue hasn't been seriously discussed since the time of the Founders, we pretty much operate according to the idea of deterrence, which states that if magicians engage in war alongside regular humans, it will lead to mass casualties and possibly mutual destruction because of how powerful magic can be."

I nodded, remembering what I'd read in the Founders' essays earlier. "But if that's still true, why would a war break out suddenly?" I asked.

Esten shrugged. "Because deterrence isn't used in non-magical politics. In Europe, some governments claim they don't have enough resources and that others have been profiting unjustly, especially those with larger industries. So they think they have no choice but to seize what they want by force before they fall further behind. Some even think that the United States had gotten too lucky with our big territory full of riches. And it doesn't help that our government is openly picking sides and mobilizing the troops."

I considered that. Maybe from the other side of the world it seemed that way, but in my small community, everyone had to work hard to stay afloat. There had never been a summer my siblings and I hadn't spent working in the fields from early morning till the sun was down. And it wasn't like all that work made us rich either. I'd never seen an icebox or a blimp up close until a few days ago, and only a few streets in our town had electric lighting. Maybe some parts of the United States were wealthy, but not where I was from.

Humans. Never enough, Oi grumbled beside me as though commenting on both Esten's words and my thoughts. I nodded sadly.

Esten didn't appear to hear Oi again. He sighed and rubbed his eyes, and for the first time, I noticed how tired he looked. All of this must have been weighing heavily on his mind. At least that probably explained some of his snappishness . . . or so I hoped.

"Did Probos mention anything else?" I asked before Esten could decide he was done chatting and ditch me again.

Esten's silver eyes locked with mine and didn't look away for a long moment. Then he replied, "No. Nothing else," thanked me for the pie, and retired to his room.

~

I barely slept that night, just lay awake and thought over everything Esten had told me. It had been nice being treated like a fellow magician instead of a nuisance for once, and so I decided I should try to act the part. Of course, I was still inexperienced, but it's not like Esten knew what he was doing either. And now that Master Hanska had gone missing and Esten had decided I wasn't a spy after all, maybe I could help with Esten's assignment? So much was happening in the world outside; what was the point of me staying cooped up in the house and doing nothing?

Despite Esten's warning not to make deals, I bargained with Oi again. In exchange for the promise of another pie, Oi told me which room was Esten's.

The moment the sun was up, I headed straight to his door, hoping to catch Esten before he left...

I knew I shouldn't feel crushing disappointment when minutes passed and my knocks went unanswered. I knew I should expect as much from him. But still, I *really* wanted to kick something—I had been ditched again.

CHAPTER 7
ESTEN

I leaned over the porcelain sink and splashed ice-cold water on my face, getting ready for the day. I needed to get my thoughts in order. I didn't regret talking to Kieren last night. To be honest, it had felt good to vent a little. It had been a long time since I'd had anyone here I could speak with freely. Of course I talked with Master, but I never complained to him about things. I wouldn't waste his time with needless gossip or grievances. Chatting with Kieren had been different. Easy. But I wasn't going to blindly trust him just because Probos wanted us to be friends.

I sighed, patting my face dry with a towel, and then returned to my bedroom to get dressed. At least my conscience was *mostly* clean. I had followed Probos's orders; I had been pleasant with Kieren for a whole dinner. But I didn't have the time to babysit him when I had the sludge to worry about and Master was still missing. Finding Master was my priority. And if the sludge outbreaks were connected to his prolonged absence, then I'd be damn sure to get to the bottom of what was causing them. Besides, it was safer—not to mention easier

—to keep Kieren confined to the house while I was busy. How much damage could he do here anyway?

So when Kieren came looking for me, I ignored him, straightened the collar of my jacket, and transported myself to the location of the most recent sludge outbreak.

∾

This time the sludge had hit a city neighborhood—and hit it hard. Even two days later, the whole area was still cordoned off by police officers. A group of onlookers had congregated nearby, watching.

I didn't want to attract their attention. So I went around the crowd, maintaining my distance, presented my credentials to the police, and they let me in to inspect the damage.

Even though most of the sludge had been removed, I could see its effects. The grass had wilted, and the ground was scorched. A thick web of cracks covered the pavement and the foundations of the buildings; the paint on their walls looked bubbly and eaten away, as though it had been splashed with acid. The longer the sludge was allowed to remain in an area, the more it rotted everything it touched. The previous outbreaks had ruined patches of woods and marshland and destroyed acres of farmland, but it had never touched an actual city before. Everything had its turn, it seemed.

Grimly I walked past the ruined buildings, approaching the last remaining puddle of sludge and the magician working on it. I knew Wyckett Foxx well. He was a dark-skinned man in his thirties dressed in striped pants, a vest over a tailored shirt, and a bowler hat, all in matching shades of sage green. Wyckett had grown up in Jamaica but had apprenticed with an American magician and stayed in the country afterward, eventually taking over the Rhode Island branch.

"Morning, Esten! Are you here to relieve me?" Wyckett asked, and managed to produce a charming grin, which didn't do much to mask how tired he looked.

"I'm afraid not," I said apologetically, and stepped closer. "Just happened to pass by. Is it bad?"

Wyckett sighed, holding his arms up to maintain the flow of magic. "I'm the third shift, and it's still not gone."

As if on cue, the glob of sludge convulsed and tried to stretch an angry tendril at Wyckett. He flicked his wrists. A bunch of roots sprouted from under the ground, surrounding the glob and forming something akin to a live cage. The tendril hit the roots and burst into tiny droplets. Trapped inside the cage, the droplets slowly broke apart and disintegrated as their magic ran its course.

So far, this was the only method of combatting the sludge. Directly attacking it with magic had proven to have no effect. It was as if the sludge simply ate the magic that came at it. Instead, whenever the sludge appeared, multiple magicians had to trap it, stopping it from spreading. Then they waited for its violent magic to decay until it collapsed into a pile of viscous, tarlike waste, still poisonous but easier to manage. The whole process was very time-consuming. At this rate, it would take even a strong magician like Wyckett Foxx at least another half a day. I felt for him.

"Any clues as to what's been causing it yet?" I asked.

Wyckett shook his head. "All we know is that it suddenly broke out and started raging in the area around that barbershop over there. The owner and his assistant died, and several people were injured before any of us got here." Wyckett pointed to a brick building that looked like it had been showered in acid. The bricks were starting to crumble; the shutters had turned into sawdust. Surprisingly, the sign in front had survived and was still legible, but the shop would probably never open again.

I closed my eyes, trying to feel the magic. There was a steady pulling kind of motion that came from Wyckett's efforts; there was my own magic, which felt calm and at rest; and then there was the sludge...

I opened my eyes and frowned. "I really don't get it. It feels so... *foreign*, somehow."

Wyckett's eyes widened at that. He carefully glanced around and whispered, "You don't think European magicians have sent this thing here, do you?"

The question caught me off guard. "What? No. No, that's not what I meant," I corrected quickly, making sure no one was within earshot. We didn't need to fuel those types of rumors. With all the uncertainty and political tension, many a wild theory was being tossed around, including that the sludge had been sent here by hostile governments.

I didn't want to believe that. Master Hanska always said that the most tragic day in the history of magic would be the day magicians decided to turn on one another.

I took a moment to clear my thoughts and then explained, "I meant that this doesn't feel like a spell. It's magic, but it doesn't feel like any magic I've encountered. There is *something* familiar about the way it eats away at things, though . . ." I watched the destructive droplets, unable to place the feeling.

I was about to speak again when somebody hollered at us, "Hey, magicians!"

Wyckett and I glanced over our shoulders to find a small crowd of onlookers standing in an alley just outside the secured perimeter. There were no police officers nearby, only the rope to prevent people from entering.

A disgruntled, round man with a bald head and a goatee addressed us. "When is this mess going to be gone from our streets, huh?" he shouted. "We haven't been home for two days. We have the right to go back!"

"Yeah!" someone else in the crowd agreed as a few more people appeared from the adjacent alleyways and joined them.

Wyckett and I exchanged glances. There was a protocol for dealing with these situations, and Wyckett was the senior magician. Despite his utter exhaustion, Wyckett continued to pour magic into the root cage while he turned around to face the growing crowd. He tipped his hat and smiled widely, getting ready to put on his best Wyckett show. Everyone who knew him joked that had Wyckett not manifested magic, he surely would have been a musical entertainer or a famous actor.

"Don't worry, kind sir," Wyckett declared charmingly. "We will be done here in no time. This area has been restricted for your own safety. Thank you for your patience."

But even Wyckett's charisma didn't have much effect on this crowd.

"Patience, my boots!" some other man yelled. "We've got no other choice here!"

"Yeah!" the goateed man agreed. "Me and Hank weren't just forced out of our homes—our businesses are taking a hit. What customer will ever want to come back to these cursed ruins, especially after Johnny and his fella were mauled by that thing?"

Wyckett's smile wavered, and the root cage shook a little, but he held it in place before the sludge could escape. "I'm deeply sorry about your neighbors. But I am certain there will be efforts to help their families and rebuild your property when it is safe to do so. The state government has established an emergency fund to compensate citizens—"

"Lies!" a third person butted in rudely. "We've heard of farmers in the Carolinas who never returned to their lands.

Everything they owned was ruined. All because of your damn magic!"

I froze.

A murmur rolled like a wave through the crowd, which had grown even bigger in the last few minutes. The newspapers hadn't reported all the horrid details of the previous outbreaks to keep the general public from panicking, so not everybody knew that those farmlands would be out of commission for a long time. But now that the truth had been spoken, hostility and dismay became palpable in the crowd.

This wasn't something either Wyckett or I was prepared to deal with.

"I am very sorry to hear that," Wyckett said, now looking for a way to end the encounter. "I assure you all, the authorities are doing their best, and I need to return to my—"

"We ain't done talking, magician!" The goateed man climbed over the rope and pointed angrily at Wyckett. "Must be nice living off our taxes while we're being lied to and forced out of our homes. How do we know it's not *you* who caused this damn sludge?"

Wyckett flinched, and my stomach dropped. Was I hearing this right? Was this man seriously accusing magicians of causing the outbreak? In the course of my apprenticeship with Master Hanska, I'd seen all kinds of reactions to magic, from awed fascination to mistrust. But never had I been accosted like this before. Wyckett was about to collapse from trying to save what was left of these people's homes, and *this* was how they showed their gratitude? Despicable!

Protocols be damned. I scowled and opened my mouth to give them all a piece of my mind when two police officers pushed through the crowd.

"Now, now, Mr. Williams," one said, addressing the goateed man and putting an arm around his shoulders. "We've explained already that you will be allowed back into your home the moment it is deemed safe. Please step back and let them magicians do their jobs, right?" The officer threw a glance at Wyckett and me, all but saying that we had better return to the sludge cleanup instead of getting into verbal disputes with civilians. Like any of this would've happened if they'd been doing *their* jobs patrolling the perimeter!

Mr. Williams grumbled something in annoyance but didn't dare fight when the officer nudged him back past the rope. After leveling a few more stares at us, the rest of the crowd started to disperse as well.

I was still fuming. I hadn't been planning to spend my day like this, but now I had no choice but to stay and help Wyckett break down the remaining sludge. Even with the police present, I felt uneasy leaving him alone in case the crowd became rowdy again.

It was becoming clear why Probos wanted the phenomenon investigated, even with everything else urgent happening in the world. Except I still had not the faintest idea why of all magicians, Probos had chosen me for the job.

CHAPTER 8
KIEREN

"Oi, I want to help find Master Hanska. Please teach me to transport," I said after breakfast. Oi and I had indulged in honey toast with cheese and apple cider. It was splendid.

Oi made a noise that sounded suspiciously like a burp, considered my request for a second, and then outright refused me. *No can do.*

"But why not?" I asked, astonished.

No ready, Oi replied simply.

I frowned. "Why not?"

Because no ready, Oi repeated matter-of-factly, and burped again.

I shook my head, wounded. I couldn't help resenting Esten for continuously leaving me out. And now even Oi refused to help. Had Esten put him up to this?

"Fine," I huffed. "I'll teach myself, then."

With that, I marched out of the kitchen. How difficult could transporting be anyway? The lights were easy. Oi had already told me that magic was everywhere and all I had to do was direct it. I could do that again.

I got to the foyer, closed my eyes, and wished to be transported to the garden in the front yard.

Ten long seconds passed, but nothing happened. Not even an inch of movement.

Frustrated, I wished *harder*—transport magic must require more effort than I'd thought.

But still nothing happened.

I gritted my teeth and tapped my foot on the floor impatiently. Maybe the problem was that I was aiming too far for my first attempt. Maybe I should try just getting myself over the threshold first.

I took a few steps toward the door, closed my eyes again, and *strongly* wished to appear on the porch. After a few seconds of strenuous effort, the magic in the air thickened, and the house started to vibrate around me. I smirked. "Come on, now, almost there," I whispered, coaxing the magic to work, and—

Nothing.

Absolutely nothing.

I glowered at the door, my frustration mounting quickly. *What a stupid door. Still here, still in my way. All I want is to get to the other side. Why won't it listen?*

Angrily, I let my head fall forward, and my forehead hit the doorframe.

BAM! Something exploded and knocked me several steps back. The door tore violently off its hinges and flew forty feet into the front yard, where it finally stopped upon colliding with a big hydrangea bush and its luscious mops of purple flowers.

I gaped—*oh, no!*—and then took off after it.

∽

It took some effort to drag the heavy oak door back to the porch, all while trying not to let the stone pathway scratch its expensive-looking finish.

Oi surveyed me and my accomplishments unsympathetically. I propped the door against the wall, where it sat, appearing utterly forlorn. The metal hinges looked like they'd exploded, and half the branches of the beautiful hydrangea were broken. Esten was probably going to kill me when he got back home.

In utter defeat, I plopped onto the porch steps, wiping sweat from my forehead, which now ached dully as though the bone underneath was bruised.

Esten bad listener. You sometime worse, Oi grumbled, and then appeared on the steps next to me. The bugger was totally flaunting the ease with which he could magically transport. Unlike a certain newbie magician.

I tried not to let it add to my sullen mood. What was I thinking, trying to go find Master Hanska by myself when I couldn't even manage the basics of magic? But what else was I supposed to do? Nobody had wanted me at my old home once I'd manifested, and now I was stuck in this new one where no one seemed to want me either. What would happen to me if Master Hanska never came back? Would I be assigned to a new magician, moved to a different state again? Esten would hardly keep me around even if his rank were high enough to take on an apprentice. Would anybody else accept me, especially now that I had a history of destroying people's property? I wanted the ground to open up and swallow me whole. I had completely botched my one shot at proving myself useful and helping with the investigation.

"I meant to ask you, Oi," I said, trying to keep my thoughts from spiraling, "how come Master Hanska and I can understand you, but Esten can't?"

Oi made a humming sound like he was reminiscing. *Hanska —great magic. Always listened. Always helped. Esten not bad but not good understanding.*

I tried to decipher what Oi meant. "Not to make excuses for Esten," I said carefully, "but your speech is a little unusual, Oi." Oi's eyebrows might have been painted on, but I could almost imagine him quirking one. *I speak fine. Your translation bad.*

I frowned. "Translation? Do you mean you're not speaking English right now?"

Dolls speak English? Oi asked wryly.

I looked at him sideways. Was this a trick question?

To my relief, Oi continued without waiting for me to respond, *Magic speak magic. Magic translate magic. You translate not well—maybe someday. Esten speak well but listen not. Young.*

I chewed my bottom lip. Oi's way of speaking was still mystifying, but I had a strong suspicion that what Oi had shared with me was important. If only I knew how.

"Oi, what *are* you?" I asked hesitantly.

Oi stared into the distance, past the broken hydrangea bush and the stony pathway, past the woods beyond it and into the resonant blue of the October sky.

I'm huuungry, he said longingly. *Pie time, Kieren. Promise deal?*

I sighed. Magic wisdom was not free, and deals had to be honored. "Pie time," I agreed, and stumbled tiredly to the kitchen.

CHAPTER 9
KIEREN

"What did you do to the front door?" were the first words out of Esten's mouth that evening. He looked flabbergasted.

I winced. I'd spent the second half of the day trying to figure out how to explain the door incident to him as well as making two pumpkin pies—one for Oi, and another to serve as a peace offering for Esten, should things go south.

Ultimately I had decided that the best strategy was simply to come clean. "I tried to teach myself how to magically transport to the porch," I said. "But it didn't work. Sorry."

Esten's nostrils flared. He didn't even look at the peace pie. "And what? You just decided to be a brute and blast the door instead?"

Oi eyed us both from his spot on the kitchen table, looking amused and not defending me.

"Well, the door was an unfortunate side effect," I muttered in shame, and busied myself with staring intensely at my feet.

Esten shook his head. "I cannot believe this. I simply

cannot believe this!" he groused under his breath, and marched out of the kitchen.

I followed him at a safe distance.

In the foyer, Esten rolled up his sleeves and immediately got to mending the damages. With painstaking precision, he bent the exploded hinges back into shape, very slowly guiding the metal with the movement of his hands. His calm, strong magic was the complete opposite of his annoyed grumbling. "Like I haven't already spent most of my day breaking down the sludge. And what do I come home to? Another disaster!"

My ears perked up from the big burgundy velvet armchair I'd perched on. So *that* was what Esten had been up to.

Esten continued his grousing. "Let this be a lesson to you: it always takes much more time and effort to fix things with magic than to break them. Probably took you less than five minutes to vandalize the mansion's entrance."

That was a surprisingly accurate assessment, but I decided not to acknowledge it out loud. "Why so?" I asked carefully, doing my best not to upset Esten any more than I already had.

"Because," Esten huffed to show further annoyance but finally finished mending the first hinge, "when you fix things, you have to be exact. The hinges won't work unless you put them back in precisely the shape they are supposed to be. But there are millions of ways to break something. And they all yield the same result—destruction."

I felt bad. Esten hadn't broken the door, yet he was the one stuck fixing it after a long day, and I was no help at all. "I mean . . . the door can probably wait till tomorrow," I offered meekly. "I'll sleep in the foyer tonight and guard—"

"Absolutely not," Esten cut me off. "I'm not leaving Master's house in this sorry state overnight. Also, this isn't a simple door. It was reinforced with protective charms. But of course you had to blow through those too, didn't you?"

I shrank again a little. I'd had no idea about the charms.

Instead of offering another useless apology that Esten wouldn't accept anyway, I decided this was probably an okay time to sneak in some questions, since Esten was actually talking to me and wasn't going to storm off until he was done fixing the door.

"Who were the charms protecting against?" I asked tentatively. "Have people tried to rob the house before?"

Esten rolled his eyes. "Obviously not. Good luck to regular humans trying to find this place. It's hidden in a pocket of space via magic; they'd be walking in circles. That's why I let the driver go and we had to use the stone entry when I brought you in, remember?"

I listened with my mouth open. I'd almost forgotten about the magic stone trick. I'd been getting antsy inside the house, but if I left the grounds to go on a walk or something, would I even be able to find it again? The realization was unnerving, to say the least. But if it wasn't non-magical people the door was protecting against, then—

"Do the charms ward off other magicians? Does this have to do with what Master Hanska told you?" I asked.

Esten frowned but answered with reluctance. "Master Hanska holds nothing but respect for our fellow magicians. He considers magic a precious gift that unites us all; it must be cherished and fostered. That being said, with the sludge outbreaks and the mysterious Probos assignment, he suspected some nefarious business was afoot and put the protections on the door. And just so you know," Esten warned, "it is considered very rude to transport yourself directly into another magician's home, even if you know where they live."

I nodded as Esten finished mending the last hinge.

After that, he magically lifted the door and guided it back

into the frame, restoring it to its former glory and thus finally allowing me the opportunity to offer the peace pie.

CHAPTER 10
KIEREN

The following morning I woke up to banging on my door. I jumped out of bed in my standard-issue cotton pajamas, which I had borrowed from the wardrobe, and rushed to answer, thoroughly convinced some kind of emergency had occurred ... only to find Esten standing expectantly in the hallway. Once again, he was dressed head to toe in shades of midnight blue.

"Come on. It's time for your training," he announced curtly.

I gaped. "My what?"

Esten huffed like he was offering me the deal of a lifetime out of the sheer greatness of his heart. "Considering the events of yesterday, I have decided that to avoid the ruination of Master's house, I am going to have to teach you some basics. We're starting today."

Despite Esten's sour face, I found myself grinning. Maybe breaking the door and consequently withstanding an hour of Esten's annoyed grumbling hadn't been all that bad in the end.

"Yes!" I said eagerly. "But I need a moment to get proper, if you don't mind."

Esten narrowed his eyes as though just now noticing my appearance. His sharp gaze slid from my disheveled hair—which always stuck up in odd directions after sleeping—to my face, then down my neck and the thin red stripes of my pajamas to my bare ankles. Even though it lasted only a few seconds, I felt strangely self-conscious under Esten's scrutiny. Something in my stomach fluttered, and I didn't know what to say. Esten always looked so perfect and meticulously put together, from the pristine tailored clothes that hugged his body just the right way to his glossy hair, which was never out of place no matter the hour.

He must use some kind of magic for that, I thought dazedly. Even the way Esten's eyes gleamed with that metallic tint—it was too surreal and beautiful not to be magical.

Esten cleared his throat, yanking me out of my thoughts. His silver eyes didn't quite meet mine. "Hurry up, then," he said before promptly turning on his heel and marching down the hallway.

∼

After a quick breakfast of toast and coffee (which Esten graciously brewed for us both but which I found much too bitter to enjoy), Esten decided that my training should take place outside to avoid unnecessary damage to the furniture. He led me to the back of the house, past the still-blooming rose garden and the abundant hydrangeas, to the yellowing grassy field framed by tall trees. For some inexplicable reason, the field and the trees around it seemed much more prone to autumnal withering than the gardens near the house.

The day was quite warm and sunny for October, so we picked a spot in the shade of a broad golden maple.

Esten sat down on the grass opposite me, removed his jacket, and folded it beside him, taking extra time to smooth out the creases in the fabric. I watched him curiously; this morning he was even more fastidious than usual. Was he nervous about teaching me? It seemed impossible for Esten to be nervous about anything, let alone me.

I didn't get to dwell too much on that because Esten finally stopped fussing with his jacket and got down to business.

"So, let's start with the basics, shall we?" he said. "There are two types of magic. Do you know what they are?"

I had not the faintest clue. I chewed on my bottom lip before replying, "Like, the good and bad kind?"

Esten looked downright appalled. "Of course not! No wonder you go around blowing up people's doors with those ideas! Magic is neither good nor bad. It is a type of *force*, like gravity or electromagnetism. It is not a person. Please get that squarely into your head before we go any further."

"All right," I said nervously.

Esten exhaled and seemed to calm down a little. He brushed a stray lock of silky hair behind his ear and continued with an air of dignified formality, "As magic is a force, there are two types that work in somewhat opposite ways. We call them feathered and thorned. Feathered magic is aimed at support, restoration, and creation, while thorned magic is used to break down matter. Now, before you go spouting some nonsense about thorned magic being evil, consider that it is the nature of all things to perish someday. Even the grass under our feet feeds off soil made from countless dead leaves and bugs. There is no seed that didn't sprout from a fruit that shriveled up and rotted first."

I nodded solemnly, trying to wrap my mind around the concept.

Esten continued, "Both types of magic have their uses. Moreover, each magician has a natural affinity for one or the other. That is not to say that we aren't capable of both; it simply means that one comes more easily to us than the other. My inclination is toward the feathered type, as is Master Hanska's. Although his abilities are *much* greater than mine and more balanced through countless years of training," Esten added proudly.

A sudden understanding dawned on me as I remembered how Cynn had laughed at my unfortunate choice of words when I had called Esten thorny. Of course she had; I couldn't have landed further from the truth.

"Can you guess what affinity you have?" Esten asked.

I felt rather put on the spot, but denying it was no use. "Thorned?" I said, trying hard to brush away my assumptions about this sort of magic being bad or evil.

"The way you go about things, I would say that answer is likely correct," Esten said. "The thing to know about thorned magic—and this is important, so pay attention—is that it *always rebounds* in some manner."

I frowned. "How do you mean?"

"Well, every magical act has consequences," Esten explained, "but those are most immediately apparent with thorned magic. Think of it like this: if you were to punch someone, even in self-defense, your fist would hurt afterward. The harder you punch, the more it will hurt. You might even break your bones if you're not careful. It's the same with thorned magic. The impact or rebound *has* to go somewhere. If you don't know how to manage it, it will go straight back into your own body. When you blasted that door yesterday, did you feel a pushback of some kind?"

I realized with surprise that I had. It had felt like the door had smacked my forehead before flying off the hinges. And I'd been oddly exhausted from carrying it back to the porch. At the time, I'd blamed it on the door being heavy. Come to think of it, this probably explained how I had ended up with bruised ribs after manifesting as well.

"Yes," I replied.

"Thought so," Esten said. "Your problem is that neither illumination nor transportation is an act of thorned magic. You didn't know how to transport, so you defaulted to a blast of what came naturally to you. That's why you, as a thorned magician, must pay particular attention to maintaining control—not only to manage the rebound, but also to make sure your magic doesn't get out in some way you don't intend. Magic is in our very nature. As magicians, we all sometimes perform accidental magic. For example, when I was *younger*"—Esten said this with the kind of stately seriousness that made me hold back a laugh, because there was no way he was more than a year or two older than me—"I used to accidentally change the physical properties of things, like their hardness or softness, when my attention slipped, particularly in my sleep. That habit was quite a nuisance. I ruined a few pieces of furniture."

"Uh-huh," I said, also trying to come off as serious, although imagining a bed frame sagging like rubber under a snoozing Esten was rather funny.

"But in your case," Esten continued, "we have to worry about you blowing things to smithereens. Tell me everything you did yesterday that led the poor front door to its demise."

I looked down, feeling self-conscious again. "Well, when Oi taught me about the house lights, he said I should strongly wish for them to turn on and then act as if I were flipping a switch, and it worked. So I tried to apply the principle to transport magic. I closed my eyes, and I wished to appear on the porch. When it didn't work, I wished harder—"

"And?" Esten urged me impatiently, as though I was missing something important.

"I kept wishing and imagining that I was there already. But I got frustrated, so I hit the door with my forehead, and . . . well, you know the rest."

I could swear Esten looked a little pale in the face when he said, "I suppose we should consider ourselves lucky that you didn't end up with a crack in your skull. I am quite stunned about that."

I pouted, embarrassed.

Esten sighed. "For learning purposes, I'm going to let *you* figure out what you did wrong. Go on, offer suggestions."

"I got angry with the door?" I said sulkily.

"Obviously. But not just that. What was the big difference between what you did with the lights and what you *didn't* do while trying to transport?"

I had no idea.

Esten observed the lost look on my face, then let out another long measured sigh. "After all that wishing, did you actually try to *walk*?"

I tipped my head, confused. "Walk?"

"Yes, you can't move an object without motion," Esten said matter-of-factly.

"But I didn't have to do that with the lights," I objected.

"Well, you don't usually flip a light switch with your feet, do you?"

Esten was right, of course. When I did magic with the lights, I moved my *hand* like I was flipping an invisible switch.

"You wished to transport yourself someplace, but you made no steps toward it," Esten said. "In order to work, magic doesn't require only *intention*; you need to give it *direction*, set it in motion. So today, you're going to try transporting again, but add the walking part."

With that, Esten beckoned for me to get up. So I did, my stomach twisting with nervous anticipation.

"Let's start with a short distance. We don't want you to accidentally end up in Madagascar, do we?" Esten took ten steps away from me. "Try going from where you are to where I am. *Without* getting angry at anything, please."

I blew out a puff of air. Esten watched me closely, his arms folded, his silver eyes judging. I was going to thoroughly embarrass myself in front of him, wasn't I? But refusing to try would be even worse. So I rubbed my hands together and concentrated on a spot two feet from Esten's left side. Heaven forbid I land on top of him or do to Esten what I'd done to the front door. No, no, no. That would be the end of our lessons.

Shutting down that terrible thought, I closed my eyes, wished to land in the proper spot, and took a step forward.

The oddest sensation followed. It was almost like stepping into a mighty airstream—except it was made of magic, not air. It pushed me along with a *swoosh*, and by the time I opened my eyes again, I was standing a few steps away from Esten. Not exactly in the spot I'd pictured, but close enough.

"Ha!" I exclaimed in awe and shock that it had *worked*.

Esten quirked a barely impressed eyebrow and said, "Repetition is the mother of all learning. Go back to the spot you started from the same way."

I did, and it worked again. And then again. By the fourth time, I was starting to feel woozy from concentrating so hard but also brave enough to open my eyes a moment sooner, while I was still in the stream. It was just a glimpse, but it was the most fantastic thing I had ever seen. Magic swirled in all shades and colors around me like I was walking inside a rainbow.

"Not bad," Esten admitted after four successful attempts.

I tried to hold back a triumphant smirk. It felt great to finally get some kind of approval out of his sharp mouth. After days of being ignored, even two words felt like a victory.

"I think that is enough practice for now," he said. "Transport is very draining. That's why we normally reserve it for long-distance travel and never do it more than a few times in a row."

Esten was right, of course. I was panting and feeling quite lightheaded by then, but I wasn't ready to stop yet. Something had stirred inside me at Esten's acknowledgment, and I wanted to impress him even more, strike while the iron was hot. How much harm could one more act of magic do, anyway?

Just wait till you see this, I thought, eyeing a spot on one of the maple's branches. The next moment I went for it.

I closed my eyes and opened them again right before I stepped inside the magic stream. I watched with wonder as the blue strip of sky added itself to the rainbow mix. My body tilted backward, and my feet went up as I started walking through the stream.

How absolutely amazing is this? I thought. When I was little, I'd *loved* climbing trees, competing with my friends to see who could climb faster and higher. How could I have known that someday I would be able to do this via magic? A laugh burst out of my mouth. I'd been born with this, and I'd had no idea! I could travel not only up a tree but to a different state entirely, even to the other side of the world if I wanted to. Heavens, it felt euphoric to be this powerful. With magic, everything was possible; anything was doable! And it was *all* in my hands, right here, right—

Distracted, I realized too late that it was time to exit the stream. It pushed me out anyway. Caught off guard, I lost my balance, and suddenly everything began to spin around me.

With horrifying panic, I tried to find my feet, but there was nothing solid to step onto. Just air.

The world became a different kind of blur. It was the rustling of leaves and snapping of tree branches as they hit my arms and shoulders, the ground speeding toward me as my heart thudded, and then a gasp of air followed by a strong force that jerked my body to an abrupt stop.

"What on earth are you doing?" Esten glared furiously at me.

His arms were up, radiating magic that held me suspended upside down with my face inches from his. Esten's eyes glinted like polished silver knives. "Do you know what happens when you fall headfirst from fifty feet up?" he demanded, not lowering my body. "I'll give you a hint: you *die*. Very painfully."

My mouth turned dry, and I couldn't find my voice. I nodded stiffly.

"I cannot believe this," Esten scolded. "I thought it was safer to teach you than to let you explode the house trying to learn on your own. But even with all my warnings, you go and pull the stupidest, most dangerous stunt right in front of me. Have you no shame? Did you imagine yourself a bird?"

My voice still wasn't working. No, I hadn't imagined myself as anything. I had just stupidly wanted to impress Esten, which seemed so foolish now. There was no way I was going to admit it to him. But Esten didn't wait for my response. After another moment of intense glaring, he started to slowly lower me to the ground. I half expected him to teach me a lesson by letting me plunge the remaining distance, but he did no such thing. He laid me gently down, then allowed himself to slump on the grass beside me, breathing heavily.

I propped myself up, feeling dizzy and awful. Underneath all that anger, Esten looked genuinely rattled by what had happened. I probably would've died if he'd been less quick to react. The realization was a black pit in my stomach. It wasn't like I'd risked my life battling great evil or even performing high-level magic. It was a simple loss of control doing something I'd been sure I had the knack of. One mistake could've ended me, and Esten would've been forced to watch it unfold. No wonder Oi had refused to teach me transport magic. It'd been upsetting at the time, but Oi may have been right.

We sat silently for a while, me swallowing my guilt and Esten allowing his justified fury to subside. When my voice felt like it wasn't shaky anymore, I cleared my throat.

"I was wondering," I said tentatively, not quite daring to look Esten in the eye yet, "and I'm not suggesting anyone should do this for me if I'm reckless, but can you heal someone with magic? Like, if a person falls and breaks their bones and such..."

Esten sighed tiredly. "Unfortunately, I cannot. And while we're on the subject, here's another lesson for you. In addition to thorned or feathered affinity, every magician has a unique specialty. Of course we can do other kinds of magic, but a specialty is a particularly strong gift, and the talent to heal is incredibly rare. But having the raw gift is still not enough. You have to be strong, precise, and, more than anything, quick. I told you already that fixing things takes longer than breaking them. Living matter is no exception. Even if I had the ability to fix your skull should you engage in the inadvisable activity of cracking it, I wouldn't be able to heal it fast enough to save you from dying. And that's just the bone. I'm not even talking about internal damage, like your blood vessels rupturing, or your nerves tearing, or heaven knows what else inside that thick skull of yours." Esten raised his index finger and poked at my temple for emphasis. His skin was cool and smelled like flowers. Maybe he was wearing cologne.

"That's very morbid," I replied.

Esten snorted glumly, rolled his eyes, and dropped his hand. The flowery scent lingered in the air for another moment. "That's how magic is. Get used to it," he said. "Anyway, I wouldn't be able to heal you. End of story."

I nodded, mulling that over. "Is that why you haven't tried fixing the hydrangea in the front garden?"

"Basically, yes," Esten confirmed. "But I'm hopeful it will recover on its own. You probably noticed that our garden is blooming a bit longer than it should for the Northeast. It's not really on purpose. Magic helps maintain this whole place, and flowers like being next to magic, particularly the feathered kind."

"Huh," I said quietly. So Esten's presence was literally why heaps of roses still bloomed around the house. Maybe that was where the flowery smell came from, too. I thought that it suited Esten somehow. I didn't mention that out loud, though. "Should we transport back? I can make us lunch or something?" I was looking for a way to atone for the rocky finish to the lesson.

"Oh, no," Esten said firmly. "I will be the only one transporting. *You* are going to walk the way non-magical humans do and think about your actions." With that, Esten rose to his feet and within moments was gone, leaving me to trundle back to the house alone.

CHAPTER II
KIEREN

The magic lesson was only one of two delightful and unexpected things that happened that day; later in the evening, Esten informed me that we were going out on the town.

"Don't get too excited, though," he added strictly. "I am going as part of my investigation. But since you're a menace to leave at the house unattended *and* it will be educational for you to meet other magicians, I've decided to bring you along. So get dressed."

As I hadn't had a chance to procure any new clothes yet, I changed back into the jacket and vest I had arrived in, that being my nicest outfit. Esten, on the other hand, emerged from his room looking exceptionally dashing in a flowy, midnight-blue shirt, a velvet jacket in the same color with silver epaulets and buttons, and tight pants with velvet stripes along the side seams. An exotic, spicy fragrance that was either magic or an expensive cologne trailed after him, and his shiny earring dangled playfully from his left ear as he moved. I found myself unable to take my eyes off him. Esten certainly knew how to make a statement.

"What?" Esten deadpanned when he noticed me staring.

"N-nothing," I muttered, and tore my gaze away quickly. "Where are we going, and how are we getting there?"

"You know how," Esten said. "I taught you."

"Uh . . . a-all right." I hadn't expected Esten to let me transport again so soon after the disciplinary walk from the field. But I guessed the walk had been less about distrust in my abilities and more about Esten's frustrations regarding the tree accident.

"Don't worry," he said, "we're only going to Boston. And I will even guide you there, so we should be fine as long as you don't try to pull something stupid. Here." He extended his hand to me.

I blinked at Esten's open palm and his long fingers. Was this part of transport magic, or was Esten making fun of me? Several thoughts flashed through my mind, and some of them landed in an unexpectedly warm pool at the bottom of my stomach. Esten did not pull his hand away. Not a joke, then. I swallowed and took it. His fingers felt soft and cool, and despite my nervousness, I found myself wanting to keep holding them. "Um, so, where to exactly?" I asked.

"The corner of Charmed and Cross. Keep that clear in your mind until we get there," Esten said, appearing not at all distracted by my hand in his. I guessed this was normal for magicians traveling together after all. Maybe they all casually held hands while traversing the magic stream.

"All right, let's go," Esten announced, and I hastily reminded myself that I could not afford to get distracted either. The next moment the flow of magic enveloped Esten's hand and then my own, and I followed him into the stream.

It was a different kind of swirl with Esten's magic added to it. It felt deep, blue, and *calm*. Easy to follow, too. All I had to do was take a few steps.

To my relief, when we exited, Esten was still beside me, sadly already pulling his hand away.

I glanced around. "Is this the place?"

It was an intersection of two narrow streets—alleys, really—both of which were dark and quiet. There were very ordinary-looking brick buildings on both sides. Hardly a booming entertainment district.

"You'll see," Esten said mysteriously, and walked toward one of the buildings. There in the corner, tucked away from sight, was a red-lacquered door that Esten pushed open. Pitch darkness and eerie quiet greeted us. An uncomfortable shiver prickled the back of my neck. Were we going into a tomb?

Esten didn't seem concerned, though. "Come on." He beckoned and then went in.

Briefly, I wondered if there was any chance Esten was leading me into a haunted dungeon—perhaps he'd leave me there as some kind of delayed punishment for wrecking the front door. Just in case, I took one last look at the streets of Boston, whispered goodbye to freedom, and followed him inside with trepidation.

As soon as I stepped through the doorway, the darkness pulled away like a thick curtain, and music came roaring in. As did the chatter of the crowd and the clinking of glasses. The place was *packed*.

"Welcome to the Crow Bar!" Esten smirked. "Save for a few people who work here, we magicians are the only ones allowed in. Pretty much every magician in New England hangs out here."

"Oh. So that dark, creepy door was just an illusion?" I asked.

"Yes, to discourage any non-magicians from entering. Why? Were you scared?" Esten quirked a teasing eyebrow.

"Of course not," I said indignantly.

But I was pretty sure he could see right through me. "Follow my lead, then," he said, amused, and headed to the bar. I followed, taking in the view.

Contrary to what it looked like on the outside, the Crow Bar was big. The walls were upholstered in shiny blue brocade fabric. Crow-shaped metal sconces with glowing electric bulbs provided light. In the center was a stage that housed a small band playing a dazzling jazz tune. Many magicians were dancing on the black-and-white-tiled floor. The rest congregated around a handful of tables or mingled at the bar.

Esten found an open spot and leaned over the counter, ordered two drinks called Rookies, and whispered a reminder to me that we were here for business and not pleasure.

Just then a man in a stylish, sage-green suit and a bowler hat noticed us from one of the nearby seats.

"Hey!" he greeted Esten in a pleasant baritone voice. "Fancy seeing *you* again—and at the Crow Bar, of all places!" From the way he said it, it sounded like Esten wasn't a very frequent guest here. That surprised me. I had rather assumed that Esten was the kind of person who went out often.

"Evening, Wyckett," Esten said, approaching the man. I kept close behind. "Master just accepted a new apprentice, and I thought it'd be good to show him around. Kieren, this is Wyckett Foxx from the Rhode Island branch. We worked together on the Andover cleanup yesterday."

This information immediately piqued my interest.

"Very nice to meet you, Wyckett," I said, and extended a hand for a shake.

Wyckett took it and smiled warmly at me. "Welcome to the ranks, Kieren. Do your magic responsibly, and don't hesitate to ask your peers for help should you accidentally turn someone into a spider or send them to Antarctica. There is no shame in learning," he said, mock serious. When my mouth dropped open in shock, he added with an open laugh, "I'm *kidding*, of course!"

There was something incredibly friendly and cordial about Wyckett, and even though I was still contemplating the insanity of accidentally turning someone into a spider, I managed to return the smile.

"Has something like that ever happened?" I asked cautiously.

Esten shrugged. "Accidents do happen on the job." To my ever-increasing horror, he sounded like he meant it.

"Particularly when you go looking for them," Wyckett added, pointing at the guy to his right, who was staring dazedly at someone at the other end of the counter. "I've been trying to get it into this fella's head for the past twenty minutes that it is a *very bad* idea to go hitting on Ellis Divine. Huh, Tokio, my brother?" Wyckett elbowed him lightly.

"What? What?" Tokio said, yanked out of his amorous dreams. He was wearing a maroon silk suit and had an unfocused look in his eyes that probably came from the nearly empty drink in his hands. If I were to guess, Tokio had been trying to boost his courage to approach the object of his affection.

"I've been telling everyone about your unrequited crush on Miss Divine, and the consensus being that it should remain unrequited," Wyckett said jokingly.

Tokio looked sullen. "Do you think so too, Esten?" he asked, slurring slightly. Desperation was evident in his voice.

"Don't take *my* word for it." Esten shook his head. "But ask the last guy who dared to hit on her."

Tokio frowned. "What last guy? What happened to him?"

"That's the point," Wyckett said with an air of mysteriousness. "Nobody has seen him since." He wiggled his eyebrows for emphasis.

The expression on Tokio's face turned comically crestfallen. He downed the remainder of his drink and immediately hailed the bartender to pour him another one, strong enough to drown his sorrows. It arrived at the same time as the drinks Esten had ordered for us.

As Tokio downed his shot, I picked up my glass and tasted the drink. Not unlike its name, the Rookie turned out to be pretty mild but not bad.

"So, who is Ellis Divine?" I asked Esten nervously. Should I be afraid of her?

Esten snorted. "See that lady over there with twins by her side? She is the number-one magician in the country, even stronger than Master Hanska. The twins are her apprentices."

I followed Esten's line of sight. For the number-one magician in the country who seemed to inspire countless rumors, the woman didn't look particularly terrifying, at least on the surface. Ellis was possibly of Middle Eastern descent with olive skin and dark, expressive eyes, and unlike most magicians at the Crow Bar, she wasn't dressed to the nines. It appeared as though she had simply stopped by to have a drink on her way home from work. She wore a simple periwinkle blouse and trousers, and her thick, dark hair was pulled up in a messy bun. There was something proud about her expression though, something almost magnetic. The more I stared at her, the more I was pulled in, as though by strong magic. Yet despite that odd pull, other than the twins, who looked no older than fourteen, nobody had dared to sit down within ten feet of her.

I was about to ask Esten what made Ellis Divine the number-one magician in the country when I noticed he was preoccupied with watching someone near the entrance. It was a girl in a purple pantsuit with a bow tie and a boyish haircut. Just like Ellis, she looked more like she'd just gotten off work than like she was ready for a night of partying.

"Please excuse me, I'll be right back," Esten said quickly, not taking his eyes off her, and made a beeline toward the entrance.

I frowned. Why was he in such a rush? But I didn't have a chance to find out, because Wyckett was pulling me into a conversation. "So, how has magic life been treating you, rookie?" he asked warmly.

"It's... it's been *strange*," I said, surprised that that was the word that came out of my mouth. "I mean, it's a lot to adjust to," I added, hoping my response didn't sound offensive or ungrateful.

To my relief, Wyckett smiled wistfully. "Ain't that the truth. I remember when I manifested at twelve years old—which was a bit later than most magicians, by the way—it felt as if my whole world turned upside down. Had to move from my beloved Jamaica to a place where snow piles up three feet deep. That was something, let me tell you. Can't imagine what it's like to manifest even older. You probably had your sights set on a job already. Maybe even a sweetheart?" Wyckett wiggled his eyebrows.

I flushed. "N-no, nothing like that," I said. There hadn't been a sweetheart, though I'd taken a couple of people to Saturday night dances at the local honky-tonk, and as for a job, the truth was that I'd never felt like I *belonged* anywhere. For as long as I could remember, there had been this gap between the rest of the world and me, like I was a guest in my own life. I'd gone to school and worked on the family farm not because I'd particularly wanted to but because I was the oldest son and that much was expected of me. My father had insisted that I'd take over for him someday, but ironically, that was the one thing I'd known I didn't want. I didn't want to spend my life in the fields, even if I happened to be good at working them. So I'd waited—until graduation, and then until I was done helping with the year's harvest. I hadn't had the heart to leave my family shorthanded. Besides, I'd needed to save up to move to the big city. I was going to try my luck in Richmond or maybe Washington, DC, apply for whatever job would take me, and go from there. I'd been kind of excited for the unknown. I'd just had to break the news to my father. Which was what I was trying to do when all hell had broken loose and I had manifested magic instead.

It had never occurred to me until that day that maybe the reason I hadn't fit in had always been magic. That maybe the Service and the world of magicians was where I'd belonged all along.

Wyckett grinned, unaware of the thoughts that were passing through me. "Well, lucky you, then. All the adventure and discovery are still ahead of you." There was some sadness in the way he said it, though. His gaze flicked to the band on the stage. They had just changed the tune to something up-tempo, and more magicians were getting up to dance.

Even Tokio stumbled to his feet, now significantly more inebriated. "Are you gonna sing for us tonight, Wyckett?" he slurred.

Wyckett shrugged coyly. "If Cinnamon asks, I can never say no."

"Well, she might," Tokio said, apparently trying to point toward the entrance but instead making vague circles in the air with his index finger.

Wyckett glanced back. "*Oh* . . . Cinnamon is finally here," he said. There was a new glow in his eyes, and his mouth stretched into a bashful smile.

"Cinnamon?" I asked, confused, then turned to look at

whoever had just arrived at the Crow Bar. It was Cynn, standing by the entrance in a sumptuous sleeveless gown. It hugged her body and trailed on the floor behind her. She looked mesmerizing. Wyckett and Tokio weren't the only ones noticing.

"Sorry. Gotta go," Wyckett blurted apologetically, and took off.

"Ah, women," Tokio grumbled in apprehension and awe before he stumbled toward the dance floor.

As though men are any less complicated, I thought as I took over Tokio's unoccupied seat.

It occurred to me that the Crow Bar wasn't just a place where magicians went to unwind at the end of a stressful week. This was probably the only place they could openly meet one another. I didn't know who magicians dated or if they did at all. It probably wasn't regular people, considering the shroud of secrecy around the Service and our vastly different lifestyles. But could magicians only date one another? And what about having families? Friends? Could magicians only be friends with other magicians? I hadn't the slightest idea. There was so much about this magic life I didn't know yet.

I looked around, but Esten was nowhere in sight. Disappointment pricked like a thorn in my chest. Esten was probably still with that girl. Maybe he was even in the crowd, dancing. I stared at my Rookie. Perhaps it was time to order something with more of a kick.

"Hey, there." Someone bumped into my shoulder, yanking me out of my thoughts.

"Hi," I said automatically before my eyes zeroed in on a young man with a mop of blond hair and piercing green eyes, confidently taking the stool left unoccupied by Wyckett. He was wearing a tailored, forest-green suit with shiny lapels and a golden pendant in the shape of a dagger.

"You seem new," he said, looking at me appraisingly. "Not from around these parts?"

I shook my head. "I *am* from here. Just new. Manifested recently."

"Oh. That's a rarity," he intoned. "Who are you apprenticing with?"

"With Master Hanska," I replied, and watched the guy's expression change. For a brief moment, it was a confused kind of disbelief, but then his eyes lit up with sudden interest.

"Well, you must be pretty . . . *special*, then," he said, a grin spreading over his face. "I'm Spiht, by the way. What is your name?"

I wasn't sure what Spiht meant by *special*, but I offered my name politely. "Kieren. Nice to meet you."

Spiht propped himself on one elbow, leaning into my space a little. He smelled faintly of fresh pine needles. "So, have you been enjoying your studies with Master Hanska?"

My body went stiff at the question. Esten had warned me to keep Master's disappearance a secret, but I couldn't outright lie about it either, especially to someone more knowledgeable about magical affairs than my rookie self.

"It's been going well," I said, feeling uneasy. "But I have only just manifested; I'm still learning about everything. Do you happen to know Master?" I tried to switch the talk away from myself.

There was a strained expression on Spiht's face, but he quickly covered it with a smile. "Who *doesn't* know him? He's only the second most powerful magician in the United States."

My eyes widened, but I tried to hide my reaction. I didn't know that Master ranked *that* high. Although the simple fact that Esten had compared him to Ellis Divine and that everyone addressed him as *Master* Hanska when most magicians went by only their first names should have given me a hint.

"Well, Kieren, how about I buy you another drink? To celebrate our marvelous meeting," Spiht said, tipping his head and smirking invitingly. "That one looks *boooring,* don't you think?"

I didn't think my drink was boring; it was merely light because Esten had insisted we were here for work. Except now he was nowhere to be found. What a humbug. Had he brought me here just to dump me again so he could go gallivant with that girl?

"Sure," I said, feeling properly abandoned. "Why not?"

Spiht's smile widened. "Hey, girl! You!" He pointed at one of the bartenders. "My friend here needs a better drink—"

"No, he doesn't," Esten said, cutting Spiht off curtly.

I looked over my shoulder to find Esten staring at us with narrowed eyes and folded arms. Finally decided to show up, huh?

Spiht's face soured. "Ah. Should have expected you'd be here too, if only to spoil all the fun," he said disdainfully.

Esten didn't even flinch. "The pleasure is all yours when it comes to spoiling."

Spiht snorted and removed his elbow from the bar. "Too bad, Kieren, that our time is being cut short by the killjoy in chief himself. Let's see each other again soon, shall we?" He grinned crookedly, emptied his drink in one gulp, slammed the glass on the counter, and got up.

Esten continued eyeing him like a hawk until Spiht slipped into the crowd to join a magician in a bright vermilion coat.

"Have you no discernment when it comes to people?" Esten scoffed and sat down, pushing away Spiht's empty glass with contempt. He was visibly annoyed by the simple fact that he had to use the same chair Spiht had just sat in.

"Why? What's wrong with him?" I asked.

Esten snorted contemptuously. "A great many things. It

will ruin the rest of my evening if I start recounting them. Suffice it to say that he is a gifted magician who muddles it all by obsessing over power. Did you see that pendant he was wearing?" Esten must have been referring to the golden dagger around Spiht's neck. "He believes that trinket enhances his magic. How tacky! There are no shortcuts to getting power. He should know better by now! That's probably why Master rejected him."

I tilted my head, puzzled. "Master rejected Spiht?"

Esten raised his chin proudly. "Yes. I suppose you wouldn't know this. A while back, Spiht lobbied to apprentice with Master Hanska, but Master promptly shot him down."

"Oh," I said as understanding finally dawned on me. It made sense now why Spiht was so interested in Master Hanska, and why he and Esten had practically blown up in each other's faces. It was plain old jealousy. Esten was extremely protective of his position as Master Hanska's only apprentice, while Spiht wanted to learn from the second-strongest magician in the country and had been denied that opportunity.

Where did all of this leave me though? No wonder Esten hated my being in the house. Master Hanska hadn't even chosen me. I'd probably ended up under Esten's feet because of some clerical error at the Assembly. What would happen to me when they realized they'd made a mistake? Would Esten treat me how he treated Spiht? My spirits began to sink.

Just then, the band changed the tune again, the lights dimmed, and to my surprise, Wyckett's velvety baritone filled the room. The Crow Bar hushed.

Wyckett stood in the middle of the stage holding a microphone with the silvery spotlight directed at him. He looked so natural up there. For a moment I forgot to breathe. I couldn't believe that Wyckett had that kind of talent in him. His voice was melodious and smooth, and he crooned about love in a way that instantly commanded the attention of the entire establishment. Many of the magicians got up and started slow dancing in couples.

Esten leaned closer to my ear. "Ah, so that's where Wyckett went," he said knowingly.

I nodded, still watching Wyckett but now acutely aware of Esten's proximity. I could smell his spicy magical cologne even surrounded by all these people. "Cynn showed up and he wanted to talk to her. Are they . . . you know . . ."

"Dating?" Esten finished my question.

"Yeah."

Esten hummed. "It's, uh . . . complicated between those two." When I turned and frowned confusedly at him, he added, "Cynn is complicating it, at least as far as I know. They would be dating if it were up to Wyckett."

I couldn't imagine what was so complicated about Cynn. She'd been so lovely and welcoming when we'd met. She and Wyckett seemed like they'd be a great couple, now that I was picturing them together. And who on earth wouldn't fall in love with a man who sang the way Wyckett did? He would definitely be famous if he hadn't manifested and could pursue singing as a career. It made sense now, the longing in his eyes when he'd looked at the stage earlier. I glanced around, trying to see if Cynn was watching him, but I couldn't find her in the crowd.

"So where have *you* been?" I asked Esten, trying not to sound too sad or accusatory that he'd ditched me again. "You've been gone for *a while* . . ."

"Had to catch up with a friend in private," Esten replied simply.

"About what?" I prodded, not sure if I really wished to know about the nature of Esten's *friendship*.

But Esten only shook his head—"Not here, Kieren"—and leaned his elbow against the bar, seemingly enjoying the performance.

I watched the silvery spotlight reflect in Esten's eyes for a moment, and despite my usual self-preservation, secretly wished that I could ask him to join me on the dance floor.

I never found the guts to bring it up, though.

We stayed until Wyckett finished singing and then transported back home.

CHAPTER 12
KIEREN

The following morning, I was surprised to discover that Esten hadn't ditched me yet. Instead I found him sitting at the kitchen table, reading the latest edition of the *Boston Times*. The room smelled like a mixture of strong coffee and fresh ink from the paper.

"Just look at this," Esten said, frowning and pointing at the front-page article. MYSTERIOUS METAL GIANT SPOTTED IN NEW ENGLAND SKIES, the headline read. "It says that according to a secret memo obtained by the *Times* reporters, the government is about to finish testing a new kind of airship. It's rumored to be made entirely of steel and is powerful enough to cross the Atlantic in record time with no refueling stops. What are those idiots *thinking*? At this point, they are just goading Europe and the rest of the world!"

I couldn't tell if Esten was referring to the pompous tone of the article or the fact that the government was secretly developing a new airship, possibly to use in war. Neither of those sounded like good news to me.

I opted out of Esten's bitter coffee in favor of sweet apple cider, which Esten heated for me with a flick of the wrist. He didn't even have to look up from the paper. I was starting to get jealous of that wrist . . . maybe I could convince him to teach me the trick soon. Meanwhile I made myself a cheese sandwich and offered one to Esten. I would have made one for Oi as well, but he had yet to make an appearance. Esten had warned me that Oi came and went whenever he pleased, so this was probably quite normal.

"So as I mentioned," Esten said, finally putting down the newspaper and taking his sandwich, "I did some catching up with a friend who works as Probos's assistant."

My eyes widened. So Esten had gone to the Crow Bar for work after all.

I took a bite of my sandwich as Esten continued, "I wanted to ask Cash about tensions with Europe, but she was reluctant to discuss it when I saw her in Probos's office the other day. I was hoping she'd be a little more open if we could talk in private, and I was right. She had some concerning things to say."

"Like what?" I frowned.

"Like, it hasn't made the news yet, but apparently the president and Senate Majority Leader Harkwood don't see eye to eye in terms of our military involvement in Europe. Harkwood has always been hawkish, but his stance sends a different message to the world in times of conflict. So the Council and the senior magicians fear that an all-out war will break out soon. Magicians may be sworn to neutrality, but that's never been tested in a large-scale conflict. Europeans think we might break our promises, and many Americans are starting to distrust them because of the sludge outbreaks."

"Why?" I asked. "Aren't the sludge outbreaks a mystery that no one has figured out yet?"

"They are. But so far the outbreaks have occurred only in

our country and nowhere else in the world. In the absence of a reasonable explanation, some suspect foul play. I tried to find out if Cash knew more about the sludge than what was written in the Assembly's official announcement, but nobody has made much progress on that front. And now this damn article comes out." Esten threw a pointed look at the *Times*. "It doesn't help that our government is openly flaunting large-capacity airships. The only thing stopping the escalation is that our airships are still not big or fast enough to reach Europe and pose an imminent threat. But if the reports about the Metal Giant are true, everything is about to change."

I put down my sandwich; the last bite I'd taken suddenly became difficult to swallow. "Weren't airships originally built for civilian transport?" I asked.

"They were. But apparently that's not enough for some," Esten replied gravely. "Anyway, fears are running high. Cash said that Probos is doing everything he can to reassure European magicians that we are still neutral, but it's getting harder. Even some of the Council members on our side started demanding a formal resolution so we could defend ourselves should the peace negotiations fail. I wonder if that's why Kavender stormed out of Probos's office."

"Kavender? Who's that?" I asked.

"He's one of the Council magicians and the former chief of the Bureau of Enforcement. Cash said that a while back he tried to pressure Probos to loosen restrictions on magic and curb the severity of punishments for violators. They haven't been on good terms since."

I frowned. "Isn't that kind of the opposite of what's required of an enforcer?"

Esten snorted. "Hence the *former* chief. The Council voted him out about a month ago, but he did have support from several members."

"I really don't understand why some people seem so eager to have a war."

Esten stared at the table. "Me neither. But I think that's what Master Hanska might have been investigating."

"What makes you say that?" I asked.

Esten took a sip of his bitter coffee and then reluctantly confessed, "I told you I've been trying to retrace Master's steps. The other day I snuck into the metal forge in Grafton."

My jaw nearly dropped. "What do you mean, *snuck in*?"

Esten briefly looked up at the ceiling, then sighed. "I impersonated one of the steelworkers and went to spy on whatever shady business they were doing there."

I could not wrap my mind around the idea of the very proper and put-together Esten doing something this illegal, not to mention sullying his beautiful self with metal dust and soot. And he had the nerve to accuse *me* of being a spy? "O-kay..." I said dubiously.

"Well, based on what I saw at the forge, I'm afraid this article might be true. I found blueprints for a giant airship made from steel, just like they reported," Esten said. "Here's the conundrum, though. The *Times* said that the government is almost finished testing it, that they have eyewitnesses. But how could that be? You should have seen the thing they're building. It is *huge*, three times bigger than anything currently in the skies. Nobody in the world has the technology to make something like that fly. So how could they make it work in such record time?" Esten sounded genuinely vexed.

"You don't think... magic is somehow involved, do you?" I asked carefully.

Esten considered his coffee cup for a long moment. "The idea is preposterous, but... why would Master Hanska even be investigating this if it didn't have anything to do with magic? Government affairs aren't our concern. That's not what we do.

However, if magic is involved, that brings us to an even bigger mystery. You simply can't hide the amount of magic it would take to create and test something like this. Especially if it's thorned magic, which I suspect it is."

"I'm not following," I said. "What do you mean by *hiding* magic? Would it leave a residue?"

"Yes. But it's not just that." Esten tapped on the table as though debating something with himself, then added, "Come on. This will make for a good second lesson."

∽

I followed Esten to the field—he graciously allowed me to transport myself there via magic.

We sat down in the same spot under the maple tree. Thanks to the cloudy skies and high winds, today felt like a true October day, and I instantly regretted not bringing a jacket.

I shivered a little as Esten spoke. "Remember how I told you that every act of magic has consequences?"

I nodded.

"That holds true for both feathered and thorned magic. When large amounts of magic are performed, it leaves traces that can be felt by other magicians to varying degrees. Some of the residue gets absorbed by our environment. While feathered magic can be left to run unrestricted most of the time, thorned magic cannot. Remember how thorned magic always rebounds?" I nodded again. "If the rebound is great enough, it can kill the magician and cause severe damage to everything around them. Unless you learn to manage it, that is. Have you ever heard of the well concept?"

I shuffled through my memory, but nothing came to mind. "No."

"Stands to reason, what with your front door adventures," Esten huffed. "Anyhow, the well is a method of harnessing the rebound from magic in such a way that it won't hurt the magician. They say someone with a strong thorned affinity invented it many centuries ago. You create a space that will catch and store the rebound so it doesn't come back and hit your body. That space is your well."

I blinked in astonishment. "Is such a thing even possible?"

"Yes," Esten said. "Every thorned magician has one. Your survival depends on it."

"But how does it work exactly? Do I have to dig one in the ground or something?"

Esten snorted a laugh. "Of course not. You create one with magic. I've heard it's rather intuitive."

"You've *heard*? Do you not have one?"

"I have no need for it," Esten replied simply. "I'm not capable of performing thorned magic at a level that might kill me, and my body can absorb smaller things without much damage."

"Huh . . ." I said, stumped. I couldn't have been more wrong about Esten's magic. All those times when I'd thought he was going to curse me or blast me to pieces to teach me a lesson, I hadn't realized none of that was even possible for a magician like him. Instead, this whole time *I*'d been a menace to myself without even knowing it.

"I'm not complaining," I said after some pondering, "but is this actually fair? You said all magic has consequences, and doesn't it feel like we're cheating a little by using a well?"

Esten's eyes widened briefly, and there was some strange emotion in their silver glimmer that I couldn't immediately place. "It's not cheating," he said, choosing his words carefully. "The well is . . . it's *temporary*, Kieren."

I tried to ask what that meant, but words failed me on my first few attempts. "H-how?" I finally managed.

Esten sighed and ran his gentle fingers along the yellowing grass. He averted his gaze when he replied, "It's called the well for a reason, Kieren. You fill it up when you perform magic, and one day when there is no more space in it, it ruptures, and being hit with all that rebound magic at once kills you. That's why it's not fundamentally unfair or unbalanced. No one can wreak havoc with copious amounts of thorned magic and not eventually suffer the consequences. The well simply delays the inevitable and keeps you from having to heal broken bones and organs in the meantime. But the end result is the same."

I stared at Esten numbly. Despite what I had frivolously thought while trying to impress Esten with my reckless tree climbing stunt, magic didn't make us all-powerful or invincible—or even special, when it came to matters of life and death. And most of all, it was *never* free.

"So how do I use the well?" I asked, trying to shake the depressing thoughts off.

"From what I understand," Esten said, sounding relieved to move on from the philosophical part of it, "first you create an intention by imagining a space and strongly wishing for it to become your well. Then when the rebound comes, you give the well direction by sending the rebound into that space. Don't worry about imagining any particular place for your well. You can make it under this maple tree if you want. The rebound is not physically stored there. Your magic keeps it; you're just picturing an image to make it less abstract."

"Got it," I said thoughtfully. I didn't want to imagine my well under this beautiful maple though. I'd already wronged it by falling and snapping some of its branches. Instead I decided to imagine it under the family barn where I'd manifested while arguing with my father about my future—or whatever was left of it, that is. It seemed like a fitting place.

"If you've decided, then let's practice," Esten said. "Let's do something small that won't hurt you if you miss the mark and won't overwhelm your well if you succeed. How about you try breaking some of these?" Esten pointed at the long stalks of grass beside him. "Snap them in half with magic and put the rebound into your well."

A little anxiously, I agreed.

I imagined the grass stalks wouldn't be hard to cut, as I had easily exploded the door's metal hinges, which were much thicker. It was how dangerously close Esten was sitting to them that worried me. Knowing my propensity to overdo things, I had to concentrate and not accidentally hurt him.

I set my eyes on one of the stalks a couple of feet to Esten's right and imagined snapping it in the middle. I made a flicking gesture with my index finger. *Hoosh.* A small wind rose and collided with the top part of the stalk. It broke off and fell—and with it, all the grass within a five-foot radius. So much for not overdoing it. Instantly I felt a push of magic and a prickle in my index finger. When I looked down, a tiny red bead of blood was already gathering on its tip. Curses! I was too distracted and forgot to capture the rebound.

Esten eyed the patch of broken grass skeptically. "I didn't mean mow the lawn with your magic, but I suppose that's to be expected with you. So, did it work?"

"Mmm, not yet," I muttered guiltily. At least now that I knew what the rebound felt like, I could watch for it this time around.

I concentrated once again and made the same motion with my index finger, directing it at a patch farther away from Esten so I wouldn't worry about how many plants broke this time. When roughly ten square feet of grass stalks snapped in half simultaneously, I was ready for it. Once I felt the rebound magic head back toward me, I sent it packing to the ruins of the old barn with all my might. *Hooooosh,* the magic went.

I must have had some funny expression on my face because Esten's eyebrows arched in amusement.

"Well, it's a lot of mental juggling, just so you know," I pointed out indignantly. If Esten only knew how much effort it took to not mow down half this field and him together with it.

Esten tipped his head and grinned like he was pleased. "Finally you're starting to learn something. Welcome to the life of a magician."

CHAPTER 13
KIEREN

After more practice with the grass, I began to understand what troubled Esten about the airship investigation. Unleashing large quantities of thorned magic meant expediting the magician's own demise. Why would anyone risk their life just to make heavy airships fly, not to mention breaking neutrality and possibly pushing the country to the brink of war? It simply didn't make sense. And yet the existence of at least one Metal Giant had now been confirmed by the *Boston Times*, and Master Hanska was still gone without a trace, and the sludge was still as unexplained a phenomenon as ever.

It seemed that the only solution was to find the Metal Giant and catch the perpetrators that way. Maybe that could even give us clues as to Master Hanska's whereabouts. The problem, of course, was actually locating the ship. The *Times* reporters had spotted it somewhere in New England, but the region was huge, and the airship was hidden on the ground most of the time.

As I pondered these things with a mouthful of potato pie

that evening, a letter appeared on the dining table. Its envelope glowed ominously red, denoting an urgent communication. It was addressed to Esten and bore the seal of Probos himself.

Esten tore the letter open with nervous fingers and instantly frowned at the contents. "A magician named Katerina Stag went missing three days ago," he said. Probos believes that it's relevant to the investigation. He says that Stag's last reported location was near Sutton Pond, just north of Andover."

My stomach flipped. "Wasn't that the town hit by sludge just a few days ago?"

Esten nodded. He reread the message, unease evident on his face. I knew what he was thinking. The letter didn't contain any news about Master Hanska, but the fact that another magician had inexplicably gone missing didn't spell good news for Master's prolonged absence.

Esten folded his napkin and got up from his chair, his face determined.

I stood up too. "We're going there, right?" I said.

Esten's critical gaze focused on me. *"We?"*

My heart plummeted. Even after all these lessons and going to the Crow Bar together, he was going to ditch me again, wasn't he? "Oh, come on," I said. "Don't leave me behind. You know I'm not a spy."

Esten's frown deepened. "It's not that. You're not ready, Kieren. You barely know anything about magic."

I gripped the edge of the table, frustration boiling in me. While it wasn't my fault that I was new, it was hard to argue with Esten's logic.

But I wasn't ready to give up.

"You're right," I admitted. "I know very little. But we're investigating this in secret, so we'll keep a low profile, right? In which case my abilities don't matter. I'll keep out of your way and not try anything dangerous. I know Master Hanska means a lot to you, but solving this and finding him is important to me too." Esten's inky eyelashes flickered a little at the unexpected turn of the conversation. Earnestly, I added, "I can't just sit in this house doing nothing. I really *want* to help. I promise I'll transport myself out of there at the first sign of trouble."

Esten gave me a long, hard look. Finally he sighed. "I'm going to hold you to your promise, just so we're clear."

I barely managed to restrain the grin bursting across my face. "We're clear," I said, and ran to my room to fetch a jacket.

∽

Esten offered his hand for guidance again as we transported ourselves to Sutton Pond. According to the assignment report that had come with the letter, the area had had some heavy rain early in the week. The Merrimack River had overflowed, and Sutton Pond was connected to it. Katerina Stag had been assigned to help redirect the water before it started flooding nearby farms and apple orchards. It wasn't a high-priority job, and at least on the surface, it didn't seem like a particularly hazardous one.

We exited the magic stream into what looked like a pitch-black void save for one streak of pale moonlight that shimmered on the calm water. Esten let go of my hand, and the next moment a cold blue flame emanated from his palm, casting enough light to illuminate about twenty feet around us. I couldn't help feeling a tiny pang of envy at Esten's precise transportation magic. We had landed on the soft grass at the *very* edge of the pond. If I'd been allowed to navigate this far on my own, I had a sneaking suspicion I would have dunked us both into the water.

Esten stared at the pond's dark surface, contemplating.

The light from his palm washed over his features, making his profile look gorgeously ghostly.

"I just don't understand it," he pronounced after a moment. "How is this connected to anything? This looks like a routine job."

"Well, why does Probos think it's connected? He wouldn't have sent you the letter without a reason."

"Because it happened near Andover, I think, and because magicians don't go missing every day," Esten replied. "I've met Katerina Stag before. She seemed like a decent girl, not one to stir up trouble or become a deserter. Of course, she could have changed, but that still doesn't explain why she would go missing *here* of all places."

"What is around this pond?" I asked.

"Andover is to the south; the east is all apple orchards." Esten shrugged, sounding almost bored. "The Cochichewick River connects the pond to the Merrimack in the west, and to the north is just undeveloped land. Some forest, some wild fields, but the nearest houses are miles away."

"Maybe we should check out what's up north, then," I suggested. "Since we know what lies in all other directions."

Esten didn't seem too excited to blindly search miles of fields and forests, but there was nothing else either of us could think to do at the moment, and the night was young.

Esten let me transport myself to the northern side of the pond unguided for practice. I was delighted that I managed to reappear on solid ground instead of in the middle of the pond, and since that also landed me in Esten's good graces, I decided to take advantage of the situation.

"Is there a chance you can teach me to make a light as well?" I asked self-consciously, pointing at Esten's blue flame as we walked upstream along the Cochichewick River.

Esten's eyebrows quirked at the unexpected question, but

he didn't decline. "Why not?" he said. "This could be useful, and it's not difficult. Put your hand out and wish as clearly as you can for there to be a flame. Make sure to only think of it as a source of light. Light is feathered magic, but hot burning fire is not. It might scorch your hand unless you rebound it into your well."

"Got it." I nodded, grateful for Esten's attention to detail. I didn't want to get scorched, and I didn't want to use my well for something so trivial either, so knowing the distinction was useful.

I stuck my hand out and wished for there to be light. I thought of the bright rays of the sun, imagining how they looked as they peeked through windowpanes—warm but not hot—and felt the magic swirl around me.

In an instant, a foot-wide pillar of light shot out of my palm all the way to the sky. It illuminated half the field and was so intensely bright that it looked solid.

"Highest heavens!" Esten yelled in a panic. He quickly shut his eyes and turned away, trying to avoid being blinded. My free arm shot up to cover my eyes as well. But there was nowhere for me to hide from my own magic. "I didn't *specifically* mention it," Esten chided, "but I thought it was self-explanatory that we are trying to keep a low profile, so don't go blasting an *inferno* just because you can!"

"Sorry, I'm sorry!" I yelled, but I wasn't sure how to make the pillar dimmer. "I probably shouldn't have imagined the sun."

"You think?" Esten deadpanned. "Think of clouds or something, or nightfall. Just make it go away, please!"

I scrambled to imagine something useful to diminish the light. Squinting, I dared a peek at it, but it was still too bright, so I lowered my gaze. That's when something peculiar caught my sight.

"Wait, Esten. What's that over there?" I asked, only to earn a derisive laugh from him.

"How should I know? In case you missed it, you've blinded us both."

I imagined magic clouds then, thunderous and thick, like they'd look right before a storm. To my relief, it finally worked, and the pillar transformed into a ball of light that glowed faintly in my palm. After a few agonizing seconds, Esten and I could look at each other again, though bright white dots still danced in my field of vision.

"What were you talking about just now?" Esten asked, rubbing the bridge of his nose and blinking.

"Oh." I pointed at the ground to my left. The grass around us looked a little strange, like it was recovering from something heavy being dragged over it. Now that Esten's and my combined lights illuminated a bigger area, the contrast was visible even without my pillar of light.

Esten narrowed his eyes and knelt to examine it closely. "Something big went through here, and someone used magic to cover up the tracks," he announced after a moment.

"How do you know they used magic?" I asked.

"If you focus your attention, you will feel it too—traces of it still linger around here. Plus, look at this grass. As I mentioned, fixing living things is difficult, and someone did a sloppy job of it."

I didn't feel the magic residue, but I saw what he meant about the grass. It stuck out at odd angles like broken bones that weren't set right, but someone had forced it to keep healing and growing anyway. The illusion would have worked from a distance, but up close the grass was uncomfortable to look at.

We followed the peculiar grass and found that it stretched

north from the river. The track was so wide that it was a wonder we hadn't noticed it right away.

Eventually it led through a gap in the line of trees—some of which also looked hastily fixed—and into an open field behind them. One glance at the area made it immediately apparent that it had recently been used to store something big. The grass here was trampled all over. There were tire marks from multiple cars. Whoever had covered up the tracks must have hoped that the trees would hide the evidence in the field.

"What do you think happened here?" I asked.

"Can this be *it*? For once, your brutish and reckless display of magic was useful!" Esten declared, turning to face me. As always, he skillfully skirted the line between giving a backhanded compliment and outright berating me. I was starting to get used to it. Esten continued, "A few days ago, someone needed a way to inconspicuously transport something large and heavy to a secluded field where no one would come looking for it. That something was so large, in fact, that they couldn't easily move it by land; that's why they had to use water. Most likely, the cargo came on a ship down the Merrimack River to the Cochichewick River until they unloaded it here and had no other option but to drag it over land. Lucky for them, it was a short distance. Now, what is big and needs an open field?" he asked triumphantly.

I hesitated, lest Esten chastise me again.

"Come on," Esten urged. "You were just on one a week ago."

"You can't possibly mean that we've stumbled on the Metal Giant testing site by accident," I said skeptically.

"Well, according to the *Boston Times* and what I witnessed at the forge—which, by the way, is located near the Merrimack River—the timing would just be perfect. I don't know how Stag figures into this mystery yet, but if we're right about the

Metal Giant being tested here, then the sludge outbreak that happened on the night of Stag's disappearance might also be connected somehow."

For the sake of argument, I tried to think of other things that were big enough to require a secret field, but nothing else came to mind. The timing of these events couldn't have been a mere coincidence either, but we needed more evidence. I was about to ask if Esten felt any more traces of magic around when suddenly—

"What are you two doing here?" a raspy voice demanded. Both Esten and I jumped.

Behind us, some fifty feet away, stood another magician with a reddish flickering flame in his hand. He was a stocky man with spiky red hair, wearing a long, vermilion trench coat. There was something distantly familiar about him, but I couldn't place him.

Esten's body went tense. "We could ask you the same thing, Nogg," he parried, flicking his chin up.

This caught me by surprise. Esten clearly knew this magician, yet made no pretense of politeness.

Nogg sneered, and in the ominously red glow of his flame, he looked like he was daring Esten. "I've no desire to explain my business to a pair of yapping puppies who got lost in the fields. Shall I show you the way out?"

Well, that was unnecessarily rude. I didn't even know the guy. Why was he insulting me? I opened my mouth to respond, but Esten's free hand shot to the side as if to stop me. Whatever the source of this confrontation was, I was missing something important.

To my amazement, Esten bluffed, his tone still laced with acid. "We'll see ourselves out when we're done with our official duties. A pond flooded not far from here. We're making sure the damage has been properly contained."

Nogg narrowed his eyes at us suspiciously. "A pond?" he rasped. What Esten said wasn't entirely untrue, but that didn't mean Nogg was buying it.

"Yes, Sutton Pond," Esten said curtly. "The Assembly received flooding complaints from local farmers."

"And let me guess—you hurried here like obedient dogs?"

Esten's mouth twitched. Something cold and furious stirred in him. "If you have complaints, I suggest you take them to Probos. Maybe *this time* it'll work out for you."

Nogg's entire face contorted in a furious grimace. The red flame shook in his palm, then doubled in size, sending a few errant sparks scattering into the night. Esten's whole body tensed beside me, his free hand ready at his side. I didn't know what to think. What was even happening? Were Esten and Nogg going to *fight*?

Another moment passed, charged and dangerous, but then the pressure suddenly dropped. Instead of responding, Nogg smirked. "Well, we shall see how long a puppy can keep yapping without its master," he hissed. Then, before either of us could respond, Nogg took a step backward and disappeared into the magic stream.

Esten's blue flame shook, and all color drained from his face.

"Esten?" I said, worried and puzzled by the whole exchange.

"We're going home. Now." Esten pushed out one breath and, just like that, disappeared into the stream as well.

CHAPTER 14
KIEREN

I was so dizzy from trying to keep up with Esten's sudden transport magic that I lost my concentration and nearly knocked down my favorite burgundy armchair as I arrived back at Master Hanska's residence.

By the time I got my bearings, Esten was pacing around the foyer, muttering to himself. "He knows Master is missing. He couldn't stop himself from taunting me about it!"

I watched him go round and round, my own uneasiness growing with his every step. I'd never seen him this rattled.

"How could he know though?" Esten continued. "Is he involved in Master's disappearance? But Master is strong; that scumbag couldn't have done anything to him. He couldn't—"

"Esten, wait," I said, trying to stop him from spiraling. "I don't understand what just happened. Who was that guy?"

Esten finally stopped pacing, but there was a wild look on his face as he tried to pull his thoughts into coherence. "That was Nogg. About a year ago, he petitioned the Council that senior magicians like himself shouldn't have to deal with routine Service assignments and small stuff. He said we aren't dogs non-magicians can keep on a leash and use whenever they feel like it, and it was time to revise our Service agreement. Imagine the nerve! Of course, Master Hanska got into an open debate with him and completely obliterated Nogg in front of the Council. Since then, he's been openly hostile with Master and me."

I nodded. The confrontation between the two was starting to make sense now.

"Is that why you lied to him? Why didn't you mention Stag?" I asked.

"I had to think of something on the spot," Esten said. "That information hasn't been released to the public. I didn't want to let Nogg know that we know Stag is missing in case he is responsible."

"Okay," I said, trying to keep calm. "It certainly *is* strange that we stumbled on Nogg at the potential testing site and last known whereabouts of magician Stag, but is there any chance that Nogg's mention of Master Hanska could have been a simple misunderstanding? Maybe he was just trying to get a rise out of you. You guys don't get along, but that doesn't mean Nogg did something to harm Master Hanska, right?"

Esten blinked as though he'd just realized something. He shook his head and gave me a pitying look. "Kieren, it wasn't to get a rise out of me. The flame Nogg used wasn't feathered magic."

My insides dropped. "What?"

"He didn't openly threaten us, but he was ready to if we made a wrong move," Esten said.

The flame in Nogg's hand had looked a bit strange, but I'd had absolutely no idea it was thorned. We'd been in danger, and I hadn't even noticed. "Why would he be willing to use thorned magic on us?" I whispered, stunned.

"That's what I'd like to know!" Esten strode to the nearest

armchair and fell into it, holding his head in his hands. "I have to find that dirtbag and get the truth out of him as soon as possible," he said, despair rising in his voice again. "How could I have gotten carried away like that? What if Master is trapped somewhere? What if he's hurt? What if he's already—"

"Esten," I said softly. It was painful to see him like this, his hopeless hunched figure and shaking shoulders. I wanted to touch him, make him feel better, do something. "Maybe we can go back to the Crow Bar or the field and look for more clues," I suggested.

But Esten cut me off. "*We* are not going anywhere, Kieren." His angry eyes bored into mine. "I'm done chaperoning you. I've wasted enough precious time here when I should have been concentrating on looking for Master Hanska."

I inhaled sharply. Esten's words *stung* right in the soft spot under my rib cage. There was no thorned magic in them, but they felt like thorns anyway. Esten was justifiably upset, but did he honestly think that teaching me was a waste of his time? What about eating the pies I'd baked or going out together? And here I thought we were starting to get along, that Esten *wanted* me around, that I was becoming a part of this new magical life.

I stood there before him and didn't know what to say.

A few moments later, Esten seemed to get hold of his emotions. "I'm going to report this to Probos immediately," he said grimly. "I'll need his help if I want to find that scum." Despite it being late evening, he pushed himself out of the armchair and stepped into the magic stream without saying another word or even looking at me.

The next morning, I ate breakfast alone.

CHAPTER 15
KIEREN

Following the encounter with Nogg, the atmosphere in the house turned gloomy. Esten was somewhere investigating without me, and I wondered if this was the end of our magic lessons. The thought left me feeling dejected. Was I really so useless that he wouldn't consider my help? Even Oi was nowhere to be found.

Alone and sulking, I desperately needed a distraction. I cut up some fresh apples and pears for a snack, set up camp in the library, and plunged myself into reading about magic and the Founders.

It turned out Nogg wasn't the first magician to dispute the terms of the Service. The debate was age-old. Back in the day, when the institution was first established, magicians were often tasked with a wide variety of assignments, from trivial things like searching for lost sheep to significant magical undertakings like digging tunnels through rock formations or diverting rivers so the government could build roads and bridges.

As society and technology grew, most of the menial tasks

were replaced with large construction projects and disaster management. The unspoken rule seemed to be that if something could be easily done without magic, it was up to non-magical citizens to take care of it. But if it involved dangerous labor, magicians were called in.

The Council occasionally debated the terms of the Service and was in charge of renegotiating them with the non-magical government.

Initially the Council consisted of only the Founders, but as time went on, it was expanded to include a varying number of senior magicians, who in turn elected the head of the Council as their leader and spokesperson.

Based on what Esten had told me, both Master Hanska and Probos were currently on the Council. Kavender must have also been a part of it at some point, as he had been the chief of the Bureau of Enforcement. Hadn't Esten mentioned that he had some supporters among the Council members as well? After what Nogg had said last night, I wouldn't be surprised to find him in the ranks of Kavender's admirers. But merely raising questions about the Service didn't automatically prove that Nogg was evil or turn him into Master Hanska's kidnapper. Even Cynn had confessed to me that she felt overworked. Maybe their complaints were justified.

I ate a slice of pear, wishing I could talk to Cynn again—or any magician, really. I had a million questions about magic and no one to ask. I didn't even know where anyone lived, so using transport magic to meet up with them was out of the question. I sank into the cushy armchair and sighed. Was a magician's life always this lonely? Or was it just me?

A munching sound interrupted my thoughts. It was coming from where the fruit plate sat on the table. By the time I turned to look, both the rest of the fruit and the plate had been gobbled up, and a certain spirit doll sat in their place.

"Oi! Where have you been? I was afraid you'd left for good!" I exclaimed. That was a bit of an overstatement, but I had missed Oi and was beside myself with joy that he'd finally come back.

No left. Oi had business, Oi said, still munching. *What Kieren do?*

Since Oi wasn't inclined to give any details about his travels, I told him everything that had happened in the past few days and struck another deal with him.

Oi wasn't knowledgeable about the inner workings of the Council, so I couldn't ask him about that, but in exchange for two sweet potato pies, he agreed to teach me more about magic. This was practically a bargain. I enthusiastically accepted the terms.

~

"How can I sense magic?" I asked once Oi and I had returned to the familiar spot under the maple tree. Even without Esten, it felt right to have the lesson there.

No understand question, Oi said. The feathers around his head were fluttering gently in the breeze. *Everything magic.*

That . . . was confusing. "Do you mean everything *has* magic?" I asked.

Yes, Oi purred. *Everything. Everywhere. World without magic cannot be. Dead.*

"Huh." I tipped my head, puzzled. I'd never heard anyone refer to magic as vital. "But I always thought only magicians had magic," I said.

Oi gazed at me with those black painted eyes as though I'd just said something incredibly stupid. *Only?*

"Oh." Instant embarrassment washed over my cheeks. I

smiled sheepishly. "I guess not just magicians—you have magic too."

Not only Oi, Oi corrected me again. *Tree has. Earth has. Ant has. Pie has. Everything has. Kieren needs listen. Ask right question.*

I pursed my lips, pondering. Oi's teaching style was quite different from Esten's, as were Oi's views on magic, apparently. It was a good thing I was learning different perspectives, but it seemed I'd have to ask more precise questions with Oi.

"I guess," I ventured carefully, "what I meant is, how can I sense if magic was performed somewhere, like what Esten felt near the pond? He could even tell whether it was feathered or thorned."

Mmm . . . magic everything, Oi repeated slowly, and my shoulders dropped in mild frustration. But then Oi added, *But different things, different magic. Big small. Magicians add magic. Move magic. New. More.*

I perked up. "So you're saying that even though everything has some magic, magicians are the ones who can move it around? Which means that when someone performs magic on, let's say, a field, it ends up with more magic than it should have?"

Yes, Oi replied with satisfaction. *More and different. Field has magic but cannot move magic.*

A bubbly sense of discovery rose in my chest. Deciphering Oi's answers was starting to become rather fun now that I'd gotten the hang of it. "How do I know how much magic there should be and what kind is normal?" I asked.

Kieren new. Listen—soon you know, Oi said.

By that Oi seemingly meant that I needed to get more experience, which I could definitely work on acquiring.

"Okay, then what about the differences in how feathered and thorned magic feel?" I asked eagerly.

Oi replied, *Wind—cold warm—you feel. Trees—green orange—you see.*

"Ehh . . ." I scratched my head. "You mean that one feels like the opposite of the other?"

No opposite. Match. Second side, Oi said. *Magic need both.*

Which reminded me of something Esten had said during our first lesson: that feathered and thorned magic were complementary forces and that what thorned magic did was just as natural and crucial to the world.

Try now, Kieren, Oi suggested. *Listen magic.*

I nodded and closed my eyes. It was challenging to know what was magic at first—so much was happening all around me. There was the warmth of the sunlight and the sound of the breeze, the rustling of maple leaves and the grass. Birds were chirping nearby. I didn't know how to separate magic from everything else, so I tried to think of things I knew with certainty were magic . . . and Esten came to mind.

By now I was well-acquainted with the feel of Esten's magic, its cool and calm blueness that was so unlike his usual haughty demeanor. I tried to look for that feeling and midnight blue color in the field around me, and with amazement, I discovered that it seemed to be *everywhere*. It wasn't as strong as when Esten performed magic but more like a thin, almost-transparent veil over the field and the trees, over the garden with its still-blooming roses—and, if I concentrated hard enough, even over the house. It flowed around me, and I had to stop myself from being lulled by its gentleness.

The only thing that didn't feel like Esten was the ball of dense magic beside me.

Oi felt much *bigger* than the size of the doll he was in, and also deeper somehow. *It's probably his gluttonous stomach,* I thought with a smile. All that food *had* to go somewhere.

"Say, Oi," I asked, not opening my eyes just yet, "can I find someone's location using their magic?"

You hear Oi's voice—you know Oi speaks, Oi replied.

I turned that over a few times in my head. "Does that mean I need to know their magic in order to find them?"

Yes, Oi said. Which was very encouraging—I could practice doing that next.

"Thank you, Oi," I said earnestly.

Thank with pie, Oi corrected unabashedly, rousing a chuckle out of me. Like I was ever going to forget *that*.

CHAPTER 16
KIEREN

After baking the promised two pies for Oi, I decided it was time to put my newly acquired knowledge into practice.

I knew the feel of Esten's magic, but the notion of searching for him when he had ditched me again made me extremely annoyed. Yet the only other magicians I'd met were Cynn, Wyckett, Spiht, Nogg, and Tokio. Nogg was a no-go for obvious reasons. Assuming that Wyckett's singing at the Crow Bar hadn't been magically enhanced, Cynn was the only other person I had seen perform magic.

I opened the kitchen cupboard and located the box of bergamot tea and the teapot Cynn had used the day she'd visited. It had been almost a week, so the chances this would work were slim, but I held the tea and the pot and closed my eyes.

At first there was nothing, just more of Esten's magic swirling through the house. Ugh. But then something felt *different*. It was a faint little thread, and I carefully pulled on it. The magic that showed itself was an earthy, pleasant orange-brown and had an aroma like a confectionery—sweet, warm, and round. No wonder Wyckett called her Cinnamon. Although I suspected Cynn's magic wasn't the only reason for Wyckett's affectionate nickname.

"Got you," I announced triumphantly, and found Oi watching me curiously from beside two empty pie dishes on the kitchen table. "I think I'm going to try locating someone by her magic," I explained to him. "A friend. Would you like to come with me?"

Oi considered the invitation. *No*, he purred slowly after a pause. *Find Oi if in trouble—yes?*

I smiled and nodded. "Thanks. I will." It would be more fun if Oi came along, but I couldn't blame him for not being interested. Besides, his distinct magic would make a great beacon if I got lost or couldn't find Master Hanska's house again. Which —who was I kidding—was more likely to happen than not.

I closed my eyes and concentrated on the feeling of Cynn's magic. Imagining it as clearly as I could, I wished to transport myself near her and stepped into the magic stream.

The pot and tea shook and fell from my hands, and when I opened my eyes again, the kitchen was swirling around me. I felt dizzy, but I kept my gaze on the sweet toffee-brown thread of Cynn's magic. *Just you watch, Esten—I can do this without you*, I resolved as I followed the trail out of the stream, and—

"Ah!" I yelped. Instead of being greeted by solid ground, I plunged into deep, ice-cold water. Panicked, I flailed my arms to stay afloat. Thank heavens I knew how to swim. Of course this was bound to happen. I must have jinxed it with my thoughts about landing in the pond last night. Except this wasn't a pond. Judging by its size, I was in the actual ocean. Heavens, I hoped it was the Atlantic and not someplace really, *really* far away.

A salty wave hit my face, and I spat out a bunch of water that burnt my mouth and throat. My body was getting awfully cold. I sloshed around, looking for a way out. The mainland was a dark line in the distance, but luckily, about five hundred yards to the left sat a small island with a cottage on it. Not willing to give up my pursuit but also not trusting my magic to transport me somewhere safe, I swam toward it. I could decide what to do once I was on solid ground again.

By the time I crawled onto the gray rocky shore, I was shaking and shivering from head to toe. Water had soaked my clothes, and my limbs were going numb. Belatedly, I wished I'd asked Esten or Oi to teach me how to get dry, preferably without setting myself on fire in the process. But that train was long gone. It looked like my best bet was to ask whoever lived in the cottage for help. Groaning, I pushed myself upright when a voice yelled a warning.

"Stay right there, or I'll send you right back into the water!"

I spotted Cynn staring at me from some distance away, her arms raised, intense magic swirling around them. Despite her hostile stance, relief flooded my chest.

"I'm s-sor-ry! I-I was just—" I tried to speak, but my teeth were chattering so badly I could barely form words.

The expression on Cynn's face turned astonished. "Kieren? Oh, good heavens!" She dropped her arms and rushed to me.

~

"So, is this your house?" I asked, peeking out of the large sitting room window. Below it was the gray rocky beach and the vast, shimmering ocean. The view was spectacular, if a little austere.

"Used to be my teacher's, but she passed away, and now it's all mine." Cynn handed me a cup of hot black tea and joined me on the brown chesterfield. "Would be a waste not to use it."

Cynn had dried my body and clothes with magic in mere

seconds, but a deep chill from swimming in the Atlantic in mid-October was still rooted in my bones. I took a sip of the tea and let the liquid warm my throat and chest. It was surprisingly strong and a bit bitter, not unlike Esten's morning coffee. What did New England magicians have against sugar? Still, a hot drink was good.

My thoughts must have shown on my face, though, because Cynn raised a curious eyebrow. "Don't like it?" she asked.

I quickly shook my head, trying not to appear rude. "No, not at all. Just, if you have any sugar, I'd love some."

Cynn snorted a strange kind of laugh that was almost as bitter as the taste of the tea. "Haven't you heard? Sugar isn't good for you."

"Oh," I said, slightly stumped by Cynn's reaction. Had I offended her somehow?

I was going to apologize, but already Cynn's mouth was stretching into a grin. "I'm just kidding, Kieren. Have as much as you like." With that, she extended her right hand and tapped the lip of my cup with her index finger. I could almost smell the sweetness of her magic working. "Better?" she asked.

I tasted the tea again. Whether it was magic or sugar, I couldn't say, but the tea tasted *so much better*. It made me happy somehow, like I'd gone to a candy shop and bought every single confection there.

"Yes," I said, smiling. "Sorry for the trouble."

"No trouble at all." Cynn shrugged.

I took another sip and looked around the room curiously. The fact that the cottage used to belong to Cynn's teacher made sense. It was a lovely house, full of books and paintings and photographs. But it was hard to imagine someone warm like Cynn living in such an isolated place, surrounded by a cold, wild ocean. Then again, I didn't know the precise location of Master Hanska's home either. For all I knew, I was living in some kind of wilderness as well.

"So, how did you end up here?" Cynn asked, taking a sip of her tea.

"Well . . ." I blushed. "I was just, um . . . I was practicing how to find someone with magic, and I don't know many magicians yet, so I thought I'd look for you."

Cynn's mouth opened in shock. "That is not easy magic, Kieren," she said slowly, studying me intently. "And by not easy, I mean *extremely* advanced. Hardly anyone can do that. Has Master Hanska been teaching you that?"

I'd had no idea I was doing something advanced. But I doubted a being like Oi even had a concept of what was beginner stuff and what was reserved for high-level magicians.

"Um, not exactly. Master is still busy," I mumbled, averting my gaze. I knew I was supposed to lead the discussion away from Master Hanska and his absence, but Cynn seemed to know he was gone already, so it was probably safe to admit that as long as I didn't give away any details.

To my surprise, Cynn started laughing. "Don't worry, Kieren. We've all been there. I tried a lot of inadvisable magic when my teacher was too busy to check what I was up to. No harm in that. We are magicians—what else are we supposed to do with ourselves?"

Oh. I stilled. Cynn had misinterpreted what I'd said, but I wasn't going to correct her.

"So, did Esten put you up to this, then?" Cynn prodded, smiling mischievously.

My heart sank a little. "No . . . he's also busy," I said.

There was a look of pity in Cynn's eyes. "Are you two still not getting along?"

I bit the inside of my cheek. I hadn't sought Cynn out to complain, but she was nice to me, and maybe I just needed a friend. So I let the words of disappointment slip out of my mouth.

"Not really. Esten is . . . he's preoccupied with other things, and he is very attached to Master Hanska. Honestly I feel like I'm a third wheel there or something." The moment I said that, I felt guilty. But the guilt didn't make my feelings untrue. I'd been wondering why I'd been sent to a place where nobody wanted me. It wasn't like whichever magical authority had assigned me to Master Hanska knew that he'd gone missing, but still.

Cynn took a long pause, sipping her tea. "It's not unusual to feel this way," she said eventually. For once the playful amusement disappeared from her face, replaced with a thoughtful, pensive expression. "Every single one of us was taken from our families to be raised by our teachers, whom we'd never met before. The moment we manifested, our normal lives and childhoods were over. It's just that in your perhaps lucky case, you've done most of your growing up while still with your family. But Esten had quite the opposite experience."

"How do you mean?" I asked. I stopped sipping my tea, instead cradling the cup in my palms to warm them.

Cynn sighed. "I don't know the details, and it's not my story to tell, but Esten manifested very early. Word is that Master Hanska was called to assist with a disastrous mudslide in the Sierra Nevada and found a boy near the ruins of a house. Unfortunately, by the time he arrived, the boy's family was already dead, crushed by debris and buried in the mud. But the boy had manifested magic and survived. Master Hanska decided to take him in as an apprentice. Esten was barely five years old then. So you see, there are reasons why Esten is so attached to him."

I listened to the story with my mouth open. Well, that

finally shed some light on Esten's behavior. Not only was Master Hanska his teacher, he was Esten's only family.

"But that hardly explains why he hasn't grown out of his bratty attitude." Cynn's tone went back to its amused lilt, and a teasing smile returned to her face. "But don't worry, he'll get over not being the only cat in the house. Everybody does eventually."

I couldn't help but chuckle at that.

"Look here." Cynn got up from the sofa and fetched a framed black-and-white photograph from the nearby side table.

I took a look at it. In the middle of the photo stood a tall woman in a dark dress with a high collar and a ruffled skirt. On one side of her was a younger Cynn, and on the other was a blond boy with a proud chin and piercing eyes.

"Is that . . . that's Spiht, isn't it?" I asked, incredulous.

Cynn's eyes widened. "You've met him already?"

"Yeah, at the Crow Bar the other night."

"Oh, good. Well, you probably don't know that he was my teacher's other apprentice," Cynn said, surprising me even more. "A bit of a handful sometimes, if you ask me, but you're no stranger to that yourself."

I was immediately reminded of how much open animosity there had been between Spiht and Esten, but I supposed there were certain similarities between their cocky attitudes.

"Anyway," Cynn said, "I was close to finishing my apprenticeship by the time Spiht arrived, and still it wasn't easy to accept another magician in the household. Took a long time for us to stop trying to one-up each other and vying for our teacher's attention. I know it wasn't our fault. We both felt like we needed to prove ourselves in this world that demanded so much from us. We magicians don't get to choose when we manifest or which teacher will take us in. There is a lot of uncertainty that comes with that, and a lot of pressure that not everyone is prepared for, especially being so young . . ." She trailed off and shifted her gaze to the rolling cold waves below.

I nodded. After meeting Spiht and hearing Esten berate him so much at the Crow Bar, it was strange to hear Cynn talk about the same person like he was her baby brother. I related to the sentiment. I had a younger brother and two sisters, after all. We had often fought for attention, but at the end of the day, we were family and loved one another. Until I'd manifested, that is. After that, I wasn't anyone's brother anymore. Why did it have to turn out that way? If only I'd manifested in a less violent way. Or never manifested at all . . .

But there was no point in thinking about that now. I couldn't change anything.

At least my situation with Esten wasn't as uncommon as I'd thought. If he still treated Spiht as a rival, there was no way he'd be happy about me being in the house.

Carefully I asked, "Is it true that Spiht wanted to study with Master Hanska but Master rejected him?"

"Something like that," Cynn said. "Master Hanska was conflicted about it though. When my teacher died, I had already finished my apprenticeship, but Spiht hadn't. I didn't have enough experience to take him on myself, and he really wished to study with the number-two magician in the country. But after much consideration, Master Hanska decided that they were not compatible and that it was better for Spiht to learn elsewhere."

This did not sound like the dramatic story of rejection Esten had spun for me.

"So who took him in, then?" I asked.

"A magician named Kavender did," Cynn replied.

I stiffened at the mention of the name. "Did it work out well?"

Cynn smiled an easy smile. "I think Kavender was a great match for him. Spiht has grown a lot since then. Makes me quite proud."

I smiled politely as I wrestled with a sense of bafflement. Maybe Kavender wasn't as terrible as I'd been led to believe? Cynn certainly didn't think he was. Maybe Esten was just being dramatic again. Either way, I supposed it was best not to draw hasty conclusions about people without actual proof, especially when I still knew so little about magic.

So I stayed with Cynn a bit longer, asking her more questions about the lives of magicians, but soon she received an urgent correspondence and had to leave. I thanked her for the tea and for rescuing me from hypothermia, and transported back to Master Hanska's home.

CHAPTER 17
ESTEN

"I'm sorry, Esten, but I cannot allow you in." Ali towered over me, blocking the entrance to the Assembly. His broad shoulders, clad in a carmine silk blazer, were the human equivalent of a brick wall.

I couldn't believe this. "What do you mean, you can't let me in? I have to see Probos. I have urgent news about... about an assignment he gave me." I bit my tongue before I could blurt out something unnecessary about Master being missing or Nogg's disgusting insinuations. My mission was still top secret. But I needed Probos's permission to go after the scumbag.

Ali did not budge an inch. He folded his arms and said pleasantly, "Sorry, Esten. I got my orders. The Council is in session, and for security, no one can come in."

I gaped. This was utter nonsense. What need was there for security? Who could threaten the ten strongest magicians in the country? Besides, I'd never been denied entrance before. For some reason, I was being given a flagrant runaround, now of all times. "Listen, I have information I simply must relay to

Probos," I begged, abandoning any shred of dignity. "Please, Ali." But Ali's face remained perfectly impassive. I should have known that neither pleading nor bargaining would work on him. Ali would never have gotten the guard job otherwise.

"In that case you can write him a report," he said encouragingly. "It will reach him as soon as the Council meeting is over."

Bitter anger rose in my throat. Master's life was in danger, and he wanted me to write a *report*? I looked around in a panic. Ali was the only guard at the entrance, but there was no way I could storm the Assembly just to get to Probos. I'd end up getting arrested, and by the time I explained myself, Nogg would be long gone.

"Fine," I gritted out.

Ali smiled, completely unconcerned, and gestured to a small station in one of the alcoves that held a stack of golden envelopes and ink pens. "You can help yourself to the stationery over there."

I stormed to the table, grabbed an envelope, and furiously scribbled a report about the Sutton Pond incident, asking for Probos's permission to pursue Nogg. The letter vanished as soon as I sealed it, and I sped down the Assembly's marble steps, trying to figure out what to do next.

I'd barely made it to the National Mall when a letter bearing Probos's seal flashed red in the air in front of me. I was stumped. A response already? Wasn't he busy in a Council session?

I tore the letter open and read:

Esten,

A trusted magician will keep their eye on Nogg and investigate the matter. Until then, stay on the sludge mission.

Probos

I reread the message several times, unable to believe my eyes.

I wanted to tear the paper to shreds. Who cared about the sludge right now? That scumbag Nogg had all but confessed to harming Master! He must be arrested on sight. Why was Probos dragging his heels?

I kicked the sand under my boots and sat heavily on a nearby park bench, trying to stop my thoughts from reeling.

Logically I understood why Probos would send an Enforcement employee to watch Nogg—I had no means of locating the traitor and no experience conducting an arrest. But if anyone was allowed to pursue someone who had harmed Master, it should have been me! Why was I tasked with investigating the sludge instead? Where was the urgency in that? The only outbreak vaguely connected to the Metal Giant and Master had been in Andover. The other three had occurred hundreds of miles away. The New Missouri and Idaho ones were so far from civilization that it had taken days before they'd even been discovered. I couldn't make any sense of this.

My head sank into my hands as my lungs filled with despair. After all this time, I was still not enough to solve anything—not smart enough, not talented enough. No matter how hard I tried, how much I studied, I always ended up so awfully inadequate. Why had Master Hanska picked me as his only apprentice? He could have chosen anyone he wanted. I'd rejoiced whenever he rejected a new potential candidate, but I wasn't delusional. I'd always known there were many he could've chosen instead of me. Magicians who possessed ten times my talent, who would have made him proud. Not someone who would sit here sobbing on the National Mall, abysmally powerless and floundering in his own misery. My shoulders shook. I'd never even had the courage to ask him, *why me?* I had just hoped that someday I'd do something to deserve the honor of being chosen by him. But I hadn't, yet again.

And the worst of it all was that I'd had the stupidity to be distracted by a *boy*, of all things. By his brutish magic, his silly country freckles, his homemade pies. And all the while, Master was out there, missing. Alone. What was I thinking, gadding about the Crow Bar? Wasting time on magic lessons when the single most important person in my life was gone without a trace?

"Pathetic," I muttered, and wiped my eyes with the sleeve of my jacket.

I had to rein myself in. I had to find Master, no matter what it took. I couldn't get distracted again. Not when Master's life was on the line.

CHAPTER 18
KIEREN

It was early evening by the time I returned from visiting Cynn. I called Esten's name, but no reply came. I listened to the heavy silence hanging in the air and let out a frustrated sigh. What was I expecting? That Esten would suddenly appear in an armchair and tell me about his day? That he'd involve me in his investigation? It was like we'd gone right back to where we'd started: two strangers living in the same house who had nothing to do with each other. Except unlike back then, I realized, I wasn't actually *stuck* inside Master Hanska's residence now. I didn't need Esten's help or permission to go somewhere. And that didn't just apply to my personal business.

I assessed the idea. I could transport wherever I wanted and search for magicians using remnants of their magic. Probos hadn't assigned me a mission, but he hadn't explicitly prohibited me from going on one either. So what if I didn't have proper training? I was still a magician, and I wasn't useless. I could help with the investigation whether Esten wanted me to or not. I too had a stake in finding Master

Hanska, if only to ask the man why on earth I had been sent to his house.

Resolutely, I closed my eyes and started walking around the foyer, trying to get a feel for Master Hanska's magic. Maybe it was because he'd been gone for a while, or maybe I just wasn't good at this yet, but all I could find was more of Esten's deep-blue magic saturating everything. I huffed, annoyed with both myself and Esten. But I didn't want to give up yet. There were more things to try. If I couldn't find a sample of Master Hanska's magic, maybe I could locate Stag instead. She must have done a fair amount of magic to keep the Merrimack from flooding. If I was lucky, I might be able to find some remnants of it at Sutton Pond.

With that in mind, I pictured the pond's shore and stepped into the magic stream.

To my immense relief, I didn't land in the water. But doing transportation magic this many times in one day did make me feel lightheaded and wobbly, so I plopped down on the golden grass for a few moments.

The place looked beautiful in the light of the setting sun. Unlike the garden around Master Hanska's house, the trees here dutifully followed the seasons and had started changing, and the leaves burned bright red and burgundy, reflecting in the shimmery surface of the pond. I inhaled the chilly autumn air, willing myself to feel steady again. Once I was ready, I moved to the very edge of the pond, knelt, and put my palms to the ground, searching for Stag's magic.

I sensed a faint remnant of something. It felt glittery, like a jewel, and the color of it reminded me of a shrub with clusters of fragrant flowers that bloomed in the late spring. What was it called again? Ah, that's right—lilac. It reminded me of lilacs.

I had, of course, no way to ensure that this trace of magic

belonged to Stag, but what else was there to do but find out? Cautiously, I followed the trail into the magic stream.

Several seconds later, it dumped me out onto a dirt driveway. I scrambled to my feet, feeling even more exhausted and dizzy from transporting again. Patting the dust off my knees, I looked around. I had no idea where I'd landed. It seemed like the outskirts of a town. The weather didn't feel different here, and the trees looked to be in the same state of change as the ones by the pond, so I was probably still in New England. I could smell wetness in the air; perhaps a river was close by. At the end of the driveway stood a huge red hangar surrounded by a couple of industrial-looking buildings. All three were eerily quiet and appeared deserted. But the magic had led me here for a reason, and I had to find out why.

Stealing glances over my shoulder, I approached the hangar. Its massive front doors were shut, so I snuck along the perimeter, staying close to its wooden walls and crouching low to the ground. Maybe there was a back entrance I could use. But before I could make my way to the very back, I heard something and went still. A muffled voice was coming from inside the barn. No, not a voice—two voices.

I looked up. I was right under one of the hangar's big sash windows. Its panes were made of thick, smoky glass to prevent people from looking in, but one was busted.

With my heart pounding, I rose up and peeked through the broken glass. The hangar was mostly empty, save for heaps of paper scattered on the floor and two people arguing by one of the structural pillars. Their voices echoed around the cavernous space. My breath hitched—I recognized them both.

"I don't know what you're up to, but you're not keeping good company, my youth," Wyckett said sternly. There was frustration on his face, so different from his charming, smiley demeanor at the Crow Bar.

Spiht cocked his chin daringly. "Oh, yeah? Are you my babysitter now, Foxx?" Apparently Esten wasn't the only magician Spiht didn't get along with.

Wyckett shook his head. "Of course not. You're old enough, Spiht. And you never once listened to anything I had to say anyway. All I want is for Cynn not to get her heart broken. Please don't involve her in this."

Spiht laughed dryly. "You know my sister doesn't want anything to do with you, right? Why won't you accept that and get lost?"

Wyckett flinched as though Spiht's words had poked into a deep, open wound. But despite that, he refused to back down. "Whatever you're doing, think hard about who you ally with. Some things you can never take back. *Never*, no matter how powerful a magician you become."

Spiht pressed his mouth into a stubborn line, but I saw the slight hesitation in his green eyes. Little seeds of guilt. "I don't know what you're talking about," he said, taking a step back. "And someone like *you*, who has no respect for the absolute power of magic, has no right to be giving me advice on what kind of a magician I need to be. I am proud of who I am, Foxx." With that, the hem of Spiht's forest-green coat flew up, and he disappeared from sight.

Wyckett stood motionless for a moment, his shoulders tense with worry, but then he too took a step into the stream and was gone.

I stared into the empty hangar, not knowing what to make of the exchange. Why was Wyckett arguing with Spiht? Who was Spiht's bad company? And how had I ended up here when I was looking for Stag?

It was possible I'd misread Stag's magic by the pond or gotten it mixed up with someone else's inside the stream. I needed more practice with this skill. Even when I'd searched for Cynn earlier, I'd ended up some distance from her home, and when it came to Master Hanska's magic, I hadn't been able to find a shade of it at all. One thing was clear: Stag was not here, if she'd ever been.

I took one last look at the surrounding buildings. The sun had nearly set, and the air was getting colder by the minute, making me shiver. Exhausted and more confused than ever, I decided it was safer to mull things over at home than hang around this abandoned place.

CHAPTER 19
ESTEN

I was knee-deep in mud, scouring miles of the countryside around the Merrimack River, looking for the Metal Giant and finding absolutely nothing—no clues, no traces of Master or that scumbag Nogg. It was like the airship had vanished into the ether. Whoever was behind this, they were good at keeping their tracks covered. Even the original forge had ceased production—I'd checked. That had been the first place I'd gone. But by the time I'd arrived there, the blueprints had disappeared, and so had the engineers. And now I had no more leads on where to find Master. Cold fear seized in my chest, threatening to suffocate me.

That's when a message from Probos found me.

Dear Esten,

Magician Nogg is officially wanted for questioning by the Assembly. You may find him at East Potomac Park in Washington, DC. You have several minutes before this announce-

ment is sent to the Bureau of Enforcement. Proceed with extreme caution.

Probos

For a few seconds I simply stared at the glowing red letter in disbelief. Probos had come through. He wanted me to go after Nogg when I'd all but thought he was trying to prevent me from finding Master. This didn't make sense. Why would he refuse to meet with me, insisting that I pursue the sludge instead, and now do this? Something didn't add up here, but I had no time to question Probos's motives or look this gift horse in the mouth.

Mud squelched under my boots. I was on my way to the capital with the very next step. If I was lucky, I could question Nogg before any other magicians arrived on the scene. As furious as I was with Probos, I couldn't deny that he'd put me in an advantageous position. Instead of blindly searching for Nogg all over New England, I actually knew the scumbag's location.

I exited the magic stream in the park, whipping my head around in search of Nogg, but an intense whirlwind of magic forced me to stop in my tracks.

"What in the world is this?" I scowled, deeply unsettled by the sensation. It seemed to be coming from the direction of the river, and there was something dangerous, something destructive and *unnatural* about it. It made the little hairs on my neck rise.

I shook it off. No matter what this disturbing magic was, it was my only link to finding Master, and I had no choice but to head toward the source.

I sprinted across the grounds, weaving between trees until I spotted the familiar vermilion coat at the edge of the park.

Nogg was standing close to the water, his back to me. His body pulsed with a staggering amount of thorned magic. There was a shimmer in the space in front of him, a tear of some kind that seemed to be closing. I had never seen anything like it. Whatever Nogg was up to, it couldn't be good.

"Stop right there!" I yelled, trying to break Nogg's concentration and interfere with his magic.

Nogg threw a glance over his shoulder. "Of course. Who else but the nagging little puppy?" he jeered, appearing not at all concerned by my presence. It was almost like he was waiting for someone to show up. The next moment Nogg spun around, and fire erupted from his hands. "Eat this!"

I barely managed to skid out of the way. I fell to the grass as Nogg's flames shot through the air and hit a tree behind me. In an instant, it was engulfed in flames, its bark crackling and splitting. I gasped—Nogg had really gone for it. No warning, no declaration of battle. Just pure intent to kill. I gritted my teeth and willed myself to calm down. No one had ever tried to kill me before, with or without magic.

I needed a way to protect myself, and fast. I scrambled off the grass and conjured the first thing that came to mind. A plume of water erupted from the river and floated in front of me, forming a thick shield.

"Good try, but that won't save you!" Nogg yelled, amused. His next burst of murderous flames hit my shield head-on.

The blast was so enormous that it evaporated nearly three-quarters of the water, exploding it into clouds of steam. It blew into my face, burning my eyes and lungs, and for a second I couldn't breathe or see.

Still blinded, I raised more water to strengthen my shield, but I was hit again immediately. I tried to redirect the vapor away from me, but the shield took most of my concentration. The vapor scorched my skin and made me cough. Heavens, I hated dealing with fire, and the magic ones were the worst.

Despite how much I'd trained and sparred with Master Hanska, none of it came close to the urgency of real battle and making decisions on the spot. The water had been a quick defense, but this was no way to win. Nogg was going to steam me alive before I could demand answers from him. I desperately needed a plan—and I had an inkling of one.

I waited until the next blast came, but this time I threw my shield forward, meeting the fire halfway. Again it exploded into a hot cloud, but I didn't replenish the lost water. Instead I lunged to the side, past the densest steam, so I could finally get a good view of Nogg. He had moved, and now we were only about forty feet away from each other.

Nogg sneered—"There you are!"—and fired another blast.

Instead of water, I raised a wall of dirt between us—along with the grass and shrubs and everything else that grew from it. No doubt Probos would make me write a lengthy report explaining this destruction of public property, but right now what mattered most was getting to Nogg and squeezing the truth out of him before anybody else showed up. Soil was just as good at stopping fire as water, if not better. It was good at stopping *everything*. The dirt shield hardened and cracked from the heat of Nogg's blast but barely released any steam. I had no intention of seeing how long it would hold, though; I had only a moment before Nogg fired again. It was time to take risks. After all, attack was the best defense.

Abandoning my position, I raised another wall of soil, but not to protect myself. Instead I chose the spot right next to where Nogg was standing.

Thorned magic thickened around Nogg's arms as he got ready to fire, but he didn't have the opportunity.

At my command, the ground shot up like a wave. Dirt swirled and climbed around Nogg, immobilizing his arms and then cocooning his entire body up to his chin, forming a small mound around him.

"Curse you, dog!" Nogg yelled, spitting dirt from his mouth. He tried to fire a blast into the mound around him. It shook, and the earth dried and cracked, but the shape held.

Not wasting another second, I ran up the slope, stopping a few feet from Nogg's head.

"Shut up," I hissed, struggling to keep my mind from spinning. It took a monumental amount of concentration to keep Nogg trapped. With his arms pinned underground, he could only do so much damage, but he could continue to blast away at the dirt. I knew my work wasn't going to last. I had to interrogate him now before I lost my chance.

I opened my mouth, trying to steady my breath, when another voice called my name.

"Esten?" Cynn stood some twenty feet away, looking alarmed. "What's going on?"

Momentary confusion seized me. What was Cynn doing here? But then I realized Probos's announcement must have gone out by now and other magicians were coming for Nogg. Soon the park would be flooded with Enforcement employees —the Assembly building was barely a mile away. Which meant that I was running out of time.

"It's all right," I shouted, panting heavily. "I have orders from Probos to engage. Stay back, Cynn." I turned to Nogg again. "I'm going to give you one chance," I warned, temporarily increasing the pressure of the dirt around him. My palms started throbbing painfully as the balance of my magic tipped into the thorned territory. "What did you do to Master? Where is he?"

Nogg winced, but only for a second. Then his mouth

stretched into a defiant grin. "What do you *think* I did to him?" he said unhurriedly, like he was savoring it.

A chill ran up my spine despite the heat still hanging in the air. I found myself unable to respond.

Nogg enjoyed that. "Well, since you've turned into a silent little puppy, I guess I'm going to have to tell you myself—I *killed* that dog!" He burst out laughing. "Put his nosy nose right into the ground where he can't go sticking it into other magicians' business."

I froze. Cynn gasped, and the mound of dirt I'd raised shook under my feet and started to crack. I forced myself to concentrate, increasing the pressure again. I couldn't lose it. Not now. "You're lying, traitor," I said through gritted teeth.

Nogg's eyes bored into mine with deranged intensity. "Am I, puppy?"

"Of course you are!" I snapped back. "Master Hanska is the number-two magician in the country. Scum like you couldn't have put a scratch on him!" But despite my words, panic swirled in my chest, mercilessly clawing at my throat. Nogg's eyes looked certain; they were challenging me.

He cackled. "And yet I *did*. Sometimes even the number-two magician can be as stupid as a dirty mutt," he spat, relishing in my despair. "And you take after him. Look at what you've gotten yourself into."

Before Nogg finished the sentence, the air started crackling and buzzing around us.

"Heavens, Esten!" Cynn yelped, pointing at the place by the river where I'd originally spotted the traitor. "Look!"

I tore my gaze from Nogg. Some bizarre magic was happening. It was as though someone had ripped an opening in the fabric of space itself.

My face paled. A giant, mucky glob of intense magic poured out of the rift. It roared madly and landed on the ground, thrashing its arms and legs as though in the middle of a seizure. Its hungry mouth opened, ready to destroy. *The sludge*, I realized with horror. Had Nogg summoned the sludge?

Taking advantage of my lost concentration, Nogg unleashed another fire blast into the mound, and this one finally succeeded. The dirt exploded under my feet. I tumbled down, landing on the ground and relinquishing the last bits of pressure on Nogg. The remaining pile around him crumbled, and the scumbag broke free.

"No!" I screamed, desperately attempting to trap Nogg again, but Cynn was right beside me. She grabbed my arm, yanking me up and out of the debris just as the sludge glob collided with a nearby tree and barreled violently past us.

"Esten, the sludge is on the move," she warned. "We're in the middle of DC. We *must* contain it!"

The sludge roared again and took off through the park, instantaneously reducing the nearby trees to piles of rot and turning the land and water black with poison. To make things worse, it was rapidly galloping north—straight for the National Mall and the government buildings.

I forced my gaze away from the poisonous glob to find Nogg's triumphant, goading face. Master's murderer was using this distraction to get *away*.

"No! Let go of me!" I shoved Cynn's arm. Rage and hopeless despair surged through me, mixing with magic and setting my skin alight with one desire: to tear Nogg apart for what he'd done, sludge be damned.

But it was too late.

"Good luck with that one, puppy!" Nogg mocked, and disappeared into the magic stream just as the Assembly reinforcements finally started to arrive on the scene.

CHAPTER 20
KIEREN

When Esten returned home late that night, his usually pristine clothes were smeared with dirt. His silver eyes looked devastated and hollow, and his voice barely rose above a whisper.

"Master is dead," was all he said before locking himself up in his room.

∼

The weather turned bleak the following morning. The skies became a solid gray. Cold rain came down in sheets, drumming against the windowpanes and blurring the world outside beyond recognition, as though the skies themselves were grieving Master Hanska. To make things worse, a fresh edition of the *Boston Times* manifested on the kitchen table next to my breakfast plate, its front page covered with horrific pictures of the sludge outbreak in DC. The contamination had spread all the way to the National Mall before magicians managed to trap it.

At least I wasn't completely alone—Oi had come back too sometime after Esten had.

"Can this be true about Master Hanska?" I asked him. There was nothing about Master in the *Times*. News about magicians rarely made the pages of regular newspapers.

Yes, Oi said mournfully. However Oi knew, he sounded certain.

I nodded and picked at my sandwich.

Not surprisingly, Esten didn't join us for breakfast; he never came out of his room. I tried knocking on his door, even brought him food, but Esten didn't respond, and the door didn't open.

He was there, though. I could feel his midnight-blue magic in the room and around the rest of the house. Always Esten's and nobody else's.

If only I'd heeded Oi's advice—*listen, ask the right questions*—I might have noticed sooner that Master Hanska's magic was already gone from the residence, that Master might have been dead even before I arrived. But I hadn't been looking to find that answer, and so I couldn't see the truth hiding in plain sight. *Esten bad listener*, Oi had said, but maybe I was no better.

CHAPTER 21
ESTEN

15 years ago

I lay in bed, mutely staring at the wall. I hadn't moved in hours, or maybe days—I didn't know. The man called Hanska had brought me here to this big, unfamiliar room, told me I was a magician, told me other things—I hadn't listened. All I could hear was the tumbling of rocks and snapping of tree trunks as the hills crumbled and the ground shifted, dirt rolling down the slopes and destroying everything in its path. My clothes were still saturated with the wet smell of it.

The man called Hanska insisted on bringing food and leaving it on the table beside my bed, but I refused to turn around and touch it.

"Esten, you *must* eat something," Hanska said eventually, his voice soft but commanding, "or you will die."

I did not reply.

A long, heavy silence followed. Then I heard the sound of Hanska's boots on the wooden floor.

Good, I thought. He was going to leave, leave me alone.

Instead I froze as two big, warm palms scooped me up, lifted me out of bed, and sat me on the edge of it like I was nothing more than a kitten.

I stared, wide-eyed. Hanska was a tall man with long, dark hair and high cheekbones. He was dressed in a vibrant emerald-green suit, and he was gazing at me with eyes that seemed older than the sun.

"You need to eat," Hanska repeated patiently. "And then you need to step out of this room and get some fresh air. The garden is beautiful." With that, Hanska picked up the bowl of soup he'd brought with him and offered it to me.

My lips trembled. *Garden? Beautiful?*

"I DON'T WANT IT!" I shouted, and hit the bowl, making the soup splatter. My throat hurt from how loud I screamed.

"All right," Hanska said, unperturbed, "we can do it in the opposite order if you wish. Let's start with the garden."

To my horror, Hanska placed the half-empty bowl back on the bedside table and went to pick me up again.

I revolted. "No! I don't want it! Leave me alone! Get out!"

I fought, flailing my arms, trying to punch and kick Hanska. When that had no effect on the man, I grabbed his long hair and pulled with all my might. But I was exhausted, hungry, and weak, and Hanska was strong—he held on. Misery and helplessness swelled inside me like a devastating wave. I shoved my hands against Hanska's chest and screamed.

Wham! Something shot out from my palms. Hanska recoiled as though he'd been shocked. The fabric of his jacket where my palms touched it thickened and cracked like it was made of clay. A moment later, my hands seared with pain.

~

"That is why you must eat, get well, and start learning soon," Hanska said, bandaging my hands. His jacket and the shirt underneath it were ruined, but he hadn't bothered to change out of them, tending to my wounds instead. We hadn't made it to the garden, but Hanska had coaxed me to the kitchen, where the medical supplies were kept. The mudslide that had destroyed my home and family hadn't bruised an inch of my skin, but whatever strange thing I'd done to Hanska had left angry white blisters on my palms.

"I don't want to learn anything," I said, looking away from Hanska's hands.

"Esten," Hanska said, ever so patient and kind, "magic is a very special gift that must be treasured. Do not deny it."

My throat was a bitter knot. What kind of gift was it if I couldn't use it to save my family? Why had magic chosen to manifest in me at all? Maybe I should have let the mud bury me alive instead of making that cursed shield. I didn't even know how I'd done it—I'd been asleep when the ground had broken. How I wished I could have spread it over my mom and my siblings, but by the time I'd realized what was happening, it was already too late. The wave of mud had crashed into our small wooden house, taking it down. The walls had caved; the roof had collapsed, mercilessly trapping my family under the rubble. Everyone except for me. The mud and pieces of the house had never broken the safe bubble around me. The dirt had cocooned me and carried me to the surface while burying my family alive.

Hanska let out a long sigh at my silence. "Esten," he said, "magic *is* a gift, and that gift itself is perfect, but our use of it is regretfully not." His voice was still warm and kind but also sad. "I would give anything to be able to traverse time so I could stop the mudslide before it got to your family. But although my gift of magic is strong—one of the strongest in our country—I still cannot do that. I *can* do a great many other things, however. That's why we magicians must always strive to learn magic. To make ourselves better at it, to make the world better *with it*. It is our responsibility as the ones who had been chosen by it. Here—I have something for you." He produced a small velvet pouch from his pocket. "I went back to your home. Unfortunately, most of it is still buried, but I was able to find this. I cleaned it up and repaired it as best I could." Hanska took my bandaged hand and let what was in the pouch slide into my palm. "You can have it back if you promise not to use thorned magic on me anymore. It doesn't suit your feathered nature."

My mom's silver star earring was resting in my palm—the only thing left of her, of my family. My eyes stung with tears, making Hanska's ruined emerald suit a blur of green.

I closed my hand, holding the precious earring securely in it. "What's feathered?" I asked, wiping the salty streaks from my cheeks.

CHAPTER 22
KIEREN

"Esten, please come out," I pleaded, and knocked on Esten's door for the umpteenth time. "We need to talk."

"Go away," came Esten's coarse answer.

I leaned my forehead against the door in frustration. Was it a good sign that Esten was acknowledging my attempts to get through to him, or not really?

"I won't leave," I said stubbornly.

But no more replies followed.

I paced outside the door for a few long minutes. I'd been prepared to wait, to give Esten the time he needed to sort his feelings, but Oi had had a different idea.

Esten need talk, he'd said, and by the tone of his voice, I'd known not to question his instructions. Except that hours after I'd first knocked on Esten's door, he was still dead set on ignoring me.

I took a deep breath. There seemed to be no choice but to use magic to get in.

I concentrated on the door's lock, not wishing to accidentally destroy the whole thing or blow off the hinges again, and flicked my index finger. Despite my best effort to keep my magic contained, it *whoosh*ed like a gust of wind. The door burst open, bulldozing over the doorstop, and slammed into the wall with a loud *BAM*!

Esten sat up in bed, startled, as I peeked inside, anxiously surveying the damage.

Esten's room was similar to mine, though with a different color scheme. The same midnight blue Esten favored in his clothes was the color of his walls and bedding. The bed looked rumpled and unkempt, and there was a large pile of magical correspondence atop his bedside table, some of it overflowing onto the floor and none of it opened. One glance at Esten explained everything.

His face looked ashen. There was red around his eyes, and his cheeks glistened wetly. Even his hair was a mess for the first time since I'd met him.

I stepped inside. "Esten, we need to talk," I said. "There are letters for you. Probos is probably waiting for a report, and we need to figure out what's next."

"I don't care," Esten pushed through his teeth.

"You don't care about what?" I asked carefully.

"Anything," he muttered back.

I frowned at Esten's hunched figure. No matter how dejected he felt, he couldn't possibly be serious. We couldn't give up on the investigation now.

"Do you not care about the sludge outbreaks?" I asked, gently trying to talk some sense back into him. "Magicians are going missing. Someone is using magic to incite a world war. Are you telling me you only got involved because you wanted to find Master Hanska and now that he's gone, you're going to quit?"

Esten did not reply, just stared past me blankly. My spirits sank.

"I thought you were a strong magician," I said quietly, feeling my cheeks flush a little at the confession. "I looked up to you. I thought we could solve this thing together."

"I never asked you to look up to me or follow me," Esten said icily.

The words stung more than I would dare to admit aloud.

"So . . . what? You want me to leave, then?" I asked, not expecting the reply that followed.

"Yes. Your apprenticeship is over. There is no one here to teach you anymore."

My stomach dropped.

"Esten, it's okay to grieve," I said, trying to remain calm, though my lips shook a little. Surely this was Esten's emotions talking. He wouldn't throw me out now. "I know Master was your family, but—"

"He was my *everything*!" Esten's scream stunned me into silence. "Don't pretend you know what I've lost or anything about my grief!"

I swallowed; a heavy stone lodged behind my ribs, making it suddenly hard to breathe.

But Esten wasn't done venting his anger at me. "You never met Master. You've never had a teacher. What can you possibly know about what it feels like? You are barely a magician. A week ago you were some country boy living a boring farm life. Have you ever come close to losing everything that mattered to you in a single day?"

Something inside me gave way at that. The hurt and rejection that had been piling up in my heart turned into fury. For days I'd been trying to be part of this household. For days I'd felt like I didn't belong. And yet never once had I thrown a fit or threatened to quit.

"Yes!" I yelled back, the word sharp and satisfying on my tongue. "I lost everything the moment I manifested. And for what? Do you think I *want* this life? This life where you treat me like an nuisance, only to kick me to the curb whenever you're done with me? If this is what magic is, I'd like to give it to anyone who'll take it from me and go back to my *boring* farm life . . . except that I can't! Even if I were released from the Service, I'd have nowhere to go, no home to return to. Every person in my town hates me. None of my friends or neighbors who've known me since the day I was born would speak to me now. Even my family disowned me. What do *you* know about that?"

I was starting to choke on my words, my heart pounding, but it was like an invisible dam had broken in me, and I couldn't stop myself from lashing out. "Magicians are not the only ones who can get their hearts broken, who can die, who have to make sacrifices. Regular people have to make hard choices too. But most of them don't have the privilege of pouting in their bedrooms and calling it quits. We all have jobs to do. Someone still has to bake that bread that shows up fresh in your pantry, and make fancy clothes for you to wear, and build roads and towns and airships! Do you think none of those people ever lost anyone they loved?"

I was shaking so badly now that I barely noticed how Esten was staring at me with alarm.

"Kieren," he said. "Kieren, please—"

"Please *what*?" I yelled. "*Now* you want to talk to me?" But that was when I noticed it too. I wasn't the only one shaking with anger; the whole house was trembling around me. The furniture rattled; tiny cracks ran across the ceiling. All the unread letters fell from the nightstand and landed in a heap on the floor.

The outside looked even worse. It wasn't just the heavy

rain; the wind had picked up and was swirling hard too. Esten's window blew open, shattering multiple panes and making us both jump in shock. Then the wind burst inside the room, lifting the papers and spinning them around me like a vortex.

Oh, heavens—I took a panicked look around—*not again*. This was exactly like the day I'd manifested. I had to warn Esten. Now.

"Please, get away!" I shouted through the wind and rain that was getting dragged into the vortex from the broken window. Drops collided with my skin and clothes, quickly soaking them.

But Esten didn't move. His dark hair became wild in the wind, and he was glowing with intense blue magic. "Kieren, you have to calm down," he said, keeping his voice level even in the midst of the storm. He pushed himself away from the bed and stepped toward me.

"No! I don't know how," I yelled desperately, and took a step back. "Please get away. I might kill you if you don't!"

"No, you won't," Esten replied calmly, and moved toward me again, breaking through the vortex. Instead of colliding with his body, the papers skidded out of the way as though trying to avoid an invisible bubble around him. "You know what to do," he ordered. "I taught you, and you practiced. Stop feeding the storm and then put the magic in your well."

But it was too overwhelming. Too late. I backed against the wall in a panic. "Please, Esten, get away before I destroy this house."

But Esten didn't. His silver eyes remained on me, and he stepped closer still—so close now that he could put his hands on my shoulders.

Blue magic enveloped me like a calm, steady shield, and my own violent magic ceased to rage in response to it. The wind slowed too; the floor shaking ebbed. It was like being submerged underwater. *Peaceful*, I thought, wishing I could stay in this feeling forever.

"In your well—*now!*" Esten shouted, snapping me back to the present.

I only had a second to react. Jagged spikes of rebound hit me in the chest with such force that I dropped to my knees, howling in pain as everything around me went white.

Before I passed out, I thought I caught a glimpse of Oi beside me. Except Oi wasn't a doll anymore, he was something . . . someone else. He opened his mouth, and—

CHAPTER 23
KIEREN

The next morning I awoke in my bed—and every inch of my body *hurt*. If I didn't see the house still standing with my own eyes, I would've assumed it had collapsed and buried me under the rubble, just like the day I'd manifested.

Slowly I scanned the room and found Esten sleeping in a chair, elbow leaning on the desk. The memories of what I'd done to his room came flooding in. I stiffened with horror. No wonder Esten had stayed here. Was his bedroom even reparable after the stunt I'd pulled?

I winced in shame. What grounds did I have to chastise Esten for sulking when I had completely lost it? At least Esten's mood swings didn't ruin the house.

My stirring must have woken him up then.

"Are you all right?" he asked, groggily pushing his hair out of his face. He looked disheveled, like a sleepy lion.

"I'm okay," I said, not wanting to confess how awful I really felt. "Thank you for not running away last night and for talking me through it..."

"Wouldn't be much of a magician if I hadn't." Esten snorted, briefly returning to that cocky manner of his, then suddenly went quiet and looked away guiltily. "I'm sorry," he whispered. "And not only about yesterday." I stared at him in shock. "I shouldn't have neglected teaching you," he continued. "I should have been the one to take care of this house and everyone in it in Master's absence instead of being flustered about him being gone. Master always said that magic is not only a gift but also a great responsibility, and I ran away from mine. That won't happen again. I give you my word."

Even though it felt like most of Esten's apology was actually meant for the late Master Hanska, such sincere remorse from him felt both astounding and momentous.

"It's okay," I found myself saying. The pitiful look on Esten's face gave me an almost irresistible urge to comfort him.

"No, it's not," Esten said sternly. "I know now why you were assigned to Master. I didn't want to admit it, but whoever decided that your apprenticeship should be with the second-highest magician in the country was right. Why didn't you tell me about how you manifested?"

It was my turn to look away. This was an unfair question. "It never came up," I said defensively. "And it's not like you told me about yours, either."

"Well, *I* didn't raise a mile-wide tornado," Esten deadpanned. "Would have been nice to know you were capable of doing such a thing."

Oh. Was that what the sheriff had put in the official report, then? I had suspected the storm I'd manifested was big, but I didn't know the full extent of it . . . or rather, I had *tried* not to know the full extent of it, because of the shame and guilt it brought me. My tornado had leveled our barn and nearly destroyed our home. But it hadn't stopped there. I'd heard the nurses whispering about it outside my hospital room. At the time, I hadn't wanted to believe them. But then the sheriff had said the same thing. After my tornado had destroyed the barn, it had ripped through multiple neighbors' farms and orchards, injuring five people and destroying several families' livelihoods. And all of that had happened because of a single argument, because I hadn't been able to convince my father that I could lead a worthy life outside the farm. Looking back on it, I hadn't even been *that* angry. It was one word after another, and a tiny moment when those words had turned too sharp and too careless and I'd lost my temper. So inconsequential and stupid in the grand scheme of things. I was leaving anyway; I had already decided. What did it matter if someone didn't approve of it? But that small moment of anger had been the moment magic chose to pour out of me for the first time.

"My tornado hurt people," I admitted quietly, keeping my eyes trained on the floor. "I didn't know how to stop it. I couldn't believe it was me doing it. I lost consciousness when the barn collapsed, but the tornado went on until the magic ran out. I had no idea I was capable of something like that."

Esten was silent for a moment. Then he sighed heavily. "You're not the only one, Kieren."

I dared to look at Esten again, surprised to find a rare shade of regret cast over his usually proud features. "Magic can be powerful and dangerous," he said. "Especially when you don't know how to harness it. My whole family died the day I manifested, and sometimes I can't help but wonder if the mudslide that killed them had anything to do with my magic or if it was just a terrible coincidence. I try not to think about it too much because I'll never know the truth. However, accidents *do* happen with magic. Every magician has stories like that. It's something we all learn to live with. It's the responsibility that comes with our gift. That's why we study and practice—to prevent such disasters from happening."

I nodded slowly. Cynn had told me that Esten's family had died when he'd manifested, but I'd had no idea that Esten blamed himself for it. He was always so careful, so studious. It must have been hard for him to admit this aloud.

"Last night," Esten continued, "we got lucky, because shields are a specialty of mine. You probably would have torn the house off its foundation had I not stopped you. I think Oi did something to help too, though I'm not sure what exactly. It's a miracle your injuries aren't more severe. Did you put *any* of the rebound in your well?"

"I . . . think so?" I said. But the uncertainty in my voice was a dead giveaway. It was unlikely that I'd used my well at all. I'd been so overwhelmed that I'd forgotten to even think of it. The rebound must have gone somewhere, though, at least in part. Because despite how awful I felt today, I *wasn't* in the hospital.

Esten shook his head. "It's clear to me now that without proper supervision, you are a danger to yourself and others. For that reason, I must ask that you refrain from using thorned magic until we've trained you more. Can you promise me that?"

I swallowed. Esten sounded gravely serious. Concerned, too, which I could hardly blame him for. Even Oi had had to intervene. I could only hope that my accidental magic hadn't hurt Oi too. "I promise." I nodded solemnly and then ventured with a little more hope, "So does this mean you're not kicking me out yet?"

Esten let out an indignant snort. "Obviously I'm not. As Master Hanska's apprentice, it is my duty to assume Master's responsibilities, which apparently include making sure that you don't unleash a bunch of tornadoes on New England.

Although I can't imagine you won't be assigned another teacher now that word about Master being dead has got out..." Esten frowned and trailed off.

I could see how much it pained him to say the words out loud. Not to mention that Esten's apprenticeship wasn't over yet, so he would probably be reassigned as well. This left my heart heavy and uncertain. Would we end up with different teachers in completely different parts of the country?

"Anyway," Esten added after a moment, "I don't think it will happen right away, with everything else going on. In fact, I'm expected to testify before the Council about my fight with Nogg. Now that you're awake and they've finished cleaning up the sludge, I can't delay it any longer. I must be off."

My eyes widened. "You fought with Nogg?"

Esten huffed and stood up. "Long story."

But there was no way I was letting him go like that. "Wait!" I said. "Can I come with you?"

Esten tilted his head and folded his arms, clearly expecting nothing less than a stellar explanation for why he shouldn't leave me here so I wouldn't go around menacing myself and the world.

I made one up on the spot. "I don't know much about the Service and the Council, and if I'm going to get reassigned, it would be good for me to at least glimpse the senior magicians. Don't you think?"

"Are you even well enough to stand?" Esten asked skeptically.

I propped myself up, plastering a smile on my face and ignoring the protest of what felt like every bone in my rib cage. "Yes, absolutely."

Esten contemplated for a moment but gave in. "All right. We won't have much time for sightseeing—and they might not let you in, just so you know—but be ready in an hour."

"Will do!" I grinned and waited for Esten to leave the room before collapsing back onto the pillows. Pain surged through my ribs, and I winced horribly.

Maybe I could make myself presentable in five minutes and spend the rest of the hour in bed trying not to die.

CHAPTER 24
KIEREN

My good clothes were pretty much out of commission after the tornado I'd raised in Esten's room, so I had to resort to the standard-issue linen shirt and pants with suspenders that I found in my armoire. They were a bland, brownish color, but somehow the fit was good.

When Esten and I reconvened in the foyer at the top of the hour, I was promptly greeted with a snotty look.

"We really need to get you to the tailor soon," he said.

I squirmed self-consciously. "Why?"

"Don't you feel weird in those clothes?" he asked.

Notwithstanding the debacle in his room and the night propped against my desk, Esten's face looked dewy fresh. His glossy hair was in perfect waves above his shoulders, and he was once again dressed impeccably in tall, shiny boots, skin-tight trousers, and a double-breasted jacket with three rows of buttons. How did he always manage to do that?

"Well, I'm not fussy like you," I muttered, and looked away, trying not to blush. My eyes had lingered on the rows of buttons for too long as I accidentally wondered how much effort it would take me to unbutton them all and if I'd quit being careful halfway through. "I'm fine looking simple. I don't need to blow my whole government allowance on a dandy new wardrobe."

"That is not what I meant at all! And I am *not* fussy," Esten replied, obviously offended. "We need to get you into your color. These garments are all over the place. I don't know how you can stand it."

Huh? I examined Esten's ensemble again, giving myself permission to stare freely. All the pieces he was wearing were shades of midnight blue. From the boots on his feet to the trousers hugging his hips to the ascot under that proud chin of his—always midnight blue. A realization dawned on me. "The clothes—they reflect the color of your magic, don't they?"

How had I not put two and two together until now? Every magician I'd met dressed in shades of one color, which was also the color I followed when I searched for their magic in the stream.

"Duh," Esten said, flicking his impossibly long eyelashes. "A magician can't help the pull of the unique color of their magic. I'd lose my mind if I were forced to wear anything else."

I pondered the revelation. "Well, I'm not sure yet what my color is. Is there a way to know?"

Esten tipped his head, puzzled. "Mmm. It should come to you rather instinctively. I'm surprised it hasn't yet. Anyway, let's head to the meeting, and if all goes well, we can swing by a tailor not far from the Assembly afterward. Maybe looking at different fabrics can help you figure it out."

Excitedly I agreed, and we transported to Washington, DC.

When I stepped out of the magic stream and onto the broad marble steps of the Assembly building, my ears were immediately assaulted by an angry, roaring chant.

"No more sludge! Get your magic out of our lives! No more sludge! Get your magic out of our lives!"

I spun around to find several hundred people gathered in protest. They'd taken over the front lawn and were standing dangerously close to the steps I'd landed on. Some were brandishing signs demanding that magicians be held responsible for the destruction of the National Mall. They weren't armed, but once they spotted me, I became the sole target of their anger. "We don't want your dirty magic ruining our city! Get out, magician!"

I froze. Esten hadn't guided me here, allowing me to transport on my own for practice. I'd seen pictures of the Magicians' Assembly, so I'd thought it would be easy to get to. And I had come to the right place, but Esten must have exited somewhere else, leaving me alone to face this crowd.

Noticing my confusion, a wave of protesters decided to push onto the steps and throw their signs at me. I flinched and stumbled backward in an attempt to get away, but the crowd and the airborne signs appeared to collide with an invisible barrier at the bottom of the stairs.

Quick steps descended behind me.

"What are you doing?" Esten hissed, and grabbed my shoulder. "Get inside!"

Wide-eyed, I hastened to the doors.

"Did you know this was happening?" I asked, anxiously glancing around the cavernous marble lobby. Its floors were covered with a plush red carpet. A line of ornate pillars supported a high ceiling that was decorated with a colorful mural of the Founders. Several magicians had gathered at the windows, watching the protest nervously. Even the security guards looked on edge.

"No. The notice must have been buried in that pile of letters in my room. Otherwise I would've told you to transport inside," Esten said, ushering me through the security checkpoint. "I saw people upset about the sludge in Andover, but never a full-on protest like this. To be fair, this *was* the biggest outbreak in a city."

"Why do they want all magicians to get out of their lives, though?" I asked, following Esten up the marble staircase.

Esten shook his head in disappointment. "Because nobody knows who is responsible for the sludge, so it's easier to blame all magicians alike. Never mind that without us, they'd have no way of containing the outbreaks." That was frustrating but true. Even my tiny town had been abuzz with sludge rumors, but hardly anyone had commended magicians for helping to fix the damage.

After walking through a wide, well-lit hallway, we arrived at the spacious greeting room, and I instantly recognized the person at the desk as someone Esten had talked to at the Crow Bar: Probos's assistant, Cash. Although I could have sworn Cash was a girl . . . but maybe I was wrong. Because today he clearly looked like a boy.

"Howdy," Cash said with a short nod. It seemed he was also on edge about what was happening outside. "They're deliberating in the Council chamber already, so go right in." With that, Cash got up from his desk and opened the double doors to his right.

When we stepped inside, nobody noticed us at first; the entire grand room was engulfed in a heated discussion. Ten magicians sat around a large, semicircular table, all wearing elaborate robes, dresses, and rich-colored suits. The space vibrated with the sheer collective strength of their magic.

"You can't with all seriousness recommend that we simply ignore this mayhem," a tall man in a pewter-colored suit demanded angrily. He had long, dark hair and angular, uncompromising features.

"Certainly not," Probos replied diplomatically. I recognized him right away from the newspapers. Unlike everyone else present, Probos didn't seem to be riled up, even though the chanting from the front lawn reached all the way inside the Council chamber. "But we shall not use magic on these protesters. It would undermine the trust we've been trying to maintain with the civil government."

The man in the pewter suit laughed disdainfully. "So we should let them have at it?"

"As utterly annoying as it is," a third person said—a woman with a bun of silver hair held by an ornate pin and a matching silver robe with a wide sash—"they do have a constitutional right to protest on federal lands, which includes the lawn outside. We cannot deny their rights. Unless we *want* to incur trouble with our neighbors on Capitol Hill, Kavender."

I stiffened at the name. So the man in the pewter suit was the infamous Kavender.

Kavender *tsk*ed. "That's the point, Ginko—*their* constitutional rights. Those rights do not apply to us magicians, and they have no right to harass us outside of our place of government."

Ginko folded her arms and shook her head as though she couldn't believe what Kavender was saying. "I do not think this is the appropriate time to resurrect the rights discussion. We have bigger issues to deal with."

"But if not now, when?" a fourth magician interrupted melodramatically. He was a short, round man dressed in a garish orange suit. "Just listen to them. One outbreak is all it took to turn them into a mob. I shudder at the thought of what might happen if these outbreaks continue. We must safeguard ourselves."

Some magicians shook their heads, but others nodded in agreement.

Ginko regarded the man in the orange suit sternly. "They are just *people*, Oris. People who are angry and scared after witnessing a glob of monstrous magic raiding their city. We, on the other hand, are the ten strongest magicians in the country. Eleven, if you count Ellis. We hardly need protection against *regular* people. Let's keep our priorities straight."

"That's where you're wrong, Ginko," Kavender challenged. "You think it is politically inconvenient to deal with them now, but mark my words, politics will be useless when they decide to *turn on us* en masse. Complacency could get us all killed."

Kavender's words had a startling effect on the Council. For a moment, no one spoke.

"Now, now," Probos said, attempting to dispel the tension. "That is a little too apocalyptic, Kavender. You might scare our youth." With that, Probos gestured toward Esten and me, still standing by the door, not daring to interrupt the discussion.

All ten magicians' gazes snapped to us, including Kavender's.

"Who's that?" he demanded, pointing at me with a scowl. There was something intensely sharp and cold about both him and his magic. I wondered what his specialty was.

Out of the corner of my eye, I saw Esten open his mouth, ready to explain.

But it was Probos who spoke first. "Everyone, you already know Esten—we've invited him to testify. And beside him is Kieren, the late Master Hanska's new apprentice. I granted him permission to be present at the hearing as well." Probos smiled politely at me.

The fact that he even knew my name came as a shock. I

nodded, silently returning the greeting. Something shifted in the way Kavender looked at me then. While the rest of the Council gazed at me with sympathy for the loss of Master Hanska, Kavender narrowed his eyes as though dissecting me. I could swear the blood in my veins prickled. Feeling uncomfortable, I looked away.

"Well, how kind of our witness to finally arrive," a fifth magician pronounced. She was sitting in the middle of the table and was dressed in a dark orchid-colored dress. Her long, ebony hair was in a thick braid, and wreathlike tattoos adorned her hands. "Shall we start now? I don't suppose Ellis will show up." She glanced at the unoccupied seat beside her, which must have been reserved for Ellis Divine. There was another empty chair next to Probos. It must have been Master Hanska's.

"Let us proceed, then. Esten, if you please," Probos said, gesturing to the spot in the middle of the room where a small lectern was set up.

Esten nodded and walked up to the lectern while I claimed one of the chairs along the back wall.

"Our condolences for the loss of your magnificent teacher, Esten," Ginko said with sincere sadness in her eyes. "Master Hanska will be deeply missed. It is not often that one magician possesses both such strength and such virtue. Would you please relay in detail the events of the night you learned of his passing, as well as any other relevant information?"

Esten took a long breath and did so, starting from the moment he'd received the letter about Nogg being on the wanted list and leading up to the sludge outbreak in East Potomac Park. It took a while for me to notice what Esten was *not* saying—he carefully omitted both his secret assignment from Probos and the true reason for our excursion to Sutton Pond, where we'd first stumbled on Nogg.

Confused, I glanced over at Probos, but he didn't correct Esten. He didn't even blink at Esten's omissions. Despite everything that had come to light, he must have decided to keep the investigation a secret, which could mean only one thing: Probos did not trust the Council. Or at least not every magician on it.

The thought that the eleven strongest magicians in the country could not be trusted was deeply unsettling.

Once Esten finished talking, the lady in the orchid robe spoke again.

"So, Esten, if we understand you correctly," she said skeptically, "instead of immediately containing the sludge, you tried to pursue Nogg, allowing the sludge to rage on the banks of the Potomac River until reinforcements arrived?"

I blinked. Wait a second—was that really what the Council lady wanted to focus on? Given everything Esten had just told them, she most wanted to know why he hadn't immediately thrown himself at the sludge?

Esten frowned but didn't object.

"Well, my fellow Council members"—the lady in orchid robes sighed, casting her gaze heavenward—"we can blame it on the inexperience of youth, but it seems we've found someone responsible for that rambunctious gathering outside."

Some of the Council murmured, expressing their annoyance; some shook their heads. Only Probos's face remained blank.

I could see the effort it took Esten to remain calm. "I understand that every second counts, considering how devastating the sludge is," he said once the chatter subsided. "I might have misjudged my priorities, Reverent Nandana. But I knew there was a connection between Nogg and the outbreak that followed. Therefore it made sense to pursue him."

The chamber fell completely silent at once.

"What makes you think so?" Reverent Nandana asked, her face devoid of amusement.

"When I arrived, Nogg was performing thorned magic unlike anything I'd seen before. It looked and felt almost like . . . like his magic had ripped a hole in the fabric of space," Esten said, struggling to describe the scene. "The outbreak occurred immediately after."

A grim murmur spread through the Council.

"But other than your *feeling*," Reverent Nandana said carefully, "you do not have proof that Nogg brought on the sludge, do you? Were you able to see what was beyond the so-called *rip*?"

Esten considered. Every Council member was observing him closely. He said, "No, I don't have proof. However, Nogg strongly implied that he had something to do with it. And as for the rip, I didn't see anything beyond it."

I wasn't sure if I was imagining it, but it seemed as though the Council members relaxed a little. Which was confusing. Were they that afraid one of the American magicians was responsible for the sludge? Would they prefer it be someone from Europe? But the Council provided no explanation, and neither Esten nor I was in a position to question them.

Esten was dismissed shortly after that, and the Council declared that they must discuss his testimony in private.

As we were ushered out of the chamber, I caught one set of eyes still focused on me: Kavender was watching me again.

CHAPTER 25
KIEREN

Because of all the protests outside the Assembly, we scrapped Esten's plan to visit the tailor in DC and transported home instead.

"What do we do now?" I asked once we were back in our foyer.

Esten shrugged tiredly. Reliving the memory of the fight with Nogg and learning of Master Hanska's passing seemed to have worn him out. "I'm not sure," he said. "I haven't received any instructions from Probos."

"He didn't correct you when you didn't bring up what we discovered near Sutton Pond," I noted.

"I know," Esten said, unbuttoning his jacket and loosening the ascot around his neck. I was surprised to learn that it took only one row of buttons to get the jacket loose. "That was a gamble, but I guess he is still keeping the investigation a secret."

"Do you think the Council magicians can't be trusted, then?" I asked.

"Whatever is happening with the airship and the disappearing magicians would require powerful magic, and those eleven are the strongest in the country. I think we can't be too careful. What truly baffles me is how Nogg, who doesn't even rank high enough to be on the Council, could take down Master Hanska."

"Could he have used the sludge to do it?" I asked.

"It's possible," Esten replied, not sounding very convinced. "But it takes multiple magicians to deal with an outbreak, so how could Nogg have controlled it single-handedly?"

"Maybe he's much stronger than we thought," I said.

Esten shook his head. "That's what I don't understand. Nogg had been around for a while; everybody knows his level. Has he been hiding huge amounts of talent from us all this time? It's not like a magician can acquire it overnight. It takes a lot of training to gain the strength and ability to harness the natural gift you have when you manifest, not to mention the limitations that come with being a thorned magician."

I hummed, mulling it over. "It's strange how the Council dismissed you so quickly after you told them about Nogg and the sludge. Like they were uncomfortable with the idea of him causing it. Or like they were hiding something from us."

"I had that feeling too," Esten sighed. "Something odd is happening with the Council. Let's see if Probos sends us directions and go from there."

With that, Esten excused himself to fix the disaster I'd made of his bedroom. Feeling thoroughly guilty, I wanted to offer to help, but it seemed that Esten wanted to spend some time alone, so I let him go.

～

I didn't see Esten again until it was time for dinner, for which I had made another pie. I had briefly considered diversifying my menu if I was going to continue cooking meals for Esten and Oi, but the truth was that no one had yet complained about my simple pies. Oi seemed to be quite a fan, and I vowed I would bake him something as a thank you for helping stop my tornado—whenever he came back, that is.

When Esten finally reemerged, he was carrying two crystal glasses from the china cupboard in the dining room and a big brown bottle of something I suspected to be of an alcoholic nature.

"What's that?" I asked.

The look on Esten's face was downcast again, probably from spending the afternoon alone with his thoughts. But at least he didn't push me away.

"There won't be a funeral since we don't have his body," he said quietly. "There will probably be a gathering at the Assembly, but I don't want to go. Let's raise our glasses to Master here instead."

That was right—another lonely fact about the lives of magicians. There had been no mention of Master Hanska's death in the papers, and there wasn't going to be a funeral either. Only people who knew him and cared about him would remember him. It seemed wrong; he'd done so much for the country.

"Okay," I replied.

Esten nodded solemnly.

It was a chilly evening, so we took a tray with plates and the pie and set up on the plush rug in front of the hearth in the parlor. Esten got the fire going before pouring our drinks, which turned out to be cherry brandy.

"To Master," he said, raising his glass.

"To Master Hanska," I echoed.

Esten downed his glass and immediately poured himself another. I drank mine in small sips instead. We ate the pie in respectful silence for a few minutes, watching the flames dance and the logs hiss and crackle underneath. It was comforting in more ways than one.

"I didn't know we had brandy," I said finally. I'd never seen it in the pantry, and it hadn't occurred to me that there might be a liquor cabinet somewhere else in the house.

Esten snorted. "We have much more than brandy. Master always kept spirits for the guests."

"Really? What guests?" I'd assumed the house didn't have many visitors, with it being so isolated. But apparently I was wrong.

"Because of Master's high rank and his position on the Council, we used to host foreign magic delegations sometimes," Esten said. "Non-magical politicians and wealthy businessmen always tried to weasel their way in here, too. Most of them never made it because of the magic, but Master occasionally had to play politics. That's why he had to put that stone in the woods for entry. The president used it once."

I gaped. "You've seen President Thibault in person?"

Esten chuckled. "Only from far away—she and Master talked behind closed doors."

Still, that was impressive. The house must have been much livelier back when Master Hanska was here. I wished I'd had a chance to know him.

"Sorry for asking," I said, "but what did Master Hanska look like? I've never seen his photo. Is he in any of the portraits in the hallway?"

Esten looked shocked. "You're joking, right?"

"I'm not," I said defensively. "How would I know? His picture was never in the newspapers, only Probos's."

"Oh . . . right," Esten said, once he took a moment to think and realized that I honestly had no way of knowing, growing up the way I did. "I guess Master didn't appear in front of the press very often. Magicians are kind of like the Secret Service that way. Civilians know Probos because he is in charge, but everyone else stays out of the public eye."

I'd noticed that. I'd never understood why magicians were like that, but after being accosted at the Assembly today, I couldn't blame them. "So is Master Hanska in any of the portraits or not?" I asked.

"No . . . no, he isn't," Esten said with an affectionate smile. "Master wasn't the kind of person who wanted portraits painted of him. I do have something, though. Here." With a flick of his wrist, Esten conjured up an old framed photograph, which appeared in his lap. I put down my half-empty glass and scooted across the carpet to look at it. I vaguely remembered glimpsing the frame in Esten's room last night. I was so glad I hadn't ruined it with my outburst. He'd probably never have forgiven me.

The photograph was of an exceptionally tall, stately man with dark hair and eyes so strikingly deep that I could've sworn the picture was enchanted with his magic. It was difficult to look away from the intensity of him.

Beside the man stood a boy. He barely reached the man's chest, and his hair was shorter than it was now, but his sharp, silvery eyes were unmistakably Esten's, though they projected less confidence than Esten did today. Looking at them side by side from the distance of years, it was both strange and endearing to realize how much of the way Esten presented himself was his awkward attempt at imitating his teacher. Except for the brattiness, of course, which seemed to be entirely Esten's own.

My lips curved into a smile. "When was this taken?"

"I must have been around ten," Esten said, slurring a little. His second glass was nearly empty, and he finished the remainder in one gulp, reaching to pour himself another.

Esten didn't seem to hold his alcohol well. Or maybe he simply didn't want to, not tonight. A faint pink was spreading over his cheeks, made more pronounced by the warm glow of the fire. Absentmindedly he reached up and unbuttoned the top two buttons of his loose shirt, exposing his flushed neck. I was suddenly *very* aware of how close we were sitting. As Esten continued to stare at the photograph, lost in his memories, I found myself unable to look away from him.

I didn't want to admit it to myself, but it felt *good* that Esten had sought out my company, that he hadn't chosen to be alone tonight.

But there were still so many things I didn't know about him. He'd had all those years of growing up with magic and adventures he'd shared only with Master Hanska, the one person I'd never have a chance to meet. It was so unfair, starting with this kind of unbridgeable knowledge gap. Confusing, too. A part of me admired Esten's devotion to his teacher. But that admiration came with an unexpected pang of jealousy. My cheeks heated at the thought. That's right—I was *jealous*. Jealous of what Esten had had with Master Hanska, of how easily Esten fit into this life of magic. I wanted the same for myself. I wanted to be accepted. And not only by other magicians—I wanted Esten to accept me. All of me.

My heart did a yearning flip in my chest. Why was I thinking these things now? Maybe my tired brain was conflating everything because I felt uncertain and heartbroken. Or maybe I just really *liked* holding Esten's hand whenever we transported. And maybe I wanted to move closer and unbutton Esten's rows of buttons and let myself dive into his midnight sea of magic. Maybe I had wanted that for a long time.

Before I could stop myself, I leaned in and pressed my lips to Esten's cheek.

Esten went very still beside me.

For a panicked moment, everything was quiet, save for the thudding of my heart, as I became acutely aware of what I'd done. There was no way to scoot away and pretend nothing had happened. Esten was grieving, and I'd found the worst time to behave like an inconsiderate, lovesick bumpkin. Oh, mercy... I had to apologize. Esten wasn't just going to berate me this time. He was probably assembling all the thorned magic he could muster to obliterate me.

Or at least that's what I thought, until Esten slowly raised his chin and looked at me—for the first time, *really* looked at me.

The expression on his face was not what I was expecting. His silver eyes were wide, but not with anger. Curiously they swept over my features, dispelling every mortified thought except how unbelievably beautiful Esten was in this moment as the fire reflected on his skin and warmth bloomed in his cheeks.

I never got a chance to blurt my apology, because Esten's eyelashes dipped, and he kissed me back.

His lips felt like velvet and tasted of cherries and spice. I panicked. Was it the three shots of brandy that were making him do this? Or did Esten really want to kiss me?

Slowly Esten's hand found its way to the back of my neck, tilting my head. *I should ask him*, I thought as my mouth parted for him, *before this goes any further.* But the next moment, Esten's tongue met mine, and all my questions fell away into a jumble of nonsense. My hands found his waist and pulled him closer. He shuffled clumsily, moving the photograph out of the way, and rose to his knees so he could straddle me instead.

A whole new feeling swelled at the bottom of my stomach as Esten's hand popped the lower buttons of my shirt and slipped under the fabric. I shivered at how unexpectedly cool his fingers were on my skin. I could almost feel his magic through them. And I wanted more of him.

Esten clearly liked my reaction. His kiss turned deeper, needier, like he was trying to forget that the world around us existed. His open palm traveled down my chest, and when his fingers grazed the waistband of my trousers, I could no longer think of any reason why we shouldn't be doing this. I arched into his touch, pushing my hips into his palm. A low moan escaped my throat, making my head swim with the need to be closer to him. My hand cupped Esten's chin, and my ring finger brushed against the delicate shell of his ear. His breath came out with a shudder. Greedily, he pushed me down onto the carpet, his mouth on mine—

Horrible pain shot through my ribs, and I winced. I'd gotten so used to hiding the effects of yesterday's rebound from Esten that I'd barely noticed the continuous ache in my bones until his sudden push caught my ribs off guard.

Startled, Esten pulled away. "You okay?" he asked, slurring noticeably. His eyes were glazed, his hair a mess, and he was completely out of breath. We both were.

What a question, I thought. *Okay* was hardly the word to describe the state we were in: Esten's flushed face, his hand on my bare stomach, my knee pressed tightly between his thighs.

"Yeah," I murmured, robbed of any coherence or ability to articulate.

"Okay," Esten said, and licked his bottom lip. I watched the tip of his tongue. All I could think of was how much I wanted it back inside my mouth and on the rest of me. When I found no more words to say, Esten dipped again, clumsily hovering over my lips before kissing me, eager to return to where we'd left off. I tasted cherry brandy again. Now that my brain had had a moment that wasn't taken over by the feel of Esten's skin, I knew what I had to do. It wasn't right not to ask.

"Wait," I said, and gently pushed my palm against Esten's chest. Esten broke the kiss and looked at me with a slight frown, expecting a prompt explanation for the interruption. "Are you . . ." I fished for words. *Sober?* Well, I couldn't ask *that*. Esten would probably flip out at the suggestion . . . but I had to know. If he were to wake up tomorrow and realize he never would've done this without half a bottle of brandy in his stomach, I would sooner die from guilt and embarrassment than forgive myself for taking advantage of the situation.

"I think that . . . you might've had a bit too much to drink," I said awkwardly.

Esten's face flickered with indignation. "Mmhaven't," he said. But his words slurred even more this time, betraying him. "I'm not . . . *drunk*, Kieren," he repeated, trying to enunciate while still hovering above me. The effort colored the tops of his cheeks a deeper red. His lips were slightly wet and the same color, although that was for a different reason.

"You should see your face," I said, holding back a smile and ignoring the renewed twist of longing in the bottom of my stomach.

Esten squinted and then brought his face within an inch of mine, as though searching for something in my eyes. Our noses bumped. A lock of his glossy hair slid from behind his ear and tickled my jaw. Esten made no attempt to tuck it back in.

"Um. What are you *doing*?" I asked slowly as Esten continued staring at my irises like they were a science experiment.

"Trying to see my face in 'em, of course," Esten replied without blinking.

"Oh, heavens, you *are* drunk!" I said, mortified. This was so much worse than I'd thought.

"Mmmnoooot!" Esten protested. "And if I were, it wouldn't

mean I don't know what I'm doing or what I want. Mm not a child, Kieren."

Well, that was a relief. At least drunk Esten didn't find my crush embarrassingly one-sided. Although there was no way I was going to tell him that. I continued to stare him down stubbornly.

After a few seconds of the silent standoff, Esten's face turned more serious. He didn't try to kiss me again. Instead he blew out a disgruntled puff of air and scooted down to lie beside me on the carpet, letting his head plop onto my shoulder. His body pressed against mine, and his hand rested on my waist. The embrace caught me even more off guard than him wanting to kiss me. I wrapped my arm around him and waited as he gathered his thoughts. I suspected that whatever was on his mind was the real reason for the three shots of brandy and the unabashed kissing that had followed.

"Mmm, just . . . I'm not sure what's going to become of this place," Esten finally said. His voice was a quiet, slow murmur against my collarbone. I shivered at the intimacy of it. "Master always had answers, even if he didn't always share them with me. But now . . . now 's like the whole world is unraveling, and I don't know who I'm supposed to trust."

I swallowed. I wasn't expecting such honesty out of him. Maybe I'd shattered more than Esten's bedroom door and his windows last night. "You know you can trust *me*."

Esten snorted against my chest. "Mmm, yeah, except for when it comes to my som . . . sob . . . so*briety*, apparently," he said, finally getting the word out.

The irony made me chuckle. "That's precisely the reason why you *should* trust me," I said. Esten only purred something incoherent in reply.

A moment later I spoke again—my own feelings weren't that dissimilar to Esten's, and maybe I desperately needed to hear something like this too. "Don't worry about other things for now. We're not alone. We have Probos and Oi. And even though the Council has its agenda, I'm sure there are more good magicians out there than bad ones. Of course, none of them could ever replace Master Hanska, but we are not on our own. We'll figure things out."

"... Mm-hm," Esten murmured after a pause, either deeply contemplating my answer or already drifting away into a comfortable, brandy-induced sleep. Either way, he didn't say anything after that and made no attempt to let go of my waist.

CHAPTER 26
KIEREN

I woke up to the soft sound of snoring against my skin. Esten's face was pressed tightly into the crook of my neck, and I wondered how he could sleep like that and still manage to breathe. Trying not to disturb him, I gently moved his head to the velvet pillow I'd dragged off the nearest armchair last night before falling asleep myself.

In the gray light of early morning, Esten's face looked as beautiful as it always had despite the messy state of his clothes and hair. I knew with certainty then that my previous assumptions about Esten had been wrong—it wasn't magic that gave him his enchanting looks. Unless he weaved it even in his sleep.

As though on cue, Esten made some unintelligible sound and threw his arm over the pillow, squishing it and burying his nose in the fabric. My mouth curved into an involuntary smile.

I sat up and looked around. The fire had gone out, but the room had stayed warm and smelled pleasantly of smoke. We had left quite a mess on the carpet, though—dirty dishes, shot glasses, the photograph, and the half-empty bottle of brandy.

Wincing at a kink in my neck from sleeping on the floor, I carefully picked up the photo and headed to the kitchen to fix some breakfast. The dishes could wait till Esten was up.

∾

He was awake before I finished cooking. He stumbled groggily into the kitchen and froze upon finding me there.

"Morning," he said sheepishly, looking down and tucking a loose strand of hair behind his ear.

"Morning," I said back with matching awkwardness. I had no idea where we stood after last night or how much of it Esten even remembered. At least he didn't seem angry or regretful or too badly hungover. "I'm making frittatas, if you'd like some," I offered, hoping breakfast would put us in neutral territory until we figured things out.

Esten nodded—"Thank you, that would be great"—and then proceeded to the table, rubbing his face like a sleepy cat.

Endearing, I thought, feeling something warm take up residence in my chest. I didn't dare voice it, though. Instead I said, "It's no problem, it'll just be another minute," and took the opportunity to busy myself with the frittatas. Both were turning a nice golden-brown color.

When I was brave enough to peek over my shoulder, I saw that Esten had picked up the framed photo I'd left on the table and was gazing quietly at it. Despite all the kissing and brandy and talk of comfort last night, it would take a lot more for Esten to heal. Time had to pass. There was no denying it.

"I tried searching for him, you know—for Master Hanska," I confessed, hoping it would make Esten feel better somehow. "But I couldn't find a sample of his magic."

"What do you mean by 'searching'?" Esten asked, suddenly alert.

"Uh, well, Oi taught me when you were gone," I explained, pulling the frittatas out of the oven and placing them on the counter. A mouthwatering aroma filled the kitchen, and my stomach growled audibly. "If I can find remnants of someone's magic, then I can use it to transport myself to them."

A long pause followed. When I turned around, I found Esten's silver eyes staring at me with awe and bewilderment.

"Kieren," he said slowly, struggling to get his thoughts in order, "this is an incredibly rare and valuable skill. I don't know how you learned it, but for your own good, please don't go telling anybody else about it. The Bureau of Enforcement employs some magicians who can do that kind of thing, but their identities are kept secret because most of us don't like being easily found. It's enough that the golden letters follow us around without fail."

Oh. It was my turn to be surprised. I didn't know that magic searches violated people's privacy. "Honestly I'm not very good at it," I said bashfully. "It only worked once anyway. I managed to find my way to Cynn, but when I tried to find Katerina Stag, for some reason I ended up at this hangar where I caught Spiht and Wyckett arguing. No idea why the magic took me there, because neither of them was Stag. Maybe I lost the trail in the stream."

Esten looked at me like I'd grown a second head and promptly demanded that I tell him about the outside excursions I'd been going on in his absence.

I sat at the table opposite him and spilled everything. By the time I finished talking, Esten seemed a lot more awake.

"I cannot believe you didn't tell me sooner," he said. "We should test this skill of yours."

"I won't be able to find Nogg without a sample of his magic," I warned him. I was afraid Esten might rush after him, considering what had transpired in DC.

"No, he's a no-go anyway." Esten dismissed my concerns, but I could see the glint of restrained anger in his eyes at the mention of Nogg's name. "It's too dangerous to go after him with just the two of us. You don't have enough experience, and I don't know what he's capable of. We can't ignore the fact that he's connected to the sludge outbreaks. Maybe let's try for Stag again, if you can."

I agreed. "I still remember the color of her magic. I should be able to find it again inside the stream without going back to Sutton Pond first. Should we go right now?"

Esten pursed his lips and said, sounding slightly embarrassed, "Can we have those frittatas and some coffee first? I'm famished, and my head feels like the inside of a ringing bell."

Oh, yes, the frittatas! I jumped up and rushed to get them out of their pans. I'd all but forgotten about them. Luckily, neither had gone cold yet.

∼

Breakfast helped with both Esten's hunger and his hangover, and after changing into less crumpled clothes, we were ready to set out.

"Do what you need to do, and I'll follow," Esten said, and slipped his cool fingers into mine. The gesture was so casual that it sent flutters through my chest. Maybe this time he actually wanted to hold my hand when we transported as opposed to it being a necessity.

I couldn't afford to get distracted by those thoughts, though, if I didn't want to embarrass myself in front of him with magic gone wrong. I squeezed Esten's hand, remembered Stag's magic as vividly as I could—the color and the feeling of it—and stepped into the magic stream. It took a few seconds of intense concentration to find the right shade, but once I did, I followed the thread.

This time we exited in a grassy field. I sensed it right away—there was magic being performed here, and there was a magician nearby. But it wasn't Stag. When the world finally came into focus, I saw Spiht standing some distance away with his arms raised over the golden stalks of grass, his equally golden hair messy in the wind. The silky fabric of his forest-green coat gleamed in the bright October sun. There was something suspended in the air beside him, shiny and metallic. Not an object exactly, but rather many little pieces of one. They hovered in the shape of a cylinder, with more pieces floating up from the ground as though Spiht had been collecting them.

While I was still puzzling over why my search had again taken me to Spiht instead of Stag, Esten decided he wasn't going to waste time. "What are you doing here, Spiht?" he demanded with an amount of animosity that could level a mountain.

Spiht's arms remained raised as though he couldn't figure out what else to do with them. The cylinder continued floating beside him. "Nothing I have to explain to you, killjoy," he shouted back, raising his chin defiantly. But despite his bravado, the look on Spiht's face was one of undeniable panic.

Noticing that, Esten pressed on. "Really, now? Would you care to explain it to the Council instead? What is the purpose of that object? Are you trying to cover something up with your half-assed magic?"

Spiht's eyes darted to the cylinder. Whatever the object was, he didn't want to get caught with it.

"The Bureau of Enforcement wants you for questioning," Esten bluffed, taking a step toward Spiht. "They know you've been up to something. We're here to bring you in."

Several different emotions flashed on Spiht's face—rage, fear, and then determination. "Like I'm going to let you do that, you spoiled brat," he yelled, and before I knew what was happening, hundreds of blades of grass snapped from their roots and rose into the air, buzzing with intense magic.

"Kieren, get down!" Esten shouted as he raised his arms.

The next second the grass stalks flipped, aiming their jagged tips at us, and then Spiht flicked his fingers and fired them. The stalks zipped through the air like arrows.

Confused by Spiht's weird display of magic, I froze. But luckily, Esten didn't lose his composure. The ground rumbled under our feet, and the soil rose in front of us like a wall. The stalks crashed into it before they could reach Esten or me. Was that what Esten had meant when he'd said shields were his specialty? We ducked behind the dirt wall, but to my shock, it wasn't thick enough to protect us. The stalks didn't bend or break upon colliding with the dirt. Instead they continued to drive into it, piercing through like sharp needles.

"Curses!" Esten spat, already adding another layer of soil to the inside of the shield.

"I don't understand," I shouted over the sound of dirt squelching, trapping and mincing the stalks within it. "How are they so sharp and strong? It's grass!"

"He's using magic to hone the stalks the same way I'm manipulating the hardness of the soil," Esten said, grimacing in concentration.

"Is he seriously trying to kill us with grass?" I said, appalled.

"Either that or it's a diversion."

"How do you mean?"

"I think he's terrified we might find out what that metal cylinder is," Esten yelled over the buzz of more stalks snapping and rising to fire at us. "Listen, Kieren—it's too difficult to maintain multiple shields at the same time. I might have to drop this one and raise a second one to capture Spiht if he decides to run, so stay close to me, and when I say 'move,' you move with me. Got it?"

I nodded anxiously. "Got it."

No sooner had Esten said it than I heard a dip in the onslaught of buzzing stalks. So Esten was right. He stuck his head around the wall and shouted, "Move, Kieren! He's trying to get away."

With that, Esten dropped the wall, burying the remaining stalks in the heavy dirt, and sprinted toward Spiht, who had collected the pieces of the mysterious cylinder and was already swirling with transport magic. I did my best to keep up. As Spiht tried to take a step into the magic stream, Esten raised the ground around Spiht's legs. The soil swallowed him up to his knees.

"Agh!" Spiht yelled, nearly falling on his face. But he wasn't going to surrender that easily. "Your dirty tricks won't work on me!" he shouted, raising his hands again. A ray of sunlight in front of him converged and sharpened as though focused through a lens. The beam aimed at the hardened soil that trapped Spiht and cut right through it, swiftly pulverizing a chunk of dirt.

The air filled with brown dust. I accidentally inhaled some and started coughing.

"Bye-bye, killjoy!" Spiht shouted, his legs now free, and transported away before the dust cleared, taking the mysterious cylinder with him.

"Dammit!" Esten cursed, wiping the dirt from his eyes. "We can't let him escape. Kieren, can you track him down again?"

I spat dirt out of my mouth. There was no shortage of Spiht's magic around here to follow. I said, "I can, but are you sure you want to do this? Shouldn't we ask Probos for help first?"

"Yes and no. Spiht is obviously hiding something, and he's blasting thorned magic like a fool. But he's not that strong, and he won't be expecting us to follow him," Esten reasoned. "If we wait, we'll lose the element of surprise. Next time we find him Spiht might not be alone."

I nodded stiffly—Esten was right. It was best to strike while the iron was hot. I took Esten's hand again and concentrated on Spiht's magic. Unsurprisingly, I discovered that it matched the green color of Spiht's clothes. There was a sharp spruce smell to it too, not at all like Stag's flowery lilac. *Why on earth does the search for Stag keep taking me to him?* I wondered as I followed Spiht's trail.

Just like the last time I'd attempted to do it twice in a row, tracking left me drained and disoriented. I stumbled to my knees when we exited the stream, sinking onto something bright and soft. When my skin made contact with it, it prickled with sudden cold. My lungs filled with frost.

"Are you all right?" Esten whispered, still holding my hand.

"Yeah," I replied dizzily as the scenery came into focus. "Where are we?"

We were kneeling in thick snow, surrounded by a forest of giant evergreens. A veil of gray clouds shrouded the sun, and in that lighting the trees appeared almost blue.

"I don't know," Esten said, white puffs of air escaping his mouth. "Somewhere up north but in roughly the same time zone, if I were to guess. But that's not important right now. Your magic worked, Kieren—Spiht is here." Esten let go of my hand and gestured to the spot about a hundred yards ahead.

Spiht was standing with his back to us. The metal cylinder was gone, and his body thrummed with aggressive thorned magic as the air in front of him started to shimmer and *tear*.

I shivered. It looked like Spiht was trying to make a rift in the air itself, exactly like what Esten said had happened in DC the night the sludge broke out.

Esten's expression turned grim, confirming my suspicion. "If this is what I think it is, we can't waste another minute. We need to distract him before he summons the sludge."

Quickly so as not to draw Spiht's attention, Esten stood up. With a flick of his wrist, he raised a thick wave of snow and hurled it at Spiht. The wave crashed forward, knocking Spiht down before he knew what had hit him. But then something unexpected happened. Instead of collapsing and burying Spiht in the snow, the wave kept rolling, as though it were being sucked in by the magic of the rift. It went right into the shimmery tear and disappeared.

I gasped.

"Dammit," Esten cursed under his breath. For the second time today, he'd failed to trap Spiht, thus losing whatever advantage we had over him. Now the fight was unavoidable.

Spiht wasted no time getting to his feet. "Not you again." He shook his head in disbelief.

For a moment the rift behind Spiht stopped growing, and the shimmer dulled around the edges. Was that enough to stop the sludge from coming? Neither Esten nor I could be sure.

Esten stepped forward. "Of course it's us again. You're underestimating magic, Spiht. We will come for you as many times as it takes."

Spiht's face contorted with disdain. "Get off your high horse, Esten. It's you who's underestimating magic! The only magic you're capable of performing is the pittance they *allow* you." Spiht flicked his chin at something in the distance.

I was confused by this, as was Esten. "*They?* I've no idea who you're talking about."

Spiht snorted. "Of course you wouldn't. What dog wants to admit it's got no will of its own, only that of its master?"

Esten flinched at the vitriol in Spiht's words. I'd heard Nogg throw a similar insult at him and Master Hanska. But Esten wasn't going to stand there and take it. "Cut the hypocrisy, Spiht. Is that what you thought of us when you *begged* Master Hanska to take you in? Because all I remember is how badly you wanted to be one of us until Master rejected you."

Genuine bitterness passed across Spiht's face. "I was naïve back then. I thought Hanska was powerful. I thought he was free. But all he did was spread the same lies about magic that we've been told since birth. Someone finally opened my eyes and showed me the truth about the world."

Esten scowled. "And who was that eye-opening magician? Nogg the murderer? Is it easy to ignore Master's blood on his hands? Or were you so jealous that you actually helped him kill Master?"

Spiht blanched at the accusation, and it took him a moment to compose himself. "I did not kill him," he gritted out. "I'm not that kind of magician."

Esten huffed. "Right, and you didn't try to impale us with those grass blades either. Give me a break."

Spiht wavered, conflict evident in his green eyes. "It's not like that," he said. "It wasn't on purpose. Hanska got trapped in the sludge. What was I supposed to do?"

Esten's breath caught in his throat. "It wasn't on *purpose*?" he echoed, his voice hollow. "So you didn't do it with your own hands, you merely stood there and watched him die?"

Something broke in Spiht at that. Unlike Nogg, he didn't try to use Master Hanska's death to intimidate Esten. Guilt washed over his features. "I already told you, it wasn't like that! He should never have followed us to the damn Carolinas, all right? I warned him. I didn't want a magician to die. But as always, Hanska was too damn righteous. He thought he could capture Nogg and me and battle the sludge at the same time. He should have let it go . . . *you* should let it go, Esten." Spiht pointed at Esten, his gaze hardening. "This is your last chance. Don't make me do this. If you're not on our side, turn around now, and no magician's blood needs to be spilled."

"Shut up!" Esten spat, his voice raw with fury. "You've got no right to talk about magician's blood when you're the disgrace willing to spill it. We're done here. For the crimes of abetting Master Hanska's murder and conspiring to cause the sludge, I am bringing you to the Council."

Spiht shook his head bitterly. "I warned you, Esten . . . I really did," he said, and flicked his fingers.

Instantly the ground began to tremble, and sparkling snowflakes appeared in the air. Except they weren't falling from the sky; they were coming from the shaking tree branches.

"Kieren, move!" Esten yelled. Before I could register what was happening, he raised a wave of snow. It circled my feet and swept me out of the way at the same time that the giant evergreen closest to me snapped in half—just like the stalks of grass earlier—and came crashing down.

For a moment, the roar of the enormous trunk colliding with the ground was so loud that I couldn't hear anything else. Heaps of snow tumbled off its branches, and flurries filled the air, making it impossible to see clearly. I scrambled to my feet, disoriented from being dragged by the snow wave, and dashed in a panic to where I'd last seen Esten. As I climbed over the tree wreckage, the splitting of another trunk made a pitiful howling sound. All I could see was a long shadow falling some distance ahead of me.

"Esten!" I screamed, but my voice was drowned out as the

second tree hit the forest floor with a deafening *crack*. The ground shook, and I almost lost my footing, but I continued to move, frantically looking from side to side, begging that by the grace of magic Esten was safe, that the tree hadn't hit him.

Finally, after a few moments filled with agony, the flurries cleared enough for me to see. Esten stood about a hundred feet ahead of me. The fallen tree was to his left, but several branches had snapped and landed near him. A trickle of blood ran down his face, and the way he was leaning on his right leg told me there was something wrong with it.

My stomach churned. Esten had used magic to push me out of harm's way but had allowed himself to get hurt.

The eerie sound of splitting wood resumed, louder this time. This wasn't just one tree's dying cry; it was at least four more evergreens. If they all fell on us at the same time—

"Esten!" I screamed again.

Esten finally noticed me. "Stay there, Kieren! Don't move any closer!" His head whipped around as he urgently tried to come up with a plan. But it would take a whole lot of power to stop these trees from crushing us both to death.

I opened my mouth to shout that we needed to leave, that it was too dangerous to pursue Spiht now, that it wasn't worth it—and that's when I noticed something gold shimmering in the distance behind Esten's back. Whatever it was had a thick halo of forest-green magic around it. I squinted, trying to make out the shape. Spiht was no longer near the mysterious rift he'd been making; he'd retreated farther away from us, keeping clear of the area where the evergreens might fall. The glow came from the little golden dagger on his necklace, which was hovering beside him, pulsing with more thorned magic than what Spiht had used to break any of the trees.

My heart jumped into my throat. The trees were a diversion; the golden dagger was the real weapon. The words died on my tongue.

As all four evergreen trunks broke simultaneously, the dagger shot toward Esten—Esten, who was wide open; Esten, who couldn't see it coming, who was going to die unless I—

There was only a split second to react. *I'm sorry, Esten. The promise I made you after the tornado in your room—I have to break it now.*

I thrust my right arm out and flicked my fingers.

I wasn't precise and inventive like Esten or experienced like the other magicians. I could think of only one thing—*erasing* the harm coming Esten's way no matter the cost. Erasing the magic directed at him, the trees, the dagger—all of it.

The wind rose, howling and spinning the snow into a thick vortex. Everything around me became a blur of brilliant, violent white. I couldn't see past the brightness of it. I was the eye of the storm. Then suddenly the howling stopped, and when the vortex ceased, all the trees within a mile radius were gone, as though ground into dust. The dagger and the snow were gone too. Esten stared at me with wild eyes from the middle of a now-empty field.

A laugh bubbled up in my mouth—I'd done it! I had no idea how, but Esten was safe. I almost started to smile. *Almost* . . . and then the rebound came. It slammed into my right hand, and the most horrible pain I'd ever felt surged through my muscles and bones. I screamed.

Get away from me! I begged in a panic, trying to summon the image of the old barn. My hand felt like it was being shredded into tiny pieces. But no relief came. I pushed against the rebound with all my will as the pain grew and grew past the point of being unbearable, blinding me, tearing my throat raw—until the world went blank.

When I opened my eyes again, the pain was gone. I was

sitting on the ground with Esten kneeling next to me, holding my shoulders.

"Oh, Kieren," he murmured with cold, shaking lips. His eyes were wide and his face as pale as the snow. "I'm so sorry. I should've sent you home. I got carried away—I . . . I didn't think he was capable . . . oh, *Kieren* . . ."

I blinked the blurriness out of my vision and looked at my right hand—or rather, at the place it had been before I'd cast my magic—and found nothing.

My heart stuttered. My right hand was *gone*, leaving only a singed, black stump of a wrist in its place. I wanted to throw up. But I'd tried putting it in the well, hadn't I? I'd tried to redirect the rebound! Had I been too late again?

Esten continued murmuring apologies, seemingly as shocked by what had happened to me as I was, until Spiht's sudden, guttural scream pierced the now-quiet field.

Both our heads whipped around at once toward the noise—right at the edge of where the trees were still growing, untouched by my violent magic, Spiht was crawling backward through the snow, unable to get up. "No! No! I'm not ready! Get away!" he begged as a semitransparent figure shaped like an exact copy of Spiht advanced on him.

"What on earth is that?" I whispered in horror, and tried to prop myself up.

But Esten's hands squeezed my shoulders, holding me in place. "No, Kieren," he said, his voice trembling. "There is nothing we can do for him now. That figure is Spiht's well, the rebound he's been storing inside. It has come for him."

I gaped. Was that what it looked like, a thorned well that had gotten too full and broken?

Spiht was sobbing like a child and begging, but the figure didn't stop advancing. It continued to stalk him like a predator stalking prey until it was standing at the very tips of Spiht's boots.

A moment before the figure dove down on him, Spiht's head snapped to the side, and his eyes found Esten and me. "You made me do this!" he cried, his face agonized. "You made me—"

He didn't get to finish. The well did not wait.

Spiht screamed and screamed as the figure descended on him, and his body started to convulse, bones bending and breaking and skin ripping. Blood soaked the snow around him with bright, bright red.

So this was what happened to a magician who used too much Thorned magic. This was the retribution that awaited them . . . awaited *me*. A shredded hand was merely a prelude.

I couldn't watch anymore. I looked away, squeezing my eyes shut until the screams stopped and the rebound magic ran out.

It took a long moment before Esten and I could talk or move again. Flurries started to fall from the sky, landing softly on my shirt. This time it was actually snowing.

Finally Esten nudged me. "Kieren, we must go before we freeze. Someone needs to look at your hand, and we need to report what happened."

I nodded numbly.

By the time we got up, the rift that Spiht had opened was nothing more than a slight, shimmery distortion in the air. It was easy to miss entirely if you didn't know it was there. No sludge had come out of it, though—at least we'd succeeded at stopping that.

Per protocol, before leaving, Esten created a magical marker—a small blue light that he placed on the ground next to Spiht's body so the Assembly's employees could find it. Then he took my remaining hand. Both our fingers felt like ice.

We were about to step into the magic stream when a splotch of vivid lilac near the trees caught my attention.

"Wait." I yanked on Esten's hand. "This can't be."

Esten narrowed his eyes, trying to see what I was seeing. "Heavens," he said, astounded, as Magician Stag staggered to her feet beside the spot where Spiht's body lay.

CHAPTER 27
KIEREN

The shock of losing my hand must've worn off, because the numbness I'd felt was replaced with a chill that bored into the very marrow of my bones. My clothes were soaked from the snow, and my limbs had become slow, nearly impossible to move.

When we made it home, we settled in the parlor. Esten raised a fire in the hearth and conjured up a heap of blankets from spare rooms upstairs. He gently pushed me into the armchair closest to the fire and guided Stag onto the couch next to me, wrapping blankets around us both. Then he brought a chair for himself and sat in front of Stag.

"Stag? Stag, can you hear me?" he asked once everyone was situated.

But Stag continued to act completely out of it. Her lilac suit was tattered, her long, dark braid a mess. Since we'd found her, she had been shaking and mumbling something incoherent.

"Stag?" Esten tried again patiently. "What were you doing in that forest? Were you with Spiht?"

At the mention of his name, Stag's gaze snapped to Esten's.

Her chocolate-brown eyes were as wide as saucers. "Well," she breathed out with dry lips.

"Well what?" Esten asked, drawing back a little.

"Well . . . well days . . . stuck well days," she muttered disjointedly.

Esten frowned, attempting to decipher what she meant, then shook his head. "Stag," he said slowly, "I don't think there are wells that deep into the forest."

But Stag seemed to have retreated back inside her mind and only continued repeating the same string of nonsensical words.

Esten exhaled audibly. He was trying not to show frustration, but I could tell he was close to his limit. We'd been through so much today. We were both drained from the battle and the sheer amount of magic it had taken to stay alive. There was dried blood on Esten's temple, and I was now short a hand —and for what? What had we learned, exactly? It was difficult not to lose composure as Stag kept muttering gibberish about wells and being stuck when the only other person we could have questioned was now dead, killed by his own broken well.

"Wait," I said as a wild idea began to take shape in my mind. It took a moment to chase it down through the fog of exhaustion. "Stag," I said, turning to face her, "were you inside *Spiht's* well?"

Stag's eyes went round again, and she inhaled sharply, plunging into a terrified stupor.

A deep, worried frown appeared on Esten's face. "What do you mean, Kieren? How is that possible?"

"I don't know," I said uncertainly. "*Is* it possible? I barely know anything about magic wells—you know how awful I am at using mine. But why did the magic stream lead me to Spiht every time I tried to look for her? At first I thought that maybe I'd made a mistake in identifying her magic, but I can feel it clearly now. It's the same lilac shade I found by the pond, and that's what I've been following. This whole time she must have been near him."

Esten pushed his hair out of his face, looking overwhelmed. "What in the world is going on?" he said. "They've killed magicians; they've opened holes in thin air and let sludge out; they've made giant airships fly and trapped magicians inside their wells. This is *madness*, Kieren. Whoever is behind this is breaking every magical rule in existence."

I didn't know what to say—the idea terrified me too. No wonder Stag sounded so insane. If she'd been pushed inside a space full of rebound thorned magic and kept there for days, anyone's mind would break from that. But how had Spiht managed to do such a thing? We desperately needed more information.

"Stag," I asked, "can you tell us how you got stuck in the well?"

Stag's shivers turned into quiet sobs. "Pond," was the only word she managed.

"You were on your assignment by Sutton Pond when it happened?" Esten suggested.

Stag's face still looked as if her mind was only barely clinging to reality, but she nodded with a jerk.

"Did you by any chance see a large airship that night?" Esten nudged.

Surprising us both, Stag nodded again. Esten and I exchanged glances. It seemed that feeding her yes-or-no questions was a more productive way to go about this.

After about twenty minutes, we had determined that Stag had more or less accidentally stumbled on the airship testing site. She had then followed Spiht to the outskirts of Andover, where she'd confronted him. That was where the most confusing part had occurred—they'd had an altercation, and

Spiht had created a rift similar to the one he'd made earlier today. Stag had run up to him, but something had happened, and she'd gotten stuck in his well. No matter how much we tried, we couldn't figure out the mechanics of her getting inside the well. To be fair, Stag didn't understand it either, but it had happened *before* the sludge had broken. She also didn't know what had transpired after she got stuck or what had caused Spiht to make the rift in the first place.

"It seems we need to take another look at the places where outbreaks occurred," Esten said. "Maybe we could get more answers that way."

"Should we go now?" I asked. The rift Spiht had opened in the forest had been nearly closed by the time we'd left. If we waited too long, we might lose it altogether.

But Esten shot that idea down. "Absolutely not, Kieren. What if the sludge comes pouring out when we poke at it? Neither of us is in any shape to deal with that now. Besides, your hand . . ." Esten trailed off as his gaze fell on my singed wrist, and guilt flooded his features. I could only hope he wasn't blaming himself for what had happened in the forest. I'd followed him willingly. It was on me that I didn't know how to handle my magic.

"It's okay," I said. "I don't feel any pain." The sight of my wrist was jarring, as though my mind had yet to catch up to it being gone. But for some inexplicable reason, my arm didn't hurt—it didn't feel like anything. Maybe that was normal when thorned magic ate your limbs. I had no idea.

Esten's eyebrows furrowed, and he still looked upset with himself. "I'm glad it doesn't, but we need to get it looked at by someone who knows about these kinds of injuries. I'm going to send a report to Probos, and in the meantime let's get some rest."

I was secretly relieved. Even though I was the one who had

asked to go back, I couldn't imagine getting up yet. My hand didn't hurt, but my ribs ached from my previous mismanaged rebound, and the magic use itself had drained me beyond words. It didn't help that the warmth of the fire had been steadily persuading me to close my eyes, if only for a minute.

Once we'd decided on a plan of action and sent Stag to a safe location provided by Probos, I did just that.

∼

I woke up some hours later to the muffled sound of crunching.

I'd fallen asleep right in the parlor, too tired to move a muscle. Esten too had collapsed on the couch beside me. When I opened my eyes, I found Oi in front of the fireplace, finishing up the wine glasses we'd used last night and never gotten a chance to clean up.

"Oi," I said sleepily, smiling, and untangled myself from the heap of blankets. "You're back. Where have you been?"

Kieren, Oi said, sounding happy to see me too. *Had to leave. Indigestion. Better now.*

"Oh," I said. "I'm sorry to hear that." I could only hope that Oi's indigestion—whatever that meant—hadn't been caused by my mini tornado the other night.

No sorry, Oi said. *Cure with pie. Please?*

That cheered me up. Pie I could do. Besides, I was rather hungry as well.

We left Esten to snore quietly on the couch and moved into the kitchen, where I was promptly confronted with the reality of having only one hand.

In the absence of pain to remind me of the injury, I'd nearly forgotten about it until the simple act of peeling potatoes became an impossible task. After a few futile minutes of wrestling with the knife, I decided to leave the potatoes unpeeled and just cut them into chunks, but even that took triple the amount of time it usually did.

Kieren hand? Oi asked with concern. He'd perched on the kitchen table and was watching my struggles.

I told him all about the battle we'd had and my mismanaged rebound. Oi hummed curiously and examined my wrist but didn't say anything.

By the time I finished arranging the potatoes in the baking dishes, Esten woke up and came to the kitchen.

"Kieren, you don't have to do this," he said, instantly alarmed, and hurried to join me. He was still limping a little, but there was no more blood on his temple. "I can ask for our meals to be delivered. It will take a minute, as they still need to be cooked, but they'll get here the same way produce does."

My eyebrows rose. "So . . . does that mean we could've had someone else make our food this entire time? Why didn't you say something?"

"Well, I rather like the pies you make," Esten admitted sheepishly.

Despite everything that had happened today, I smiled. "Then I guess I'll keep struggling through another one. I've already promised Oi."

Esten finally noticed Oi as well. "So the spirit is back again," he said as he opened the oven and loaded the heavy baking dishes into it. "Does he know that Master is not here anymore?"

"Yes," I replied, leaning against the counter. "I think he might've known before either of us did."

Oi purred a quiet confirmation from his spot on the table.

Esten tilted his head, puzzled. "Can you ask him—why is he still here if Master is gone? Not that I mind, of course; he can stay as long as he likes."

That sparked my interest as well. If Oi had known about

Master's magic being gone from the house, why had he chosen to stay?

Hanska gone, yes. Oi knew, Oi replied simply. *But my deal not with Hanska. Now with Kieren.*

It *was*? I was about to ask what Oi was talking about when I suddenly remembered the deal we'd made the day Oi first talked to me, when I'd gotten scared and run off to hide from him. In exchange for teaching me about the lights, Oi had asked for pie, but that was only the first half of the deal. The second was that I would help Oi with something at a later time. It'd all happened before Esten had warned me not to go making deals with him, and I'd completely forgotten about it.

"Well, what did he say?" Esten asked impatiently, snapping my attention back to the present.

"Um, he said that his deal is with me now, not with Master Hanska," I replied.

That greatly surprised Esten. "What deal?" he said.

I relayed the question to Oi, no less curious to hear the answer.

Oi vanished from the kitchen table and reappeared on top of the oven. *Pie first,* he declared firmly, ever a stickler for the rules when it came to food and deal-making. *I tell everything when we go to forest.*

I blinked, thoroughly mystified by Oi's reply. "I think," I said to Esten, "Oi is going to explain when we go back to the rift that Spiht made. I think he's coming with us."

Oi purred in confirmation.

∽

After we had eaten the pies, the three of us reassembled in the foyer, ready to travel. My mouth nearly fell open when Esten offered me one of Master Hanska's heavier coats to wear in the snow. Considering how protective Esten had always been of anything that involved his late teacher, I made sure to sound extra grateful for the offer, although it was strange to wear Master Hanska's vibrant emerald green. I guessed it was safe to rule it out as my color.

It was late afternoon by the time we'd transported back to the forest. The morning's light snowfall had done nothing to hide the devastation our battle had wreaked on the woods. I felt an acute jab of guilt at how many evergreens, which had probably been there generations before I was born, I'd pulverized into nonexistence with a snap of my fingers. Maybe losing a hand was a small price to pay for that. I could almost hear Oi let out a sigh as he eyed the field.

Esten didn't dwell on it, though. He guided us straight to where he'd left his magic marker near the spot where Spiht had died.

By then, Spiht's body had already been moved by the Bureau of Enforcement, but blood still stained the snow where it had lain. My gaze drifted to the red before I could stop myself. It gave me another jolt of feeling that made me ill in my stomach. It was as though revisiting this place and seeing the blood again was causing a delayed reaction in me. No matter how surreal they seemed, all these things *had* happened: Spiht had almost killed us, and in return, Spiht's well had brutally killed him. Before today I had never seen a person die, and now my memory was overflowing with screams of horror and the sound of Spiht pleading for his life. I'd had no idea my mind had stored it all so well...

"Kieren," Esten called, disrupting my thoughts.

I tore my gaze away from the splatter and cleared my throat. "Is this the exact spot?" I asked, puffs of cold air escaping my mouth.

Esten nodded. "Yes."

I examined the space, walking around it and trying to visualize the rift, but all I could see now was the snow and more evergreens in the distance. "There's nothing here," I said. "Maybe it's been too long."

After a moment of peering at the same spot, Esten blew out a frustrated sigh. "Curses . . . maybe we *are* too late." I could see him questioning his earlier decision to stay home and rest.

Only Oi remained strangely undeterred.

Kieren, magic see magic, he said, gazing at me intently. *Magic know magic.*

That was what Oi had told me during one of our lessons under the maple tree. I closed my eyes, opened them, and tried again, this time prodding specifically for remnants of magic. And to my amazement, there it was—the slightest shimmery distortion to the air. It was faint, and I had to concentrate hard not to lose sight of it.

"Wait, it's still here, Esten," I said, carefully examining it. The rift wasn't big and glowing like it had been earlier. It was now a two-foot-wide horizontal tear.

Esten scrutinized the spot, then shook his head. "I . . . still can't see it, Kieren. I'm not sure why."

Bad listener, Oi noted unabashedly. I bit my lip, pretending I hadn't heard—no chance I was repeating Oi's words to Esten.

"Well, it's here," I said instead. "And Oi sees it too. What should we do about it?"

Esten folded his arms and tapped his boot, squishing the fluffy snow underneath. "I have no idea. We can try magic on it . . . though I don't know what results that would produce."

I swallowed anxiously. Blindly blasting magic at the thing that had a strong possibility of bringing about another sludge outbreak did not sound like the most appealing solution.

You go, Oi suggested simply.

"Go?" I asked.

Yes, Oi said.

Esten gave Oi a sidelong glance. "What is he saying?"

"I believe he says we should go in—into the rift, that is," I replied, shifting my weight from one foot to the other nervously.

Esten's eyes widened. "I don't think that's a good idea, Kieren. We don't know what's on the other side. Not to mention, how on earth would we get in?"

I shrugged and looked at Oi questioningly again.

Travel magic, Oi answered. *Meet on other side?* And then there was a quiet *swoosh*, and the wooden doll that used to be Oi fell on the ground as though empty.

I gaped and knelt in the snow, picking up the doll carefully with my remaining hand.

"What happened?" Esten asked, startled.

"Oi said to use travel magic and that he'll meet us on the other side. I think he left already." I didn't quite understand it, but it felt like the magic that had inhabited the doll was now gone and it had become an ordinary lifeless object. I placed it back in the snow and stood up.

Esten gave the doll a long, skeptical look. Then his eyes shifted to the empty sleeve of Master Hanska's coat where my right hand was supposed to be. "I know I've asked you this before, but please promise me you won't do anything rash with your magic," he said, locking his gaze with mine. His deep concern momentarily caught me off guard.

"I'll . . . I'll do my best," I said slowly, realizing I could hardly promise more than that. It wasn't like I wanted to worry Esten, or get hurt, or lose another limb, but I didn't regret using magic to save him. After all, Esten had used his to save me from the falling tree moments before. It was just that my magic had a different kind of price. There was nothing to be done about that.

Esten knew this too. He let out a tiny, sad sigh, and then his face took on a more stubborn, more Esten-like expression. "Just know this: at the first sign of trouble, I'll drag you out of there myself, even if you kick and scream, invisible rifts and sludge be damned."

I laughed—"I don't doubt that"—and extended my remaining hand to Esten.

He laced his fingers with mine as I focused on the rift, wishing to transport us to the other side. Then I took a step forward.

CHAPTER 28
KIEREN

The moment I tumbled out on the other side, my ears were assaulted by a deafening honk, followed by the screech of wheels against a road. Several people gasped and cursed loudly.

"Watch where you're going, idiot!" someone yelled.

"Damn tourists, I swear!" another person shouted.

When my eyes finally focused, I found myself in the middle of a busy intersection, still clasping Esten's hand for dear life. There were dozens of cars honking and people yelling at us out of their windows.

Thank heavens Esten had the presence of mind to yank me across multiple lanes and onto the sidewalk.

"Where are we?" I panted in shock as the yellow-and-black checkered car that had nearly run us over sped away, clearing the path for the traffic jam to disperse. A few passersby threw scandalized looks at us but quickly carried on with their business.

Esten and I looked around. We weren't in the forest anymore, but in a city—a city the likes of which I'd never seen.

Hundreds of cars zoomed past us, fast and sleek. Dense rows of glass-and-concrete buildings rose out of the earth and stretched seemingly all the way to the sky. There were billboards with images that flashed and changed like pictures inside a zoetrope. This place still felt like America—the driver had yelled at us in English—but this wasn't like any city in the America *I* knew. Everything was louder and more vibrant, and everyone seemed to be in a rush to get somewhere. They were so busy that no one noticed Esten and me openly gawking or that our clothes were different from everyone else's.

Only one shape stood out in the sea of people. It was floating above the ground in a slightly see-through, bright red, hooded cloak. Instead of a face, it wore a painted white mask with black lines for eyes and a mouth, not unlike the doll we'd left on the other side of the rift.

"Oi?" I said, astounded. "It's you, isn't it!"

Esten's eyes widened. "I can see him too!" he exclaimed. But Esten and I were the only ones able to do so—people kept walking past and through Oi without noticing him at all.

Yes, Oi finally responded, his voice clearer than I had ever heard it. *It me. Welcome to my home.*

∼

We moved away from the busy street and found a bench in a nearby park. The leaves had mostly fallen from the trees, and the fountain that stood in the center of the space had been emptied of water, instead covered by a thin layer of snow. Other than a couple of people walking their dogs, no one else was around. Esten and I sat on the bench while Oi hovered above the ground in front of us.

"What is this place?" Esten asked, looking around anxiously. On this side of the rift, he could hear Oi too.

Other world. Oi live here—Oi friends live here, Oi said. So this really wasn't the America I knew.

"Why did you want us to come here?" I asked, feeling as uncomfortable as Esten. "Why didn't you tell us there was another world?"

Could not tell. Gave iron word to Hanska, Oi said.

Esten frowned. "Iron word? What does that—" he began to ask.

But Oi interrupted him. *Ask later, Esten. Not Oi secret. What important is, Oi gave word to Hanska for help. Magicians used rift, poured magic into this world—poison magic. You call it 'well.'*

Esten inhaled sharply. "Are you saying people emptied their wells into this world using the rifts?"

Yes, Oi confirmed.

Esten drew back, appalled. Things were finally starting to make sense. That's what Spiht must have been trying to do in the woods before we interrupted him and also when Stag got stuck in his well on the outskirts of Andover. That's what Nogg must have done in DC, too.

"What happened when their wells were emptied here?" I asked, shivering at the thought of an entire lifetime's worth of violent rebound magic trapped in a world without its target.

For a moment Oi looked incredibly sad. *Calamity. Ruination,* he murmured. *People here not know magic. Only Oi people do. But Oi people cannot stop what not belong here. We can eat magic, so we tried. But wells—too much, no good. Poison.*

"I see," Esten whispered, his eyes slightly unfocused as though he was working through a terrible realization. "That's why it felt and looked so familiar."

"What did?" I asked.

"The sludge," Esten replied miserably. "Am I right, Oi? Your people *turned into* the sludge after eating thorned wells."

My stomach dropped. What on earth was Esten saying?

How could someone like Oi become the terrible, malicious sludge? But one look at Oi's sad painted eyes confirmed Esten's awful theory.

Yes, Oi said woefully. *We didn't know what to do. We tried jump back through rifts, spit it out, but didn't work. Too poison. Oi people go mad. Die.*

My chest squeezed. The witnesses had said the sludge looked like rabid animals. Except they weren't animals, and they weren't trying to attack out of viciousness. It was because those spirits were in pain, poisoned by the well magic. As I thought that, another realization hit me.

"Oh no," I said with horror. "Oi, I'm so very sorry. It was you who swallowed my rebound when I raised the tornado in the house, didn't you? That's why you had indigestion?"

Oi sighed. *Yes, Kieren. But no worry. Oi wanted to help. Yours was little—Oi can do. But whole well—no good . . .*

Of course one rebound wasn't the same as swallowing an entire lifetime of thorned magic, but even so, I felt awful for hurting Oi.

"Despicable," Esten said. "That's how Spiht and Nogg became so powerful in such a short time. They must have constantly overflowed their wells and then dumped them on innocent people."

Yes, Oi said. *Oi traveled with friend who ate well and died. Oi found Hanska when Hanska investigated. Asked for help. But Hanska died before he could stop thorned magicians.*

Esten's lips shook a little. "So you knew from the beginning, then, about Master . . ."

Oi nodded.

I said, "That's why you stayed and made a deal with me. You wanted us to find out who did this to your friends."

Yes.

Esten sat in deep thought for a moment. "Here is what I

don't understand," he said grimly. "If Master knew about this —about Oi—from the start, then so must have Probos. The question is, why did Probos choose to leave us in the dark? Why did he tell me to investigate the sludge if he already knew what it was? I think it's time we ask him some questions."

I couldn't agree more. Things didn't make sense—this strange world we were in, the rifts, the investigation. It seemed the only person who could shed some light on it now was Probos.

With that, the three of us walked back to the rift in the middle of the busy street. Carefully, without attracting the attention of the crowd, I guided us back to the evergreen forest, reuniting us with the doll Oi used as a body in our world, and then back to the house. Instead of the usual report to Probos, Esten sent him a letter containing only one question:

What is the iron word?

CHAPTER 29
KIEREN

The knock on the front door came less than half an hour later. Cautiously Esten and I opened it.

"So I take it you have finally found the portals," Probos said instead of a greeting. "I'm glad you have. Now, let us talk."

Esten and I exchanged glances—neither of us had expected that Probos himself would come to us, and so fast.

We took the meeting to the library and closed the doors upon Probos's insistence, even though there was nobody else in the house besides us.

"Before I tell you about the iron word," Probos said, sitting down in one of the armchairs by the window, "I want you to know that I had no choice but to involve the two of you in this matter."

Esten tensed uncomfortably at those words. We sat on the sofa opposite Probos, and Oi was perched on the armrest.

"The iron word is a kind of magic created by our Founders," Probos explained, propping his elbows on his knees and lacing his fingers in front of him. "Every magician of Council rank, including myself and Hanska, were bound by it to protect the secret we have been guarding for nearly a hundred and fifty years. If we were to utter a word about the secret to anyone who didn't already know of it, all the iron in our blood would form a needle and pierce our hearts, instantly killing us. Hence its name: the iron word."

A chill ran up my spine at how calmly Probos talked about magic that could end his life if he misspoke.

Esten frowned. "By *secret*, do you mean the world beyond the rifts? Is that why you didn't tell us about it?"

"Yes, Esten." Probos nodded. "Because I am bound by the iron word. When the sludge first broke out, Hanska was tasked with investigating it. As the second-highest-ranking magician, he knew of the portals already, and the spirit called Oi made contact with him, providing crucial details about the sludge's origins. Due to the highly guarded nature of the secret, we also knew that someone from our very own Council must have been behind the ploy to use the rifts as dumping grounds for thorned wells. However, Hanska perished before he could complete his investigation. That is why in order to find the perpetrators, I had to rely on someone like Kieren, who was not part of the Council."

I blinked, surprised that Probos had personally planned my involvement but also bewildered as to why. I wasn't anybody special. I was just a newbie who could barely do any magic.

Probos seemed to read my confused expression, because he turned to me and said, "The portals were made with very advanced magic, Kieren. Most magicians cannot see them until they reach a certain level. Under ordinary circumstances, any magician who becomes strong enough to see them must immediately join the Council and be bound by the iron word. However, our present circumstances are far from ordinary. When you manifested, it seemed your gift was already significant enough that you'd be able to see the portals on your own

—not everyone rouses a tornado as their first magical act. It was of course to our disadvantage that you lacked training, but the matter was too urgent to delay. So instead of swearing you into the Council, I had to rely on you to help Esten find the portals without my breaking the word."

I gaped. So protecting the portals was the true purpose of the Council, and somehow I had been strong enough to join it from the start? *Me?* Kieren Belltower?

Probos was surely joking.

I was about to laugh, but then I noticed how serious Esten was beside me. He was not surprised by what Probos had said, and he certainly did not find it funny.

I felt ill.

Esten said thoughtfully, "So you knew what caused the sludge and that the perpetrator was one of the Council members. And you decided to send Kieren here even though Master was not around and would not be able to teach him . . ." Esten paused as he seemed to understand something. Anger flickered on his face, and his silver eyes bored into Probos with fierce accusation. "You *knew* Master was dead already, didn't you? And still you chose to send Kieren here!"

Probos gazed at Esten, his face betraying no emotion. "I was not *completely* certain of Hanska's fate when Kieren manifested, but I wagered that as Hanska's apprentice, I could count on you, Esten, to do the right thing if our worst fears proved to be true," Probos replied. "Besides, none of the other Council magicians could be trusted to take Kieren in, and thus my resources were severely limited."

Esten's voice rose with barely contained fury. "So your solution was to send Kieren to me? Even though I'm nowhere near a high enough rank to teach him? Probos, you *know* how dangerous his magic is without training. Look at his right hand! His life has been imperiled at least three times in my care. He could've died. And all of this so we could uncover what you already knew?"

I stared at Esten, astounded. He was worried about me. He felt responsible for my magic mishaps even though they weren't his fault. At first I'd been upset with him for not teaching me, but I hadn't known back then what I'd been asking for. Magic was dangerous, and Esten was only an apprentice. It hadn't been fair of Probos to send me to him without a proper warning.

I wanted to tell Esten that I didn't blame him, that I was grateful to him for putting up with me despite my unruly magic and the fact that he'd lost Master Hanska. But I didn't have a chance, because Probos spoke again.

"Through my long career in magical politics," he said levelly, "I've found that the choices we face are rarely the easy kind and that in dire situations, we have to make do with what is available to us. That being said, don't sell yourself short, Esten. Kieren could have suffered a far worse fate had he fallen in with the wrong crowd. What happened to Magician Spiht should serve as a convincing argument. I don't regret my decision to place him in your care in the slightest."

Esten huffed in frustration, but he couldn't dispute that. His lips trembled, and he pressed them together, as though waiting for his anger to subside. "So what is so special about that secret world that we put our lives in danger to protect it?" he asked eventually.

Probos took a long breath and drew back a little, allowing himself to collect his thoughts. "What is so special about it," he said solemnly, "is that one hundred and fifty years ago, our ancestors ran away from it."

Esten tilted his head, confused. I was sure I had misheard as well. But Probos didn't correct himself. He took another pause before continuing.

"Humanity's relationship with the forces of magic has always been a rocky one. We often fear what we don't understand, and even in the most peaceful of times, some people fear magic so intensely that they would do anything to erase it from existence. From what we know, in the world you witnessed beyond the rift, the fear of magic had grown so deep that those in power waged a century-long war to hunt down every magician they could find.

"During those dark years, our ancestors did their best to hide and plead for their lives. Some even fought back. But they couldn't fight the entire world. There have always been fewer of us than there are non-magical people. Every instance of our retaliation brought on more executions. Every person accused of magic was tortured and mercilessly slaughtered, along with their non-magical families and friends. No exceptions were made. Sometimes entire villages were wiped out. Even children were burned alive, hanged, or drowned to root out the very seed of magic from the world.

"That's when a group of our ancestors decided it was enough. Around that time, a great magician, one of our Founders—Vincent the Majestic—was searching for pockets of space not dissimilar from the pocket around this house. He intended to use them as hiding places for magicians. Then Vincent accidentally discovered that some such pockets weren't pockets at all, but portals to a neighboring world. It looked similar to Vincent's own, but with one big exception: no humans inhabited it. So a group of our ancestors banded together and devised a plan to flee. They decided to use the neighboring world to create a better society, where non-magical humans and magicians could live in peace one day.

"However, it wasn't enough to evacuate only magicians. Back then, our ancestors already knew that magic wasn't directly inherited through blood, that it chose future magicians in ways we've yet to fully understand even today. Thus, to protect the future generations of magicians from the cruel fate of manifesting in the original world, the Founders decided to bring a portion of the non-magical population along with them, knowing that some of them would have magical children." Probos paused, and for the first time since he'd started speaking, I noticed the tiniest bit of unease in his perfectly diplomatic expression. "Of course, the Founders couldn't simply *ask* non-magical people to escape with them for fear of jeopardizing the entire plan," Probos continued slowly. "Which meant they had to . . . use magic to alter the settlers' memories so they believed they had always lived here and that we magicians had never been their enemies."

For a moment, neither Esten nor I could speak.

"Are you saying," Esten finally asked, stringing the words together with difficulty, "that the world we grew up in, the history we've always believed in, is an elaborate illusion? That everyone around us is a descendent of people the Founders *kidnapped* and put under a spell so they wouldn't murder us for the crime of existing?"

A heavy silence filled the air as Probos simply watched us. Then he sighed and leaned in a little. "I understand your reaction, Esten, but it's not as simple as that," he said, his voice softer. "The Founders didn't choose to flee and save only themselves. They believed it was their duty to protect future magicians from extermination. That is why they did what they did. It was an unimaginably painful choice, and a momentous magical feat. They recreated entire cities for us to inhabit. It took years of exhausting, scrupulous work, during which time they were under constant threat of being captured. But consider this: it's been a century and a half, and the charm placed on that first generation of settlers had long worn off. Most of the memories people have today are the results of their own experiences, not an illusion. Our lives are real. The ways we treat each other are based on our own shared beliefs.

"In addition, our Founders didn't just take people against their will without offering something in return. The whole system of Magic Service is our way of paying them back for their sacrifices. It is our best attempt at peaceful coexistence.

"You wouldn't know this, but the original world spent most of the past century and a half nearly constantly at war. Magicians weren't the only ones persecuted for being different. Humans there routinely massacre entire groups of people based on the color of their skin, the languages they speak, or who they fall in love with. Our Founders chose to shield us from those horrors, gave all of us a chance to start over.

"Some might argue that despite the Founders' experiment, our world has arrived at a similarly uncertain place—tensions within Europe are growing, and our non-magical government has switched its focus from peaceful science to militarization. We even have protesters at the Assembly who want to eliminate magic. Our society isn't perfect by any means, and it might well crumble before our very eyes. Yet I deeply believe that a hundred and fifty years of peace and freedom were worth it, and I, as well as the majority of the Council, intend to keep our world from collapsing for as long as possible."

From the corner of my eye, I watched Esten nod numbly, as shell-shocked by these revelations as I was. The knowledge that in the original world our families would've burned us alive simply for existing was difficult to swallow. How could people live like that?

"What happened to those who manifested after the Founders escaped?" I asked, dread seeping into my voice. "You mentioned that the Founders took only a portion of the population with them. There must have been more of us after they left."

Probos replied, "From the secret documents left by the Founders, we know that in the very beginning, they went back and scoured the original world for newly manifested magicians. Those were dangerous missions, and two of the Founders lost their lives that way. At first they were able to find new magicians and transport them to safety, but as time went on, they observed an interesting phenomenon. The manifestations grew increasingly rare until they stopped altogether, as though the current of magic had dried out in the original world. The Founders assumed it had become devoid of magic, so they stopped going back and focused solely on this world's development."

A quiet gasp escaped Esten's mouth, and his eyes filled with concern. "I understand that they were just trying to survive," he said, shaking his head, "but don't you think it was wrong for the Founders to take magic away from an entire world? To rob all its future people of it? Even if magicians were persecuted there, who were the Founders to decide that magic belonged *only* to us?"

To my surprise, Probos's carefully constructed mask broke, and he smiled a small smile. It was as though he was genuinely happy Esten had asked that question.

"When I first learned the truth," he said wistfully, "I was quite a bit older than the two of you, but I still felt like all my beliefs had been shattered. Even though logically I understood why the Founders did what they did, I was bothered by that same question. As was your teacher, Master Hanska. In fact, the two of us often discussed it in private."

Esten perked up at the mention of his teacher, as though just now realizing that Master Hanska too had had to grapple with the sheer enormity of this truth.

Probos continued, "For the longest time, we assumed there was nothing to be done about the matter. Even without magic, the original world had managed to survive. Eventually people there worked out many of their differences and found ways to prosper. We were content to let them pursue their ways until your friend here"—Probos gestured at Oi, smiling even more now—"arrived and, to our immense relief, proved us wrong. Magic hasn't become extinct there. Rather, it no longer resides in humans and manifests in other ways instead."

Yes, Oi purred. He had spent most of the conversation listening quietly, but now he had something important to say. *Magic necessary. Life. Many Oi people in world.*

I remembered then what Oi had said during one of our first lessons—*World cannot live without magic. Dead.* I hadn't truly considered the gravity of his words back then, but now I understood what he meant. For a world to be alive, magic *had* to be in it in some form, even if humans couldn't use it. For some inexplicable reason, that made me happy. Oi was living proof that magic wasn't a *thing* that could be limited, a commodity to be claimed. It didn't belong only to magicians or to humans; maybe it existed alongside life itself. And just like life, it had to be cherished and protected . . . including from the magicians who were now dumping their thorned wells into the portals without any care for those on the other side.

"Whoever is behind this," I said, my remaining hand tightening into a fist, "they must pay for harming magical beings in the other world."

"I agree," Probos said, regret heavy in his voice. "It is possible that at first they didn't know what emptying their wells would do, but by now they're well aware of the consequences, and still they continue to do it."

"They're even willing to use it to harm other magicians," Esten added gravely. "I'm certain the outbreak in DC was a distraction from whatever they're doing with the Metal Giant."

"Yes," Probos said. "I believe it might also have been an

attempt to expose how fragile our world is and how easily non-magicians can be turned against us. That is why we must find out who is behind this before they can cause more damage and kill more innocent spirits."

Esten sighed. "I understand that you need allies not bound by the iron word, but what can Kieren and I possibly do against magicians who wield all that thorned power with no regard for rules or remorse? Spiht could have killed us had he emptied his well in time. Nogg is even more dangerous, not to mention whatever Council members masterminded the whole thing. They must have found a way to break the iron word in order to recruit Nogg and Spiht."

"I suspect they found some loophole to influence young and impressionable magicians like Spiht," Probos agreed, pleased that Esten was willing to cooperate. "But I never said that I wanted you to do this alone. There is a magician you can count on. He's kept an eye on Nogg and provided us with his location in DC. And he's not the only one we can trust. After Nogg escaped, I tasked this same magician with investigating whether one of the Council members would make a good ally. I am glad to share with you the splendid news that Ellis has no connection to the sludge outbreaks, and therefore we should attempt to recruit her."

Esten gaped. "You want *us* to approach *Ellis Divine*?"

My eyes widened—wasn't that the lady magician no one had dared to sit next to at the Crow Bar?

"Exactly," Probos said demurely. "That is my next assignment for you two—to recruit the strongest magician in the country to our cause."

"But . . . but . . ." Esten stuttered. "She doesn't even show up to the Council meetings. What makes you think she will listen to us?"

"Well, you might say that Ellis is not political," Probos said evasively.

Esten laughed. "Not political? She will turn Kieren and me into frogs before we say a word."

The corner of Probos's mouth curved up, and he shook his head. "Ellis is a peculiar person and an even more peculiar magician. However, she is not unreasonable or uncaring. She will help if she knows this cannot be done without her. As for the trusted magician who vetted her, I am breaking another one of our internal rules by disclosing his identity. Please be mindful of that. He does not yet know the true nature of our world, and the two of you will have to explain it to him when he joins you. I am sorry to place this burden on you, but as you're well aware, I have no choice. Now, about finding Ellis—it is a bit tricky, so you'd best pay attention."

Esten and I sat in stunned silence as Probos explained how to get to Ellis Divine's residence.

CHAPTER 30
KIEREN

I t was strange to continue with any usual routine after the world-shattering revelations we'd received from Probos. Yet I couldn't think of anything better to do than fix some quick sandwiches for dinner before Esten and I carried on with our impossibly long day. Of course, the fixing was hardly quick, considering I had only one hand to work with. But even so, I felt much calmer engaging in something as simple and non-magical as cooking.

Oi gratefully scarfed down his portion right in the kitchen and then announced that he had some business to attend to but would return soon.

"Please take care of yourself!" I waved goodbye worriedly. Oi smiled and then disappeared. Until this morning, I'd had no clue how many ways the three of us could be hurt, from turning into sludge to being skewered by grass needles and getting crushed by giant trees. And now I had to add something as insane as being turned into frogs to the list.

"Is that even possible?" I asked Esten, stepping back into

the library, balancing both sandwich plates on my good arm. "To turn someone into a frog, I mean."

Esten was sitting on the couch, his expression troubled and faraway. When he heard me, he immediately got up to help me carry everything. But from the dazed look on his face, I could tell he'd barely noticed I was gone until now.

"I don't know," he murmured, sitting back down with his plate. "Magic is vast and complex; it's hard to say what is truly impossible. Personally I've never seen it done, but if anyone is capable of it, it's Ellis Divine."

Growing more nervous, I sat down next to him. I suspected that the main source of Esten's worries was the truth we had learned about the world. I was still shaken by it too, but it must have been even harder for Esten. Unlike me, he'd grown up among magicians; all his dreams and aspirations were based on the idea that Magic Service was essential, that magic was revered. And now everything had been turned upside down. I could only hope that the bit about being magicked into frogs was metaphorical, at least.

Esten must have sensed my apprehension. "Look," he said, chewing on his sandwich, "the reason everyone is scared to approach Ellis is because she—how to put it mildly—lives in a world of her own? She rarely leaves her residence or talks to anyone outside of it. There are a lot of rumors about her. She is also an incredibly strong magician. They can't even make her attend the Council meetings. So nothing can stop her from using whatever magic she wants on us if we get on her bad side, even if it's not *technically* turning us into frogs."

My stomach did a flip; maybe my decision to eat before heading out was a bad one. But then again, who knew—this could be the last meal we'd ever have that wasn't bugs. "Was Master Hanska scared of her too?" I asked.

"Well . . . *no*," Esten said reluctantly. "He respected her. But they weren't close friends, either. They were both too busy to hang out."

"Got it. Well, she can't be *that* scary," I said, more to convince myself than Esten. "She has two apprentices who are younger than us. And they looked normal . . . I mean, apart from the fact that nobody wanted to sit next to them."

Esten snorted a laugh. "True. But they were assigned to her because they were also very odd cases."

I frowned. "How do you mean?"

"Well, they are twins, and supposedly they share their thoughts as well as their magic."

"Huh. I wonder what that's like."

"Probably overwhelming," Esten huffed, and finished the last bite of his sandwich. "Magic is personal. I can't imagine sharing mine with someone else—like you, for example. I wouldn't know what to do with your blasting brute strength."

I found myself smiling at Esten's half-hearted complaint. I honestly loved the feeling of his magic around me. But that was probably different from having to harness it myself. Not to mention the thought sharing. What if Esten knew all the thoughts inside my head, including those that involved kissing him or wondering how far we would've gone last night had I not felt morally obligated to check if he was sober? A deep flush spread across my neck at the memory of the sound Esten had made when my fingertips had brushed along the rim of his ear and the way his legs had straddled my hips.

"What?" Esten asked, yanking me out of it.

"N-nothing," I said hastily. But it was too late—Esten's gaze flicked straight to my mouth, as mine had to his a moment earlier. Even without reading each other's minds, it was pointless to hide what I'd been thinking when we were sitting so close. Besides, a treacherous part of me was dying to know where we stood after last night. Did Esten still want to kiss me now that we were both sober?

I got my answer when Esten maneuvered his empty plate out of the way, then slowly, without taking his eyes off my mouth, leaned in and pressed his lips to mine.

"A thank-you for the sandwich," he murmured, pulling away slightly, but not far enough to signal that he was done with the kissing. "And also, just in case we *do* turn into frogs tonight."

"Oh, mercy. I guess in that case . . ." The corner of Esten's mouth curved up as I put my only hand on the small of his back and pulled him close again—there was no time to waste.

CHAPTER 31
KIEREN

Just as Probos had explained, locating Ellis's house was tricky, but not because it was on some remote mountain peak or in the middle of an ocean. Ellis resided in New Salem, a bustling harbor town north of Boston, on a regular street, among non-magical people. That did not mean, however, that her house was easy to find. No non-magical New Salem citizen would ever stumble upon it, and no neighbor would ever stop by asking for salt. Ellis had used magic to warp the space around the lot, creating her own pocket that was visible only if you stood right in front of it and looked at it backward over your left shoulder. At least Probos had given us the address: 13 Old Gallows Road.

Of course, there was no house numbered thirteen on that street at first glance. But when we positioned ourselves exactly on the property line between eleven and fifteen and looked backward, lo and behold, there it was—a narrow stone path that led to a two-story brick building surrounded by an ornate wrought-iron fence and a small garden. There were a number of lightning rods on the roof, and the iron gate had cloud-shaped decorations on the bars.

Then came the awkward task of walking backward past the fence. The moment either Esten or I got distracted and let our gazes drift away from the narrow path into the pocket, we were magically kicked back to the street as though we'd never stepped foot on the property.

Finally, after a dozen aggravating attempts, we managed to make it to the porch, where we could turn around and face the house properly. I exhaled with relief; I was starting to develop a crick in my neck. Ellis really must not have wanted visitors if she'd designed the pocket this way.

"Let me handle the talking," Esten said before knocking on the door. "It can be a little disorienting communicating with the twins."

I wondered how anything could be more disorienting than having to approach the house backward but didn't have a chance to ask, as the door had already opened. Two boys in knickerbocker suits in different shades of blue stood on the other side of it. Both had short, bright copper hair and big, curious eyes.

The one wearing the darker blue suit squinted as though trying to remember who we were, but it was the other one who opened his mouth first. "Esten?" He tilted his head quizzically.

"Yes," Esten replied. "We have met before. At Cash's graduation bash last year."

Both sets of eyebrows went up at the same time, and their mouths rounded. "Oh. We remember."

"Great," Esten said awkwardly. "Roy L. Blue, Bay B. Blue, this is Kieren. We are here to speak with Ellis."

The twins nodded simultaneously. "Nice to meet you, Kieren." Before I could politely respond, Roy said, "Ellis is too busy, though."

"She's going to be busy for a while," Bay added with a certain finality to his voice. "Come around another time." With that, Roy started to close the door. I blinked; this was a rather quick dismissal. The twins weren't rude, exactly—just plainly stating a fact that was not to be argued.

But we couldn't give up and leave emptyhanded. "Wait," Esten said. "Can you tell her it's urgent? Probos sent us."

Roy and Bay glanced at each other, then said in unison, "Nothing is urgent until Ellis finds the solution to Kellar's paradox."

I stared at the twins blankly. Esten's forehead crinkled. "Kellar's paradox? You mean the magician who tried to master time travel?"

The twins nodded. "Yes, them."

"Well, I don't think she'll be finding the solution anytime soon," Esten said. "Even Kellar couldn't solve it. They vanished during an experiment and have been gone without a trace for years."

"As we said," the twins replied, "she'll be busy for *a while*." Roy began to close the door again.

I could see the frustration building on Esten's face, so I decided to intervene. "Um, excuse me!" I grabbed the door handle. The twins halted. "It is extremely important that we speak with Ellis today. Can we please tell her why we're here, and then she can decide if it's more urgent than the . . ." I paused, forgetting the name.

Esten came to the rescue. "Kellar's paradox."

The twins exchanged glances again, tilted their heads as though having a telepathic discussion, and then shrugged noncommittally.

"I guess you can try," said Bay.

"She probably won't listen, though," said Roy.

And then both stepped aside, allowing us to enter.

"What's Kellar's paradox?" I whispered to Esten as Bay veered off, disappearing into one of the rooms, and Roy guided us through the house to the back garden.

"Something about traveling to the future without having your body automatically age the same number of years you've traveled," Esten whispered back. "Nobody has been able to do that. Somehow your body still experiences the time skip as though it has lived through those years . . . or something like that."

"Uh-huh." I nodded meaningfully as though that explanation hadn't gone right over my head.

As Roy took us through the foyer and an endless series of hallways to the back of the house, I couldn't help but notice how strange Ellis Divine's house was on the inside. It wasn't messy, per se, but there was *a lot of stuff* sitting around everywhere. Maps, diagrams, books, papers in tall stacks along the walls, peculiar objects from faraway places. It looked like a museum storage room. I even spotted a human-sized skull sitting atop a tower of books. But more than that, the house felt much larger than it appeared from the outside. I had this weird feeling that if I got distracted and lost sight of Roy for a moment, I'd become completely lost in the maze of hallways that seemed to stretch and curve with no architectural rhyme or reason. The immense amounts of magic pulsating from every surface made it much more disorienting. No wonder Esten dreaded coming here.

If Ellis noticed our arrival, she was in no rush to acknowledge us. When we finally reached the door to the back garden, we found her kneeling in front of a flower bed with a silver pocket watch in her hand. She was wearing tight periwinkle pants and a button-up shirt in the same color with ruffles on the collar and sleeves. Her thick, dark hair was pulled up in a tousled bun held in place by a pencil, and several magic lanterns floated around her in a circle, illuminating whatever she was working on. Roy moved to stand next to her and picked up a small clipboard from the ground beside her.

Esten exhaled. "Ellis?" he called hesitantly.

"Not now," she shushed him without turning to look at us. "You're distracting me."

Esten fell silent at once and drew back a little. I squinted to see what was happening. Ellis glanced at her watch as though anticipating something. Then clusters of purple crocuses started to appear one by one in the flower bed. All were already fully grown and in bloom, and for a moment Ellis looked almost triumphant. But after a few seconds, the green leaves and stalks that had been healthy and vivid upon arrival started to shrivel up and die. The flowers withered too.

"Not again." Ellis sighed and blew a loose strand of wavy hair out of her face. "Roy, batch number one forty-two is officially a failure. Looks like we're going to have to start over."

"Noted," Roy said, dutifully jotting the information down on his clipboard.

I watched, fascinated and utterly clueless about what kind of magic Ellis had performed.

Ellis wiped her forehead with her sleeve. "What happened to that hand of yours?" she asked, picking up a limp crocus and examining its remains.

I blinked—was she talking about *my* hand? How did she know something had happened to it? She had yet to spare Esten or me a single glance.

Esten used that opportunity to seize Ellis's attention. "Kieren lost it in a rebound when we were battling Spiht," he replied.

That finally made Ellis look up. "And why were you battling Kavender's apprentice?" she asked with narrowed eyes.

"That's the reason we are here, Ellis," Esten said, getting straight to the heart of the matter. "Someone broke the iron word and taught Spiht and possibly other magicians how to empty their wells into the portals."

Ellis's thin black eyebrows arched up a little as her curiosity was piqued. "Never would have considered using them for that purpose. How did it work out?"

Esten replied bluntly, "It killed several innocent magical beings and created the sludge."

A moment passed in uneasy silence as Ellis considered this. "Roy, prepare the next set of test subjects for the experiment. Esten, Kieren, let us talk in the study," she said, rising to her feet. With a flick of her hand, the dirt disappeared from her pants, and she walked toward us, the flying lanterns following her like a procession.

It was strange seeing her up close. Ellis was incredibly pretty and equally as proud. But it probably wasn't just her looks that made magicians at the Crow Bar down their drinks and recklessly try to impress her. Ellis's magic was the most intense I had ever felt. It warped the space around her like a magnet, beautiful and terrifying at once. No wonder other magicians didn't know how to deal with such force. I couldn't help thinking that if I stayed in its presence too long, I'd grow dizzy and maybe feel a little drunk.

Silently, Esten and I followed Ellis through another set of mazelike hallways to her study. It was a cozy room with walls painted light periwinkle and several mahogany bookcases full of books. Bay stood by the window, feeding three little goldfish in the aquarium. I did a double take—the fish appeared to be perfectly normal . . . except for the fact that they were floating in the air instead of water. The aquarium had no visible walls either, only four metal rods marking the corners. How was this possible? I stared at the fish in wonder.

"Bay, do you mind giving us privacy?" Ellis said, snapping my attention back to her.

"Of course, Ellis," Bay said, and promptly exited the room as Ellis sat down in one of the plush armchairs and motioned for Esten and me to join her.

We took the settee opposite her. Ellis's floating lanterns descended as well, occupying various pieces of furniture like birds on their perches.

"Now, tell me everything in proper detail," Ellis said, folding her arms in a businesslike manner.

And so we did—about the sludge and Oi, about the Metal Giant, about how Probos had led us to discover the original world, circumventing the iron word, and asked us to recruit Ellis for help after making certain she was innocent.

Ellis snorted when Esten mentioned that. "So that's who was lurking around the neighborhood, then. Politicians. Probos could have just asked if I'd told anyone about the portals. What a misuse of everyone's time."

Surprisingly, Esten seemed to agree. But something about the way Ellis had phrased her response caught my attention. "Ellis," I said, "does that mean that you aren't bound by the iron word?"

Ellis's perfectly shaped left eyebrow quirked up. "I don't need to submit to a magical oath to know that such information shouldn't be thrown around carelessly. We've worked hard to build what we have. If the non-magical humans were to turn on us with all their ships and weapons, it would be the end of our world. Only an absolute *idiot* wouldn't understand that."

Such a blunt response was unnerving. Ellis Divine, the strongest magician in the country, someone even the Council members couldn't coerce into binding with the iron word, thought the situation was dangerous enough to spell the end for magicians.

"So what is it that you want from me?" she asked then.

I glanced at Esten, realizing we hadn't discussed a plan before coming here. But as always, Esten was prepared. Unlike me, he'd taken the time to think a few steps ahead.

"Kieren has a gift for tracking magic," Esten said. "Since we already know Nogg is one of the perpetrators, we can track him and then use him to lead us to whoever masterminded the plan. We think they're close to finishing the tests on the Metal Giant, which means they will be dumping more wells into the original world soon. We need to stop them before then, but the two of us can't take them on alone. Kieren is new and injured, and we'll be going up against thorned magicians who have virtually unlimited wells. We need your strength, Ellis."

Ellis pursed her lips as though mulling it over for a moment, but then, instead of replying, she looked at my right wrist. "What did you say happened to your hand, precisely?"

The abrupt change of subject caught me off guard. "Um... I was trying to put rebound magic into my well," I said. "But I must have been too late, because it . . . *ate* my hand? I'm not sure, to be honest. It all happened so quickly."

Ellis hummed thoughtfully, then reached out and took my wrist with both hands. My body went stiff as the idea of being turned into a frog resurfaced in my mind. "I don't think that's what happened," she pronounced with a studious expression.

"Y-you don't?" I croaked.

"No," Ellis said, twisting my wrist this way and that. "Rebound magic doesn't eat body parts. It might well have shattered all the bones in your hand, but it would have left it attached. I think what happened is that somehow your hand separated from your body and you accidentally sent it someplace else along with the rebound."

"Where?" I asked dubiously.

Ellis shrugged. "I don't know. Interestingly, I don't see any trail coming from your wrist, but I am not skilled at tracking magic... yet. Anyway, I have never encountered such a case in all my studies. I'd love to make some notes." Ellis let go of my wrist, stood up, and reached for a thick journal from one of the bookshelves. She opened it, pulled the pencil out of her bun, letting the waves of her long hair fall loose, and proceeded to scribble in the journal, looking fully engrossed in her notetaking.

Esten and I exchanged confused glances.

"Ellis?" Esten said awkwardly after a minute or so of waiting. "What about the investigation? Will you help us catch the culprits?"

Ellis tore her attention away from the journal for long enough to say, "Obviously, Esten. You can't handle it without me. Let me know when you're ready, and I'll free up some time."

"Okay," Esten replied slowly. Considering all our fears about coming here and talking Ellis into helping, the result felt quite anticlimactic. Although, come to think of it, this was exactly what Probos had predicted would happen.

"What do we do now?" I whispered to Esten.

"I think we just... leave?" he whispered back.

I nodded.

"Well, thank you, Ellis. Have a good evening," Esten said, and stood up.

"Yep, bye-bye," Ellis said, not looking up from her notes. "Do tell me if that hand comes back for a visit in the meantime, won't you?"

"Um... certainly," I promised, trying to dispel the morbid picture of my detached hand popping up on Master Hanska's doorstep, and followed Esten out of the study.

~

"Well, she didn't turn us into frogs," I said with relief once we arrived back home. Luckily the magic around Ellis's house didn't require walking backward onto the street to exit, and we'd been able to transport directly from her porch.

"No, she did not." Esten shook his head, still a little dazed and puzzled by the whole experience.

Reflecting on it, I had a sneaking suspicion that most of the crazy things people said about Ellis Divine were probably misunderstandings and baseless rumors. Other than Ellis's dizzyingly strong magic and her specific fields of study that trumped everything else, she was a surprisingly unintimidating person. That didn't technically mean she wasn't *capable* of magicking people into frogs, but at least she hadn't tried it on Esten or me. Perhaps she'd be willing to use that skill on whoever was dumping their wells on Oi's friends. I didn't mind that idea in the slightest.

CHAPTER 32
KIEREN

The following day started with Esten ordering breakfast to be magically delivered so I wouldn't have to exert myself cooking. Several minutes later, a basket of fresh bagels with cheese and jam, pastries, and fruit materialized on the dining room table. With it came a fresh-off-the-press issue of the *Boston Times*, which Esten picked up and read aloud to me. Its splashy front page proclaimed that the mysterious Metal Giant had been spotted in Eastern Massachusetts skies again. The reporter speculated that it must have been the airship the government had been secretly testing for the past few weeks, and that perhaps the US's involvement in the conflict among the European nations was imminent. To add oil to the fire, the bottom right corner of the front page was dedicated to the ongoing anti-magic protests in DC and the citizens' outrage over the lack of progress in the sludge investigation.

"How long can we tolerate the Assembly's lack of response?" the article asked. "How many more neighborhoods and cities will fall victim to this criminal negligence? Taxpayers have the right to know!"

Esten scoffed, aggravated by the paper, and pushed it to the side, replacing it with a bagel and a plate of fruit. "They've got no idea what they are talking about, singing praises for a machine that will plunge us into war while simultaneously turning against magicians for something we're trying our hardest to fix. The epitome of ignorance!" Esten hadn't woken up in the most optimistic mood, and the article was only making it worse. Not to mention that it was almost time for Probos's undercover associate to arrive for our meeting, and we both dreaded having to tell someone new about the original world.

Someone finally knocked on the front door as I was about to finish my deliciously sweet pain aux raisins. Esten and I shared a look; Esten nodded and got up. I put the remainder of the pastry on my plate, suddenly a lot less hungry, and followed him to the foyer. It was time.

"Wyckett?" Esten said in astonishment as he opened the door.

Wyckett Foxx stood on the porch in a checkered sage-green suit and a bowler hat, seemingly equally surprised to find Esten and me on the other side of the door. "Well, I'll be jinxed," he said, grinning.

We led him to the dining room and offered him coffee and breakfast.

"Probos briefed me about a few things," Wyckett said, carefully arranging a piece of cheese on his bagel, "but I never imagined you'd taken over Master Hanska's investigation or that newbie Kieren was a tracker."

My face flushed at the compliment. I was happy and relieved that it was Wyckett who had been secretly working with us all along. "Thanks," I said. "But can't you do it too? You were the one keeping an eye on Nogg."

Wyckett smirked but shook his head. "As an Enforcement

Bureau agent, I have a whole bag of tricks at my disposal—none of which I'm allowed to disclose, by the way—but suffice it to say that they don't work like your skill, Kieren. You have a special talent." Wyckett paused, stirring sugar and cinnamon into his coffee. "So, what are the two of you supposed to tell me? Probos warned me that there is certain information to consider before we set out to apprehend Nogg."

I swallowed nervously. Wyckett looked serious and businesslike but at the same time relaxed. As an Enforcement employee, he was no stranger to dangerous missions, and that was probably what he expected this time as well—another tricky job, a rule-breaking magician, a mystery to solve ... not his entire worldview thrown out of the window. Breaking the truth to him was going to be difficult. I felt for Esten.

He pushed away his coffee cup and inhaled, slowly gathering his thoughts, then opened his mouth to speak—but another knock on the front door interrupted him.

Esten went rigid. I was instantly on edge as well—we hadn't invited anyone other than Wyckett. Did Probos have any more undercover associates he'd forgotten to mention?

Wyckett cleared his throat. "I'm sorry," he said, looking slightly guilty. "I should have told you right away, but I've recruited someone to assist us."

Esten's face paled. "Who?" he asked, his voice taking on an icy edge.

Wyckett's gaze flicked to the side. "It was a bit of an on-the-spot decision," he confessed. "I was the one who had to collect and deliver Spiht's remains to her for burial. I *had to* tell her what happened."

"You told *Cynn*?" Esten said in shock. "Why would you do that?"

"Esten, breathe easy," Wyckett said calmly, but there was a new heaviness in his expression. "I know it wasn't authorized, but Cynn is devastated, and she wants to find those who put Spiht up to this. I couldn't dump her brother's bloody corpse on her doorstep and walk away. It wasn't *right*."

My heart sank. I hadn't known it was Wyckett who'd had to get Spiht from what was left of that forest, not some nameless Assembly employee. My mind flashed back to the bloody stain in the snow, to the screams. Nausea crept up my throat. How could Wyckett sit here and smile and continue to do his job? He had to feel awful. Of course I didn't blame him for telling Cynn about the meeting.

But Esten wasn't in a forgiving mood. He glared daggers at Wyckett. "Well, she isn't the only one who lost someone! Family or not, you shouldn't have done that. Of all people, Bureau of Enforcement employees should know what discretion means."

Wyckett sucked in a breath, baffled by the severity of Esten's reaction.

I bit my lip. The situation was sensitive. Unlike Cynn, Esten had never gotten a body to bury or to mourn. When he'd learned of Master Hanska's death back in DC, he had also lost his head and pursued Nogg instead of stopping the sludge. Wyckett must have been aware of that but stoically did not bring it up. Both he and Esten were guilty of the same thing; it was just that Wyckett had been missing some crucial information when he'd decided to follow his heart instead of sticking to protocol.

"Esten, it's okay," I said quietly. "Wyckett doesn't know about . . . *everything*. We can't hold that against him."

"I know that, Kieren," Esten replied, frustrated. "But what are we going to do now? We can't just turn her away—she knows too much. And we can't move on without telling her the rest of it either."

"I think we can *trust* Cynn," I proposed tentatively. I glanced at Wyckett for confirmation. He was obviously still confused by our entire exchange but nodded, and I continued to reason aloud. "Cynn is a good person, and she has treated me like a friend. Besides, Probos told us to find allies. The fact that she came here must mean that she wants to help. Having Ellis on our side is great, but we don't know how many from the Council are backing Nogg. We can't be overprepared. I think it's good that she's here."

Esten huffed. There was sound logic in what I'd said; he couldn't deny that, even though he was reluctant to go along with it. But it seemed our time to make the decision had run out.

There was another knock on the front door. To my relief, Esten sighed and stood up, facing Wyckett. "Kieren hasn't spent as much time among magicians, so he might not grasp the gravity of this situation, but don't tell me you regret this later." He sighed and left to let Cynn in.

∼

Esten took on the task of methodically explaining to Wyckett and Cynn what we had uncovered beyond the rift while I watched their reactions. They didn't ask questions, only listened as the air in the room grew heavier. Despite all their experience and training and dedication to magic, neither was prepared to hear the truth of our world's origin. Wyckett put down his breakfast and didn't touch it again. Cynn's cup of bergamot tea was abandoned after only a few sips and sat cooling on the table. At some point Wyckett's hand found Cynn's, and she allowed him to hold it.

"So . . . they've been pouring their wells into the portals," Wyckett said glumly, "and now we are at risk of not only escalating a world war but also of the general population finding out where we all came from?"

"Correct," Esten replied. "The entire world our Founders built is at risk."

Wyckett shook his head in disbelief and fell silent again.

Cynn took it worse. My heart squeezed at the sight of her. She was wearing a toffee-colored dress that matched her magic, but it was adorned with embroidery of pewter rose wreaths reminiscent of the ones in funeral parlors. There was no denying it—the warm, straightforward, smiling Cynn I knew was now in deep mourning, and learning this truth about the world was yet another harsh blow.

"I'm sorry," she breathed out shakily. "I just . . . I need a moment." With that, she excused herself and fled to the powder room. Wyckett's gaze followed her with worry, but he stayed in the dining room.

Esten got up and left as well to make himself more coffee in the kitchen—the non-magical way this time, in an octagon-shaped espresso pot on the stove—to allow Wyckett and Cynn an opportunity to process their thoughts. By the time the coffee finished brewing, Cynn had returned and reclaimed her seat next to Wyckett.

"I'm sorry," she said again, and now her voice shook a little less. "Losing Spiht to his well was terrible, and now this . . . but I suppose we can't allow ourselves to cry idly. Someone took advantage of my brother's thirst for knowledge, and now he's dead. I won't forgive that."

I was amazed at the resolve in her voice.

Wyckett nodded sympathetically, ready to go along with whatever Cynn wanted. As earth-shattering as the truth about our world was, he still seemed more worried about Cynn. "Do you guys have a plan of action yet?" he asked.

"Yes," Esten replied as he made his way back to the

table, bringing the strong smell of freshly brewed coffee with him. "We're going to find Nogg using Kieren's skill and apprehend him. Nogg doesn't know Kieren can track, so we have the element of surprise on our side. But we can't go yet—we need a sample of his magic for Kieren to work with. Unfortunately the sludge destroyed the area in DC where we battled, so we can't procure one there. Do you two have any ideas?"

Wyckett took a moment to mull it over. "I know where his home is, but he's been on the run for a while. Who knows if there's any magic left there? Also, it's risky for us to show up at his place—what if he has set up a trap there?"

Esten considered. "Well, unless we can think of another way to get his magic, we'll have to try to find it there. I'll notify Ellis so she can join us."

"Wait," Cynn said. "I think I actually might have a better idea. Nogg visited me with Spiht on the day of the outbreak in DC. He had some whiskey and used magic to make a fire drink with it. I didn't think much of it back then; I had no idea what they were up to."

Wyckett's eyes widened. "That's true—I forgot. They did visit you. I was keeping an eye on Nogg at the time and tried to warn Spiht about him, but he didn't listen. That kid was too proud for his own good..."

Cynn's lips curved into a small, sad smile.

A realization dawned on me: that was the argument I'd seen Spiht and Wyckett have in the abandoned hangar. Wyckett had tried to set Spiht on the right path because he was worried about Cynn, but Spiht hadn't wanted to hear any of it. If only I'd understood what I was seeing then, maybe I could've helped convince him. Maybe Spiht's death could have been avoided.

"Okay, then," Esten said. "That's good news. Cynn, please

bring Nogg's glass for Kieren. In the meantime, I'll contact Ellis. When do we head out?"

"I think I need a bit of time to get myself together," Cynn said uncertainly. "We have a big battle ahead of us. Let's not rush it."

Wyckett squeezed her hand in support. "Yes, I'd like to prepare and grab a few things from my place as well. If our goal is to arrest Nogg, we can't go empty-handed. I propose we do it at sundown."

"I second that," Cynn said, visibly relieved that Wyckett agreed.

"All right." Esten exhaled. "Let us reassemble here at that time, then."

CHAPTER 33
KIEREN

Ellis was the first to arrive that evening. Her long hair was pulled into a French braid, and she wore a streamlined periwinkle pantsuit and knee-high boots, looking sharp and ready for battle. She didn't bring Roy or Bay with her, which probably meant she hadn't told them about the portals. That was good.

A whole day had passed since I'd learned the truth, but with everything else that was happening, it had barely started to sink in. My head was a jumbled mess; it would take time to sort through my thoughts. Had the Founders been right to do what they did? Was it really the best solution for everyone? I didn't have the answers. How could I judge them, a hundred and fifty years later, without all the facts about what they'd had to go through? Right now, what mattered most was stopping the sludge and making sure Oi's friends were safe. Everything else could wait.

"Good evening," Ellis said, and stepped into the foyer.

I opened my mouth to respond, but before I could utter a word, she noticed Oi perched on the mantel. Her face illuminated with sudden interest. Not wasting another second on greetings, she made a beeline for Oi and immediately struck up a conversation.

"Well, good evening to you too, Ellis," Esten said with a sigh, but by the look on his face, he wasn't exactly surprised that Ellis's interest in anything rare and magical completely eclipsed the need for formalities.

Next Cynn and Wyckett materialized on the front porch. Unlike Ellis, who was merrily chatting up Oi, the two looked somber, no doubt still affected by the portal revelations. Wyckett wore the same sage-green suit as before, but now he had a satchel slung over his shoulder, and Cynn had changed into trousers and a long coat in the colors of her magic.

"Are we all ready?" Esten asked, and everyone except for Ellis nodded.

"Ellis?" I called.

Ellis finally noticed that the rest of our group had assembled, said something to Oi, and joined us, taking the spot between Esten and me. "Such rare and eloquent magic," she said instead of greeting our other guests.

Cynn and Wyckett exchanged confused glances. Oh, heavens—just like Esten, they probably couldn't hear Oi and had no clue what Ellis meant. To them it must have looked like she'd been having a very animated conversation with a wooden doll. I stifled a smile.

Ellis continued, seemingly unaware, "I have read about those spirits but never encountered one in person. I would love to come back and conduct an interview with Splendid Oi of the Eastern Woodlands, if you don't mind, Kieren."

I scratched my head. Splendid Oi of the Eastern Woodlands? What on earth had Oi told her? "Of course," I said aloud. "Anytime, Ellis."

"I'll make a note in my schedule." Ellis smiled.

Cynn stared at Ellis, bewildered, while Wyckett politely shrugged, apparently content to let her be her odd, doll-chatting self.

Ellis seemed used to that kind of reaction. She nodded, and then, as though someone had flipped an invisible switch, her expression turned serious. At the same moment, her magic began to buzz around her in that uncomfortable warping manner. Idle chat was over; Ellis was ready to go.

Esten's face turned solemn as well. "Cynn, did you bring the glass?" he asked.

"Ah, yes, I've got it." Cynn fumbled in the left pocket of her coat and produced a small shot glass.

I took it from her. It felt a little nerve-wracking to work with all these senior magicians around, but I shut my eyes and searched for the remnants of Nogg's magic. And there it was—burnt red, scorching and abrasive. "Found it," I said, opening my eyes.

A moment of silence followed, the calm before the storm. Everyone was looking at the glass in my left hand, trying to concentrate and put their thoughts in order. Only Esten's gaze was on my right wrist where my hand was no more, his silver eyes filled with worry. He hadn't asked me not to use magic this time—we both knew I couldn't promise that.

But still he mouthed, "Be careful, Kieren."

And I nodded—*You too.*

Then Wyckett broke the silence—"Let's go"—and everyone was instantly in motion.

Ellis placed her right hand on my shoulder and her left on Esten's. "Lead the way," she said as Wyckett grabbed Esten's and Cynn's hands, completing the chain. I pulled on the thread of magic from the glass, wishing to follow it to its source.

Before I stepped into the stream, I searched for Oi to say one last silent goodbye, but he was no longer there.

~

We were in an open field, I realized after the moment of dizziness that always came with the use of tracking magic. The tall grass was swaying violently around my feet. A line of projector lights had been set up along the field's perimeter, blinding me to what lay beyond them and reducing the world to a blur of half-shadows. Loud buzzing and swooshing sounds filled the air.

I looked up. Directly above us hovered a massive airship—the Metal Giant Esten and I had been searching for. It was truly magnificent, sleek and shiny, reflecting the light from the projectors and hanging there so effortlessly. For a moment all my feelings of danger disappeared and I simply gawked at the machine in wondering awe. How could something so big appear so light? How could it fly like that? Childishly I wished I could ride on it.

There was a metallic noise then, and the bottom of the airship started to open, revealing its mechanical insides. I frowned. The ship was full of magic—strong magic in different colors.

But before I could sort out what I was seeing exactly, a voice that sounded distantly familiar shouted, "Fire!" and several long metal cylinders fell from the airship's open belly.

At the same instant, Wyckett screamed from somewhere beside me, "It's a trap! Get out!"

The rest of his words were drowned out by what happened next.

My eyes were still glued to the Metal Giant, and everything seemed to unfold in slow motion. A hand squeezed my shoulder and yanked me close.

Then everything around us exploded.

CHAPTER 34
ESTEN

It all happened so fast. I'd barely gotten my bearings before Wyckett shouted a warning and the Metal Giant started dropping explosives on us.

"Kieren!" I screamed, trying to locate his silhouette against the blinding lights, but it was too late. Wyckett jerked my hand, and on pure instinct, I stumbled after him into the magic stream. A disorienting blur of magic enveloped us, and then I wasn't on the field anymore but crouching under the trees, Kieren's name still on my lips.

"Quiet, Esten!" Wyckett hissed. Although what was the point? No one would hear us in this mayhem. The cylinders from the Giant fell on the field, barreling into the dirt and exploding on contact. The ground rose like violent waves and then crashed back down with a deafening sound. Dust filled the air, and the earth shook with so much force that I could hardly keep my balance. It was a horrifying scene.

"Kieren . . . w-where?" I managed to say. If he was hurt again, if he'd lost another limb because I hadn't taught him properly, because I'd failed to keep him out of danger, I didn't know what I would do.

"Ellis got him," Wyckett said into my ear. "I saw her wield her magic before we left." Several more explosions went off, raising more dust. My shoulders slumped in relief—if there was a safe place in this carnage, it was beside the strongest magician in the country. Ellis was bound to keep Kieren alive. Right now I had to trust that. But there was panic in Wyckett's voice when he added, "But I don't know where Cynn is."

Dread twisted my insides. "What do you mean, you *don't know*? You were holding her hand. Did she escape from the field?"

"I don't know." Wyckett shook his head, trying to suppress his panic. "I'm not sure. I think her hand slipped from mine when we were still in the stream, on the way from the house. I didn't see her when we exited. Maybe she got lost on the way?"

I had honestly been too distracted to notice whether Cynn had been with us when we'd arrived, but her getting lost sounded extremely unlikely. Cynn was too experienced a magician. But I kept that thought to myself. It was better if Wyckett believed she'd never made it to the field than that she'd gotten caught in the explosions. Not to mention how *well-timed* those explosions had been and how much those cylinders reminded me of the one we'd seen in Spiht's possession...

"Hey, look," I said to distract myself and Wyckett from our brooding thoughts. The dust was starting to settle, revealing the devastation the explosions had caused to the field. On the far side of it was a high observation platform, set up a safe distance away from where the explosives had fallen. There were people on it. I hadn't noticed the platform before because of the blinding lights, but now I was out of their beams. As the air cleared, I could finally make out one figure with long hair, dressed in a pewter-colored trench coat. Anger surged through me. "I knew he was involved!"

Kavender stood on the platform looking gloriously satisfied. Behind him was a row of seats, all occupied by people in suits and military uniforms. They were clapping, pleased with the presentation. I didn't recognize any of them from this distance.

"Who are the rest of those people?" I asked.

"I think," Wyckett said, squinting, "the tallest one is Senate Majority Leader Harkwood; to the right is his senior staffer Riggins. The rest I don't know. Possibly airship engineers and military brass."

My blood ran cold. "You mean all those people are *non-magicians*?"

"I believe so," Wyckett said grimly. "Probos speculated that some high-profile non-magicians had to be involved in the airship construction, but this is more than we thought. Whether or not the project is formally sanctioned by Congress and the president, at least some government officials appear to be involved."

The men in suits shook hands and congratulated one another on the successful launch.

"How could they do this?" I asked, seething. Not only had these people sought out magic to create the vilest and most destructive weapons I'd ever seen, but they had dared to test them on magicians. "We have to arrest them," I said. "They tried to murder us!"

Wyckett shook his head. "We can't worry about them now, Esten. Non-magicians are out of our jurisdiction. Probos has to work with their government to sort this out. Our job is to collect evidence and deal with our side."

I pressed my lips together, furious, but Wyckett was right.

Kavender continued speaking to the assembled men,

gesturing toward the destruction they'd caused. I wished we could hear what the scum was saying.

As though reading my mind, Wyckett said, "Let's get closer. How about behind that line of projectors by the trees?" Wyckett had picked a good position—within earshot of the platform, but far enough away to hide us from Kavender.

I nodded. "Let's go."

Once we'd transported to the new spot, Wyckett reached inside his satchel and produced an object that looked like a small black box with a lens. I frowned. "What's that?"

"Tool of the trade," Wyckett whispered, picking up the box and pointing it at the platform. It made a series of clicking noises.

"A camera?" I said, surprised.

"Yes. We need hard evidence," Wyckett confirmed quietly, and took more pictures.

I was rather amazed—I'd never thought a Bureau of Enforcement employee's job could include something like this. But it did make sense, of course. If you wanted to accuse someone of misusing magic, you had better be ready to prove it. Interestingly, the camera had only a faint veil of magic around it. I suspected it was to alter the camera's size so it would fit inside Wyckett's satchel. Other than that, it was perfectly ordinary.

Kavender started speaking again, and I strained to make out what he was saying over the noise of the airship's propellers.

"You just saw a demonstration of several of our iron bombs," Kavender declared. "This Metal Giant can carry up to sixty inside and drop them anywhere in the world at my command. There are about thirty still on the ship and another hundred in production, waiting to be personally charged with my magic."

I scowled. No wonder I'd felt thorned magic in the metal of those cylinders. Kavender must have used it to make the explosives more devastating. Another wave of anger swelled inside me. How dare he use magic for something so despicable as bombs?

The man Wyckett had identified as Majority Leader Harkwood asked, "How soon will they be completed? One ship is enough to intimidate those European fools, but you do realize we need more than that for a successful transatlantic campaign, don't you, Kavender?"

I couldn't see Kavender's expression from this distance, but I was pretty sure he did *not* like being addressed in that manner. He didn't say anything.

Instead, one of the men whom Wyckett had guessed was on the engineering side responded to Harkwood. "The main frame of Giant II is fifty percent complete, sir. We still need Magician Nogg to alter the fuel to lift it off the ground and conduct the necessary test flights, but with the success of Metal Giant I, that can likely be accomplished within two weeks."

"Do proceed expeditiously," Harkwood said, his tone strongly suggesting that both the engineering team and Kavender had better comply.

I had the most unsettling feeling. So *that* was how Nogg was involved in the whole thing. Not only had these men made a Metal Giant that ran on enchanted fuel and was stocked full of weapons, but they had an assembly line ready to produce more airships in record time. What was going to happen if those thorned weapons were deployed overseas? The world's magicians wouldn't just stand by. If American magicians were seen breaking their policy of military noninvolvement, others would do the same, creating a conflict the likes of which our world had never seen. What on earth were these warmongers trying to achieve?

Before Kavender and Harkwood could divulge more of their awful plans, something interrupted them. The ground in the spot where Kieren's tracking magic had initially brought us started shaking; then the rubble from the explosions burst to the sides, and a bubble containing two figures emerged from under it. Ellis Divine gracefully floated into the air with Kieren suspended next to her, alive and in one piece. *Alive.* All the air left my lungs in a sigh of relief.

"Should have known it would take more than a few explosions to deter you, Miss Divine," Kavender said, grinning, and then addressed the men behind him: "Gentlemen, please follow my associates while I take care of some matters here."

The non-magicians didn't need to be told twice. At the sight of Ellis and Kieren hovering before them, unharmed despite the thirty bombs that had been dropped on their heads, Harkwood and company scrambled to their feet and fled the platform, aiming for the two cars that were parked next to it. Two more magicians materialized on the ground, ready to escort them to safety. The first one was Nogg; the second—

Wyckett's face drained of color. "What is Cynn doing there?" he said slowly.

I shook my head. "I don't know," I said, too stumped to process what I was seeing. What *was* Cynn doing there with Kavender? With Nogg, the murderer? She was supposed to have been helping us!

The non-magicians hastily piled into their cars. Nogg took the driver's seat of one, and Cynn was about to take the other when Kieren's shocked voice broke through the noise of the propellers.

"Cynn!" he shouted. "Cynn, wait!"

But Cynn didn't respond. Didn't even raise her head to look him in the eye. Instead she climbed into the car and shut the door, and then both engines roared to life. My fists clenched. So that was how things were, then. That was why she hadn't been with us when we'd exited the stream. She'd led us into a trap and let Kavender test his bombs on us.

"We're going after them," Wyckett said immediately as the two cars took to the dirt road and sped through the field.

I tore my gaze away from the cars. "I'm staying with Kieren. His magic—"

"Esten," Wyckett said, and I heard the desperation in his voice, the heartbreak he'd been holding back, now ready to spill over. "Kieren is with Ellis. He will be safe with her, and I need you. I can't go alone against *two* magicians . . ." Wyckett looked down, his shoulders suddenly heavy. He clearly didn't want to believe this about Cynn, but denial could last only so long. He knew we would have to arrest her. No matter how betrayed I felt by what she'd done, it must have been a thousand times worse for Wyckett. I couldn't leave him.

Slowly I nodded. "All right, what do we do?"

CHAPTER 35
KIEREN

For a few moments I stood rigid with horror, Ellis beside me, her hand still on my shoulder. Everything around us was exploding—ground rumbling and splitting, grass and dirt flying in all directions—except inside the bubble of space Ellis had created around us. I had to fight the instinct to flinch and duck away from the debris that kept flying straight at us and then diverting away from the bubble as though repelled by a magnetic force. It was dizzying and terrifying. But even worse was that Ellis and I were in the bubble *alone*.

I tried to get my thoughts in order amid the cacophony of destruction.

"Everyone?" was the only word I managed.

"Escaped," Ellis replied, appearing deep in concentration.

My chest loosened in relief—we were the only ones caught in the epicenter of the bombardment. Although *caught* felt like the wrong way to describe what was happening. Ellis appeared very purposeful about remaining exactly where we were. I had no doubt she could've easily transported us away after Wyckett's warning, but she'd chosen not to so she could *study* what was happening from the inside. Her confidence that she could stop the bombs from blowing us both into a million shreds made me feel faint.

Ellis observed the debris flying around us with narrowed eyes, and by the look on her face, she did not like what she saw. I swallowed down my panic and looked closely too. I could just make out the pewter-colored threads of magic in parts of the cylinders. When they hit the ground, the threads exploded and shot in all directions like obscene fireworks.

"I've seen a cylinder like this before," I said. "Or rather, tiny pieces of one. We found Spiht collecting them in a field the day we fought. What kind of magic is this?"

"I presume that someone has altered the metal in these cylinders to cause maximum damage," Ellis replied, still concentrating. "Tricky work," she added, but it was clear she didn't mean it as a compliment. The idea gave me chills as well —who would use magic for such a thing?

Finally, after several minutes, the explosions died down and their ruinous magic ceased, but by then we were completely buried in dirt and debris. Things were quiet for a while, and I had no idea what was happening above us.

Ellis exhaled. "I think I know all I need to know about those explosives. Shall we come out now?" she asked.

I agreed nervously; we couldn't stay buried forever.

With that, the dirt around us started shaking, and our bubble moved upward. With a new kind of terror, I realized Ellis was *flying* us. Heavens, I wished I'd asked her what other types of magic she was capable of before we'd embarked on this mission!

Ellis continued to fly us up and forward until we were some thirty feet above the ground, directly in front of an observation platform I hadn't noticed before. My stomach dropped—Kavender, Spiht's teacher and the magician who had watched me at the Council meeting, was addressing us from the edge of the platform.

"Should have known it would take more than a few explosions to deter you, Miss Divine," he said, smirking. "Gentlemen, please follow my associates while I take care of some matters here." At that, Nogg appeared at the bottom of the platform, along with another magician...

I blinked. "Cynn?" Instinctively I tried to step toward her, but Ellis tightened her grip on my shoulder.

"Don't, Kieren. Cynn was not with us when we arrived. I don't think it's wise to follow her now," she said, then added matter-of-factly, "Also, if you step away and I let go of your shoulder, you *will* plummet and probably break your spine."

But I didn't care at that moment. My heart was already falling. Had Cynn really led us here to be ambushed? Had she known Kavender was going to drop explosives on us?

"Cynn!" I called out, louder this time. "Cynn, wait!"

But Cynn didn't look at me. Like I meant nothing to her. When she'd told me she was glad I had manifested, I'd thought I had found a friend. I had confided in her, convinced Esten to trust her, and all this time she had been... I couldn't make any sense of it.

"What do we do now?" I asked, the taste of betrayal like bitter black tea that no amount of sugar could fix.

"We stay here," Ellis replied calmly. "Kavender is the strongest magician among them; it wouldn't be prudent to leave him alone with all these weapons and the airship." I nodded silently. I was in no shape to disagree or think of another plan.

Ellis raised her voice loud enough to carry over the sound

of the airship's propellers. "Am I correct to presume that you're responsible for those nasty explosives, Kavender?"

Kavender gave a shallow bow as though pleased with Ellis's acknowledgment. "Like them?" he asked as tiny sparks of his magic started to buzz around him.

"Not one bit," Ellis replied, unimpressed. "How did you manage to break the iron word?"

Kavender snorted. "I have an affinity for working with metals, as you might have already noticed. It was only a matter of time before I learned to disarm the needle before it killed me."

Ellis frowned and said more to herself than anyone else, "Even the Founders' magic wasn't without a flaw, it seems..."

Kavender relished her reaction. "Now it's my turn to ask a question: Since when are *you* running errands for the Council? I thought you were independent, Ellis Divine."

Ellis raised an eyebrow at that, deflecting Kavender's verbal jab. "I *am*, and I have independently decided that a magician who acts this cavalier about the peace we've achieved in this world is too dangerous to be left unchecked."

Kavender laughed. "Looks like a lifetime of indoctrination has eroded even a mind as powerful as yours. Well, nothing to do but show you how outdated your beliefs are." As Kavender said that, one of the heavy safety beams from the platform he was standing on started screeching and curling up until it tore off entirely. "Shall we settle this the way our kind does, Ellis?" Kavender taunted, his expression finally turning dangerous. The metal beam hovered beside him, its jagged piece pointing toward Ellis and me like a spear.

Ellis's quick gaze scanned the platform. It occurred to me that she hadn't been chatting Kavender up for no reason—she'd been waiting for the non-magicians to leave. Once everyone else was gone, the air around us started to thicken, warping and becoming charged with strong magic that left the oddest sensation on my skin, making the hairs on my arms rise.

Instead of replying to Kavender, Ellis raised her free hand. A bolt of blue lightning ripped out of the sky and struck him where he stood.

CHAPTER 36
ESTEN

Wyckett waited until the cars had crossed the field and swerved onto the road running through the woods, their headlights quickly swallowed by the night.

"What are we waiting for? We're going to lose them," I said, confused.

"We won't," Wyckett replied with an unsettling calmness in his voice. As an Enforcement employee, he was probably more used to these kinds of situations than I was. "Let them get closer to the woods," he said. "For me, that terrain has a strategic advantage. I'll stop them there, and we can apprehend them."

I squinted at the forest and then remembered what Wyckett's magic specialty was, and I realized at once why he wanted to wait.

"If we happen to get split up," Wyckett continued, "you go after Nogg, since you have experience battling him, and I'll take on Cynn. I know her magic—she uses sugar. Be mindful of the non-magicians, though—I'll prevent them from fleeing, but we don't want to hurt them."

"Understood," I said. If magic caused any harm to the non-magicians, especially someone as high-profile as the Senate majority leader, we'd be forced to explain our actions not only to Probos but probably to Congress as well. And we definitely couldn't afford to taint the relationship between magicians and civilians any more than it already had been by the sludge outbreak in DC.

"One last thing," Wyckett said, producing a set of golden handcuffs from his satchel. "Take these with you."

Unease stirred in me. "What are they?" I asked.

"More tools of the trade," Wyckett replied. "These cuffs are enchanted to restrain the magic of the person you put them on. Be extremely careful with them—you don't want them to fall into the wrong hands. Also, the magic runs out after about an hour of use, so keep that in mind."

I nodded, gingerly taking the cuffs and tucking them into my belt. Secretly I felt better knowing that this kind of object only worked for a short while. I couldn't fathom the horror of not being able to use my magic because of cuffs on my wrists. Enforcement employees handled some *awful* things. Capturing Nogg and putting these on him would be tricky, considering how destructive he was with his fire. But I had to find a way.

Wyckett transported us closer to the speeding cars. We exited in the middle of the road, surrounded by forest on both sides. The cars were still some distance ahead. Wyckett took a deep breath and raised his arms. The ground started rumbling as though something were moving underneath it. The surrounding trees shook as many long, thin tendrils burst through the dirt farther down the road and grew rapidly, intertwining and forming a living barrier made of tree roots. Both cars swerved, spun, and screeched to a stop to avoid colliding with it. I watched in awe as Wyckett used magic to make the roots grow. This was why he'd specifically wanted to be in the forest.

The roots continued to thicken and multiply, now stretching their tendrils toward the two cars. But before they could entangle the cars completely, the drivers' doors swung open and both Cynn and Nogg jumped out.

Until that moment, I'd been trying to hold on to the fragile hope that Cynn's actions had some reasonable explanation. But then I met her gaze. In the harsh light of the cars' headlights, she looked ready for battle. Her eyes held no silent apology, nor a shred of regret for betraying us.

Suddenly all the emotions I'd kept contained since I'd seen her next to Nogg and Kavender broke through.

"How could you do this, Cynn?" I spat, rage swirling in my chest. "You came to Master's home. You convinced Kieren you were his friend. You even used Wyckett to gain our trust, and all the while you were lying to us. That's why you tried to stop me from going after Nogg back in DC, isn't it? *Right after* he confessed to killing Master. Is there no end to your deviousness?"

Cynn regarded me coldly. "I don't owe you an explanation, Esten, but I didn't know what had happened to Hanska before that night in DC either. Believe it or not, I considered him a friend, and I am truly sad that it turned out like this."

I laughed at the sheer absurdity of the statement. "So, what, your tears were genuine? You grieved Master's life as you helped his murderer escape?"

Cynn stuck out her chin stubbornly. "As I said, I don't have to explain myself to a spoiled brat like you. You've barely learned the truth about this world, and now you think you can lecture me about how I feel? Changes demand sacrifices, Esten. I've made my peace with it."

I couldn't believe my ears. "Sacrifices? You mean like your 'brother' Spiht?"

Cynn flinched.

"Esten," Wyckett hissed, and grabbed my elbow in warning.

I knew that was a low blow, but I did not care. "Just hours ago, you said you couldn't forgive those who took advantage of his thirst for knowledge. Was that a lie too?"

Conflict and grief flashed across Cynn's face, but she squished them both. "I am deeply sad that *any* magician's life had to be lost, but that doesn't change the fundamental truth. More than anything, Spiht was a victim of this unjust system our Founders bound us to," she replied. "It's the Service and the people who keep it in place that I will *never* forgive."

Nonsense! I wanted to shout. How easy it must have been to stand there and philosophize about the Service when she had blood all over her hands.

I was going to give Cynn a piece of my mind, but Nogg cut in with a sneer. "How long are you two going to keep up your chit-chat? Cynn, you know what needs to be done. We can't leave witnesses."

Cynn's mouth twitched, but she gave a short nod and raised her arms, compliant. So that's how it was, then.

"Come get me, puppy!" Nogg taunted, and took off into the woods, a small red flame in his hand illuminating the way.

"Go after him," Wyckett urged. "I'll handle Cynn."

I didn't need to be told twice. I chased Nogg as he ran deeper into the forest. When the road was out of sight and there was nothing around us but trees, he abruptly stopped and turned around. The flame expanded in his hand, ready to turn into the kind of raging blaze with which I was all too familiar.

"Chase, dog!" Nogg shouted, and fired without a warning.

"Curses," I gasped, and ducked to the ground, raising a cocoon of dirt to protect myself. Nogg's fire beam hit the tall pine behind me, setting it ablaze.

But he didn't stop at that. Gleefully he set fire to the tree next to the one that was already burning, and then another. The woods might have been advantageous terrain for Wyckett, but not for me when Nogg had so many trees to incinerate. That's why he must have lured me out here into the thick of the forest.

"Come out, come out, puppy!" he sang as the blaze raged.

I gritted my teeth. I couldn't rush into battle with this maniac. Unlike Spiht, Nogg seemed quite all right with the idea of murdering magicians with his own hands. If Master were here, he would tell me to take my time and come up with a strategy and that if I didn't have the time, I should find a way to make some first. Which was exactly what I intended to do.

Hidden from sight by the spreading fire, I dashed deeper into the darkness, ducked into a patch of ferns, and buried myself in soil again. Let Nogg search for *me*. In the meantime I could think.

Since the fight in DC, I'd known I would need a foolproof defense against Nogg's fire cannons in order to get close to him. I'd spent quite some time brainstorming ideas—I had even considered forging a shield from a combination of materials with high melting points. But it would be too cumbersome to carry such a thing in a battle, especially if it were big enough to protect my entire body. It wasn't until I'd seen Ellis float out of the ground with Kieren that an unexpected idea had come to mind. It was risky, audacious even—something only a magician like Ellis Divine would dare try. I wasn't Ellis. But I was my teacher's apprentice, and I would be damned if I let his murderer get away because I was too scared to try something.

Already Nogg was losing patience looking for me. "Come out, you human dog. Let me send you straight to your Master, since you miss him so much!" he jeered, and released another burst of flames, seemingly intent on burning the whole forest to ash.

One of the pines engulfed in the blaze snapped in half and crashed to the ground, spreading the fire to the carpet of dry needles underneath it. The temperature was quickly becoming unbearable, and smoke was filling up my surroundings. I couldn't afford to wait any longer. I had to make my move. Quietly I dispersed the dirt shield but stayed close to the ground and inhaled deeply. The air burned my lungs, but I kept it in—I'd have to make it last if this plan was going to work. To defeat Nogg, I needed a shield that couldn't catch fire no matter what, and there was only one material I could think of that never ever burned, that would smother flames the moment they hit it: I had to make a shield out of *nothingness*.

I closed my eyes for a moment, concentrating on pushing every molecule of air away from me, creating a bubble, just like Ellis had done, except that mine had no oxygen in it whatsoever. No fuel for Nogg to burn. When I was sure my shield was empty, I rose to my feet and ran straight at the scum.

Momentary surprise flashed onto Nogg's smug face. "Never thought you'd be so desperate that you'd do exactly as I said. Do you have a death wish, or did my fire scorch your brains?"

I didn't reply—I couldn't let any precious air escape my lungs. I just kept running forward, carrying my nothing shield.

Unnerved by my audacity, Nogg scowled and raised his arms again, aiming directly at me. "Well, suit yourself, dog!" He fired.

Despite my best intentions, my body betrayed me. It halted, nearly paralyzed with fear. I stared at the glowing beam of fire as it hit my vacuum shield point-blank, a blooming inferno mere inches from my face. Yet instead of incinerating me, the beam flickered out, met with nothing to fuel it, and turned into a blue glow that encircled my bubble. A dizzying wave of relief slammed into my chest. My shield worked! It had stopped the blaze! But that was only part one of the plan. The trickiest, most dangerous part was still ahead.

With renewed confidence, I sprinted forward again, bearing the brunt of Nogg's flames. There were only a few yards left between us.

Nogg was clearly caught off guard. Stumped by the sheer impossibility of my surviving a head-on blast, he dropped the flames and stared in confusion, first at his own hands and then at me. And that was the opening I needed.

Now or never, I thought as I dropped my nothing shield and raised the ground around Nogg. He caught on to what was happening, but it was too late.

"No!" he screamed as the soil knocked him off his feet and curled around his body. "Not again—" With a mouth full of dirt, he tried to wrestle himself free and angle his fires at me, but I kept burying him with more soil, smothering his flames before they had a chance to break through, leaving only a narrow patch around his wrists still visible. Not wasting a second to breathe, I pulled out Wyckett's golden handcuffs and snapped them around Nogg's wrists. In an instant, his magic ceased.

"Puhhh!" I puffed, releasing what was left in my oxygen-starved lungs, and gulped in as much air as my chest could hold. I couldn't believe I'd managed to capture Nogg without being roasted alive. I wanted to collapse on the ground from both relief and the enormous toll the magic had taken. But now was not the time to rest on my laurels.

After a few shaky inhales, I cleared the dirt from Nogg's

face, freeing him to breathe as well. As tempting as it was to suffocate Master Hanska's murderer, I needed Nogg alive for questioning.

He spat out mouthfuls of dirt, gasping for air.

"You dog—" he began before I changed my mind and clamped his mouth shut with soil again. The traitor didn't need it to breathe, and I had no desire to listen to his insults. Instead I needed to slow down the dangerous fire that still raged around us and then check on Wyckett. The fight was far from over.

I released my magic from the shield that was binding Nogg, leaving the pile of dirt in place. There was no way he could dig himself out with his hands and magic restrained by handcuffs. After that I concentrated on raising a wall of soil around the patch of burning pines. It was hasty work, but it did the job of containing the disaster for now.

By the time I was out of the woods, close enough to see what was happening back on the road, I found Cynn and Wyckett locked in a bizarre stalemate. Wyckett's roots had sprung up around Cynn's body, tangling around her like overgrown ivy and keeping her in one spot. But despite that, Wyckett wasn't winning.

A strange thing was happening to the roots when they touched Cynn's body. At first they thickened and sprouted stems and leaves as though full of life and ready to turn into young trees, but within seconds those leaves would start to rot, curl in on themselves, and die like they were poisoned. *That's right—sugar*, I remembered. Cynn used sugar in her magic. Small amounts of it acted like nutrients for the plants, helped them grow and flower, but the more sugar she added to Wyckett's roots, the more damaged the cells became until they wilted and decayed into lifeless dust. It was a stunning and sickening process to observe—magic that started as feathered but turned thorned through persistence.

My skin prickled. It was good that I'd captured Nogg first; Wyckett could use my help to break the stalemate. I quickly moved toward him but then paused again. From this distance I could hear Wyckett and Cynn's conversation.

"Is that why you suddenly wanted to get rid of me?" Wyckett asked, taking a step closer to Cynn. "You never once explained what went wrong or why you didn't want to continue seeing me."

Cynn laughed and made more roots disintegrate into dust around her feet. "I didn't want to see you because I can't stand you, can't stand how devoted you are to this system that keeps us in chains."

Wyckett shook his head in disbelief. "Heavens, Cynn. I don't understand what you mean. What chains? We are magicians; we live proudly as magicians. In this world, no one is trying to destroy us because of our magic."

Cynn pressed her lips together bitterly. "You haven't changed one bit, have you? Even after hearing what those people did to our ancestors, you still won't open your eyes. Have you ever asked yourself what kind of life this is, Wyckett? They tear us from our families when we are children and send us to live with strangers so we can obediently serve their every whim. A fire in the middle of the night? Sure, we'll come right out. A town needs to be built on top of a mountain no human has ever set foot on? Of course, let us do all the dirty work. Fix their oil spills, regrow the forests they cut to the ground. They act like we owe them just because we're born this way. There's no pride in that. How can you refuse to understand?"

For a long moment Wyckett gazed at her, stumped, as new roots grew, were poisoned, and died. "I don't recognize you, Cynn," he said with sadness. "I don't recognize you at all. Do you honestly think we do these things because we owe it to the non-magicians? If you happened to walk by a drowning person, would you not use your power to save them?" Wyckett took another tentative step toward her.

In response, Cynn mercilessly rotted all the new shoots that sprouted from the ground.

"Maybe," she said. "That would depend on the circumstances. But even if I did save them, that would be me *choosing* to help instead of me being obligated to risk my life for them. These people have done nothing to deserve such sacrifices from us."

Something snapped in Wyckett. "Obligated? Obligated?!" he said, his voice rising. "How can you possibly be so blind? From the moment we manifested, it stopped being about us or them. We owe our actions to the great force of magic that chose us, that gave us these gifts. Or did you think that being chosen was without consequence? Life doesn't work like that. You don't get to run around doing selfish and horrible things, even killing people, because you don't like feeling obligated. Grow up, Cynn!"

Cynn's lips trembled. The words that poured out of her were as laced with poison as her magic was. "I hate you. I hate that you believe it's all right to throw away our dreams for the sake of this charade our Founders created. But most of all"—she paused as though savoring the hurt she was about to inflict—"most of all, I hate your singing. You could've had music, could've gone after your dreams, but instead you chose the damn Service."

Wyckett's shoulders went rigid. He clenched his jaw, swallowing Cynn's vicious words. For a few seconds nobody said anything. When Wyckett finally spoke, his voice was quiet and resigned. "You can hate me all you want. You can be as stubborn and wrong as you want, but I'm not going to let this destroy you or our world. Murder is not how we bring about change or settle our differences. If you have concerns, you can present them to the Council at your trial. I am sorry. I am going to arrest you, Cynn." With that, Wyckett's left hand dug inside his satchel and produced the second pair of golden cuffs.

Cynn's eyes went wide. "No! Get away from me!" She thrashed inside her growing root cage, causing more and more of Wyckett's roots to rot.

But Wyckett continued to move closer. "Please don't resist, Cynn. You will only hurt yourself."

"No!" Cynn screamed again as the magic inside her started to pulse with growing intensity. "I won't give up my freedom! Not for them!"

My throat felt tight. I had been wrong. Wyckett *was* winning this battle, but he was also trying desperately not to lose Cynn in the process. Wyckett Foxx was a strong magician, a feathered magician, and time was on his side. He could bring Cynn to her knees through the endurance of his magic. But it was the opposite for Cynn, and she knew it. If she continued to fight, if she didn't give up . . .

I sprinted toward them, simultaneously raising dirt around Cynn in an attempt to help restrain her. I needed to do something, had to stop her somehow—

But it was too late.

"Don't come any closer!" Cynn screamed, and sent out a burst of magic so intense that it crumbled all of Wyckett's roots and turned my shield into a pile of dust.

"Cynn, no!" Wyckett rushed toward her as Cynn collapsed to the ground. Seconds later another figure shaped like Cynn emerged from the shadow of the woods. "No, no, no," Wyckett pleaded, abandoning every shred of dignity and caution, and cradled Cynn's body in his arms. But the figure, the magic from

Cynn's broken well, continued to move, its unwavering gaze set on her...

It was over quickly. Unlike her brother, Cynn didn't beg for her life. She knew what was coming; she'd chosen it herself. She convulsed in Wyckett's arms as magic broke her bones, tore at her lungs, and smothered her heart. She was still breathing when I got there, but her big eyes were like glass marbles, and a trickle of blood ran from the corner of her mouth.

"I don't really hate your singing," she confessed, her voice barely audible. "Just . . . it reminds me of the things we can't have . . . I loved you, and I hated that." Cynn's chest shook one more time, and she gasped for air.

"I know, Cinnamon," Wyckett whispered back, holding her head gently. "I know."

But Cynn could no longer hear him.

CHAPTER 37
KIEREN

Ellis's bolt of blue lightning ripped from the sky, aiming for the platform where Kavender stood, but before it could hit him, the spear he'd made out of the safety railing flew up and caught the tip of the charge just like a lightning rod. The current ran through it and struck the ground instead. The bright blue flash flickered and went out.

"Not bad," Kavender announced in that grandiose, conceited manner of his. His spear levitated and pointed at Ellis and me again. "Looks like the Divine moniker isn't only for show. But do you truly understand the meaning of that word, Ellis?"

Not waiting for her to respond, Kavender flung the spear at the bubble around us.

It torpedoed toward us at an alarming speed. Ellis's grip on my shoulder tightened, and she yanked us both to the side, but there was not enough time to react, and the spear tore right through the bubble a few inches away from my right hip.

I exhaled sharply. I'd been bracing for impact, expecting the bubble to hold against the spear as it had with the cylinders, but that did not happen. We remained shakily floating above ground, but the bubble was now compromised.

Ellis's eyebrows furrowed. "I'm sorry, Kieren, that spear had stronger magic than the explosives on the ship. This will need my full attention." With that, she lowered us down and released what was left of the bubble and my shoulder.

The ground we landed on was torn up and uneven from the explosions. I staggered, trying to regain my balance.

Ellis looked as graceful as ever. "Keep close to me, observe, and be prepared to dodge," she whispered, then raised her voice, addressing Kavender. "I'm not interested in small talk. You are distracting me from my studies. As such, I'll give you a minute to explain yourself before I put an end to this."

Kavender quirked an eyebrow. "Not much for patience, are you? Well, neither am I." He smirked, and the air around him buzzed. More metal pieces twisted out of shape and tore off the platform, producing an arsenal of a dozen spears. They flew up and started rotating around Kavender like lethal satellites.

"I'll get straight to the point then," he continued, thoroughly enjoying his display of magic. "'Divine' used to mean 'godlike.' That's what people believed as they waged wars on our kind in the original world—that a *higher* power ruled their lives. They were certain that someday it would manifest in all its glory and judge them. I disagree with them on many things, but I happen to believe they weren't wrong about that. They just failed to realize that *we* were the gods they'd been waiting for."

Ellis's face soured as though she found the sentiment both offensive and boring.

"I already told you I am *not* interested in empty talk," Ellis said, and the air around us flickered with tiny blue sparks that made the hairs on the back of my neck rise like static electricity. Simultaneously another pillar of lightning ripped out of the sky and struck the platform Kavender was on.

The field became so bright I had to shut my eyes. An extreme wave of heat followed. When I dared to peek at the field again, all the spears and the platform had liquefied, melting into a puddle on the ground. My breath caught in my lungs at the sheer destructive force that was Ellis's magic. Unlike the first strike, which had felt more like a test of her opponent's strength, this one had gone after Kavender's source of metal.

But it wasn't enough to stop him. Kavender had leapt off the platform just in time to dodge the strike and had landed on the field a safe distance away.

"Clever," he snorted, slightly out of breath as his heavy boots hit the ground. "But I'm not going to run out of metal, Ellis. Or *magic,* for that matter." With that, a lump of liquefied metal rose from the puddle and started to spin. Steam came off its surface as it cooled and took on a new shape.

Ellis's mouth twitched with distaste. "Why? Because you found a way to cheat the well system?"

Kavender grinned openly, pleased that he finally had Ellis's interest. "Admit it—that was a once-in-a-generation breakthrough for our kind."

Ellis deadpanned, "Considering the consequences of emptying wells into an unsuspecting world, I'm rather inclined to call it a magically wasteful instrument of murder."

"Oh, please," Kavender huffed. "Great magical breakthroughs always demand sacrifices. This is but a stepping stone in our path to greatness."

The cooling clump of metal sharpened and now resembled a tall, heavy scythe. Its blade caught the light from the projectors and glinted with the promise of more destruction.

Ellis sighed, side-eyeing the scythe scornfully. "Are you still on about your holy aspirations? Do you fancy yourself an ancient god of war? Is that why you're trying to start one with those nasty cylinders?"

The finished scythe floated over to Kavender. "Start? No, Ellis, I am merely helping it along. If you haven't noticed, those savages are quite good at starting wars themselves."

Ellis frowned. "And why would you do that? Why side with the common government you so loathe?"

"Oh, Ellis. Of course I'm not *siding* with them," Kavender said dismissively. "You've studied the history of the original world, haven't you? The war has always been inevitable. We can erase their memories, give them a fresh start, even pamper them by doing all the hard work for them. But in the end, those humans can't help but try to slaughter one another. That's what they *do*, and who are we to change the nature of an entire species?" Kavender shrugged theatrically. "That leaves us with only one logical solution. If we can't stop them, we might as well use their war for our purposes before they ruin everything and drag our magic into it."

Despite the heat that still hung in the air, a chill ran over my skin as I listened to Kavender callously philosophize about the deaths of millions of people as though it were merely an opportunity too good to miss.

"Most of our fellow magicians have grown too comfortable," Kavender continued, "too used to a life of servitude to notice the chains around their necks. If you'd ever bothered to attend, Ellis, you would have seen me raise this issue with the Council many times over, but always unsuccessfully. Those fools keep clinging to the past even as the possibility of a world war looms—a war in which we would die for those savages. I've desperately tried to open the Council's eyes to the truth. But at some point I realized mere words wouldn't be enough, that it would take a massive conflict to show them the

Founders were wrong to leave the fate of the new world in non-magical hands."

"So instead of trying to change the terms of the Service, you singlehandedly decided to damn the entire world?" Ellis said.

"Indeed." Kavender smiled. "Every world order crumbles once it becomes outdated, and our time has finally come. Back in the Founders' days, we were too weak and outnumbered. Of course it never occurred to the Founders that magicians would have been much better suited to rule. But things are different now. We can use both magic and science to overthrow the non-magical majority and take charge of this world."

"Are you implying," Ellis asked, the crease between her perfectly arched eyebrows deepening with every word, "that you created this ship and these weapons for your *own* use?"

"Glorious, aren't they?" Kavender said. "It's high time *we* started using non-magicians for menial labor. It wasn't even difficult to trick them. The government was all too eager to have their war—they were practically salivating at the opportunity to get someone on the Council involved. Little did they realize that by the time they are ready to plant the seeds of destruction, magicians will be the ones in control of their fancy murder machines. We will rise up and pass judgment on them like the higher power we were always meant to be."

Ellis stared at Kavender thoughtfully. Then she announced, "You took much longer than a minute to explain yourself, and you are still full of bull, Kavender."

Kavender laughed. "Oh, Ellis . . . because I refuse to stay in denial like the rest of you?"

"No." Ellis shook her head. "Because your argument is flawed."

Kavender cocked his head to the side, amused. "How so?"

"You seem to assume that magicians and non-magicians

belong to separate species. Believing in this false difference allows you to claim that we must compete to survive, and thus it is only natural that one must strive to rule over the other. But you're wrong. Magicians and non-magicians come from the same families. Magic aside, we are the same people with the same blood and bones—trust me, I've *checked*. It is the collective use of all our unique talents that allows the world to flourish. That's why we must rely on one another to survive in the long run. That's why the Founders brought both magicians and the non-magical people here—to create a world where we can all thrive."

Ellis delivered her argument in the most Ellis-like way. She didn't speak passionately like a politician at an assembly. Rather, she stated her case as if it were a matter of fact, an obvious truth.

Kavender's amusement dissipated. "How you disappoint me, Ellis. And here I thought I could reason with you." He shook his head dramatically and then, to my astonishment, directed his gaze toward me for the first time since the battle had started. "What about your young companion, though? He hasn't lived long enough to be brainwashed by the Council. What say you, Kieren Belltower? You've learned the truth about our world. Do you believe you're living in a fair system? Do you think non-magicians have the right to use our talents as they please?" As Kavender said this, his mouth curved up again as though he could see through me.

My stomach twisted. I hadn't been expecting the question. I'd been relying on Ellis to fight and reason her way through this situation. She was strong and bright, and what Kavender had done to us, to Master Hanska, to Oi's friends, was wrong and evil. There was no doubt about that . . . but that wasn't what Kavender's question was about.

I swallowed, opened my mouth, but no words came.

Ellis's elbow pushed softly into my side. "You don't have to answer him, Kieren," she said. "We are not here to judge our entire world. We are here to stop magicians who broke our laws. That's all. No need to trouble yourself beyond that."

I was still speechless but found myself nodding slowly. Ellis might have saved me from having to answer, but it didn't make me feel better.

Kavender abandoned his interest in me with great disappointment. "See what happens when you lie to generations of young, promising magicians, Ellis? That's why we can't let this charade go on any longer. We'll run our very best into the ground. It saddens me to lose magicians who could lead us in the new world, but you would rather be stuck in the past than admit that the Founders' experiment has failed." The scythe by Kavender's side began to spin in the air, rapidly gaining momentum. "I'm sorry, Ellis, Kieren, but this is goodbye," he said, and unleashed the weapon.

I braced, ready for whatever was about to happen, but the scythe didn't come at us. Instead it stayed low to the ground and flew toward the line of tall trees at the edge of the field. One by one, the scythe chopped them down. Then, with a swing of his hand, Kavender flung dozens of trunks at us.

I froze in the terror at the armada of pines ready to crush us. The memories of the battle with Spiht were still fresh in my mind. But Ellis was ready. The air around her hands sparked, and several lightning bolts flew straight out of her palms, striking the trees with a series of deafeningly loud *fflup-fflup-fflup*s. Halos of steam burst from the bark, and the trunks started blowing up, torn pieces falling to the ground in heaps before they could reach us. In seconds the field was covered with exploded pine wood. I had never seen anything like it.

Yet Kavender was nowhere near done. His scythe swung around and came right back like a boomerang, this time aiming at the projector lights on the side of the field. It batted at them with its hilt, sending half a dozen flying at us like some absurd version of baseball.

"Isn't this fun, Ellis?" Kavender shouted as his scythe spun around the field again. "This is what we're meant to be—letting our magic be free with no restrictions. This is our nature! Why deny it?"

Ellis gritted her teeth. "Enough with the distractions!" she shouted, pointing her left hand at the projectors and her right one at Kavender. A lightning bolt shot out of her left palm. It twisted and curved like a blue ribbon, splitting into several branches, catching the projectors in a net of electric charge. The lights went out, glass shattered, and the metal frames started to liquefy, dropping to the ground. Then another bolt shot from Ellis's right palm, a horizontal pillar of bright purple light aimed straight at Kavender.

Kavender didn't expect such a fast counterattack. He tried to summon the scythe to deflect the discharge, but it was still too busy trying to fling projectors at Ellis. The purple pillar hit his left arm, and Kavender howled in pain, collapsing to his knees.

For a moment the flying projectors and lightning strikes stopped, and there was no sound on the field besides the flutter of the Metal Giant's propellers.

"I may have underestimated you, Ellis," Kavender said gruffly. He coughed and stood up, bracing his chest with his right arm. His left one hung loosely at his side as though he could no longer control it. "But you're still wrong," he continued stubbornly. "You can't deny that the Founders made a mistake. A hundred and fifty years is not enough to change the true nature of these people, to make them forget they tried to exterminate our kind. You know they'll turn on us at any opportunity."

"No, they won't, Kavender," Ellis objected. "Non-magicians have made strides since we moved here. We are a different society now. The protests will disperse once we stop the sludge, which in time will be forgotten, just like any natural disaster."

"Are you *certain?*" Kavender insisted. His bravado was gone, and he seemed angrier now that the possibility of losing to Ellis was becoming a reality. But he hadn't given up yet. "The sludge might have been an unintended consequence, but it was also a great way to test whether they've changed their attitude toward magic, and clearly they haven't. You've seen what happened after the sludge hit DC. But if that experiment doesn't satisfy you, how about we try another one? You love experiments, don't you, Ellis? What would happen if something bigger than the sludge were to strike the non-magicians? If thirty magic-infused explosives dropped from an airship flown by magic on a city like"—Kavender paused, a cruel smile curling the side of his mouth—"Boston, for example? Would they not turn on us then?"

A chill went up my spine.

Ellis frowned. "You wouldn't dare do something so reckless, Kavender."

Kavender snorted. "You think you can stop me? Why start a war somewhere else when we can get the same results on our own soil? Let's find out for sure which one of us is right."

With that, Kavender lifted his right arm and pointed at the Metal Giant. His pewter-colored magic shot toward the airship. As though pulled by strings, the ship started maneuvering itself southeast.

I stared at Kavender in shock. Was this madman seriously going to bomb Boston just to prove a point?

Ellis blew a loose strand of hair out of her face. "Kieren, listen," she said, not taking her eyes off Kavender. "I can't strike that ship—members of the crew are likely still on it. And I can't afford to direct my attention away from Kavender either. He's injured, but we can't let him use this as a diversion to escape. I will hold him here, but you must go and stop the airship before it reaches Boston, understand?"

My eyes shot upward to the buzzing propellers of the Metal Giant, and my stomach twisted. *Me?* How on earth was *I* going to stop something so huge by myself? But there was nobody else around who could do it, was there? Esten and Wyckett were still gone, and Ellis was right about Kavender—we couldn't give him an opportunity to escape. Who knew what else he was planning to do if we didn't stop him?

"Okay," I said, and swallowed hard.

"Good." Ellis nodded. "Good luck, Kieren. I'm counting on you."

And that was all the sendoff I got. Electricity sparked in Ellis's palms again, and her full attention was back on Kavender. At the same time, Kavender's scythe spun in my peripheral vision, but I couldn't get distracted by that.

I faced the rapidly retreating airship. This was going to be dangerous. The Metal Giant was in constant motion, and I'd no idea what it looked like on the inside, which made it difficult to pick a spot where I could transport. I racked my brain, trying to come up with a plan. Back when the ship had been hovering above us, I'd spotted a small, protruding part with windows near the front. That must have been the control room. I could aim for it and hope I didn't repeat the disaster of the day I'd tried to climb a tree to impress Esten. If I fell from the sky without him to catch me, I would surely die.

I shoved my anxious thoughts to the furthest corner of my mind, closed my eyes, and stepped into the magic stream. As I willed myself to exit inside the control room, my heart pounded so loud that I thought it would jump out of my chest and get stuck inside the stream. After a few moments, however, I found my feet planted on the metal floor of the corridor inside the hull.

"Phew," I exhaled with massive relief. This wasn't the control room, but I wasn't far from it, and—most importantly—I was *not* falling from the sky.

Silently thanking the mighty power of magic for keeping me in one piece, I sped down the corridor.

When I got into the control room, it was in a state of chaos. Whatever magic Kavender had done had frightened the crew. The emergency exit door inside the cockpit was wide open, and I could see the sky through it. One of the copilots was standing in the doorway, a parachute strapped to his back. Before I could say anything, he stepped forward and was gone. I gasped in shock. The remaining copilots both snapped their gazes to me, and absolute terror flashed on their faces.

"Stay back, crazy magician! I never signed up for this!" the second copilot screamed, backing away from me.

"Wait!" I raised my arm, palm facing out in a pacifying gesture. "I'm not with Kavender. I need your help—"

But that was the exact wrong thing to do. The moment the crew saw my hand move, they thought I was about to do magic and rushed through the open door, nearly knocking each other out.

"Wait!" I yelled after them. But it was too late—both were already on their way to the ground.

"Ah . . . all right." I took a deep breath, trying to calm down. At least the crew was safe. Unfortunately, now I had to figure out how to stop the Giant on my own.

Trying my best to avoid looking down, I reached out and kicked the open door shut. Then I rushed to the control panel. My gaze swept over it, but there were far too many dials, buttons, and levers, and I had no idea what any of them did. I had only ever ridden a horse before—how was I supposed to pilot an airship?

Terrible panic rose in my chest. If I couldn't turn it around and take it somewhere safe, I needed to crash the ship before it reached a populated area, hoping I could transport out of it before the collision killed me.

Not wasting another second, I started pressing buttons and pulling levers at random. If only I still had my right hand so I could do this faster! I swung the steering wheel to the left and right, but the airship continued on course as though none of those controls had any effect on it.

"Heavens," I whispered. That's why the crew had looked so panicked. The Metal Giant was obeying Kavender's magic instead of the manual controls. The crew probably didn't know what to do with it and had decided to abandon ship before it was too late.

This was terrible news. And now the first lights were starting to appear on the horizon. I peered out the window. I'd overestimated how far into rural New England Kavender had lured us. The airship wasn't flying over woods and farms anymore; it was fast approaching a stretch of cities along the harbor—the beginning of Boston's densely populated neighborhoods. That meant that I could no longer crash the Giant without killing hundreds, possibly thousands of people.

I slammed my hand into the control panel and hung my head. I'd wasted too much time. There was no way to pilot or crash the ship, but there had to be something else I could do. *Think, Kieren, think.* Could I magically transport the Giant and its explosives away from here? I'd never learned that kind of summoning magic though. And even if I managed to figure it out in time, Kavender might still be able to activate the bombs.

Maybe instead I could *destroy* the entire ship the way I'd obliterated the forest while battling Spiht? But I wasn't sure I was powerful enough to do that either, not to mention being sufficiently skilled to manage the enormous rebound that would follow. I'd already lost my right hand. What would happen if I tried to destroy this much thorned magic at once? Would I survive?

I looked at the flickering lights ahead, at the peaceful neighborhoods that had taken so much time and effort to build by both magicians and regular people...

It didn't matter what happened to me. I had no choice but to try. If I didn't, a lot of people were going to die, and magicians were going to be blamed for it.

Resolved, I pushed away from the control panel and dashed out of the cockpit.

The ship was big, but luckily every passage connected to the main keel corridor that ran all the way to the rear. It was impossible to get lost. I found the ladder to the cargo section right in the middle of it. As Kavender had said, inside were thirty cylinders loaded with his destructive magic.

The best approach, I decided, was to destroy them one by one. That way, if I died before I finished, at least there would be fewer explosives to damage the city.

I stood in front of the first cylinder and closed my eyes. Trying my best not to overdo it this time, I wished for the bomb to cease to exist, and tapped it with my left hand. When my fingertips touched the metal, I felt pressure building around the cylinder and then a *swoosh* of air, as though a small vortex had enveloped the bomb. It swirled for several seconds, and then both the cylinder and the vortex were simply gone.

The rebound followed, immediate and brutal.

I concentrated as hard as I could, trying to stuff it into my well—the broken barn at the edge of my family farm—and this time part of it did go in... but not all. The remainder slammed into my ribs, and I fell to my knees, clutching my broken torso as pain bloomed through it.

"Get up," I ordered myself with shaking lips, not waiting for the pain to dull. "Get up. Get up." There were twenty-nine bombs left to go.

Destroying the next two cylinders was just as awful. After the fourth one, I doubled over and coughed up blood, and by the fifth I couldn't keep myself upright anymore. Every breath I took cut the cracked bones and muscles in my chest like razors.

So I crawled on my knees and reached for the sixth cylinder, desperately trying not to focus on the fact that there was no way I could destroy all thirty in time. I wasn't good enough. I wasn't strong enough, hadn't had enough practice. Esten would probably scorn me for how pathetic I was and come up with a brilliant and elegant solution that would put my brute magic to shame. *Oh, Esten.* I had promised him I'd stay safe. There were many things I was going to fail at tonight.

"I'm sorry," I whispered, and tapped the sixth cylinder, but before I could send my magic through it, a voice interrupted me.

No sorry, Kieren, it said.

"Oi!" My eyes snapped open; Oi was perched on the floor next to me. But the relief of seeing my friend was instantly replaced by worry. I had to warn him. "Oi, what are you doing here? The ship's about to explode. You need to leave!"

But Oi's demeanor was perfectly unconcerned.

Oi here to help, he said. *Oi brought friends.*

I squinted, puzzled. One by one, shadowy shapes appeared beside Oi. It was difficult to make out their outlines, similar to how I hadn't been able to see the edges of the portal until I stared directly at it. But they were here—Oi's friends, about a dozen of them. They resembled Oi the way he had looked in the other world—cloudy shapes in masks, some wearing colorful hooded robes, some sporting elaborate headgear. Some had fins and tails, and some wore fans, feathers, and beads. There was no uniform look to them, as though they came from different parts of the other world, from different cultures.

"What are you going to do?" I asked anxiously.

Gonna eat, Oi said, pointing at the cylinders.

My stomach dropped. "No! These are full of thorned magic, just like the wells. You're going to die. Please don't do this. I can destroy a few more!"

In response, the painted mouth on Oi's mask appeared to smile mischievously.

These not so bad, Oi said. *Not full like wells.*

"Are you sure?" I asked in disbelief. The rebound I'd suffered suggested otherwise.

Yes. No worry, Kieren. Make pie later. Help indigestion, okay?

I nodded. Even one-handed, I'd make a million pies if that meant Oi and his friends were going to be okay. "Yes. Anything you need."

Then deal, Oi purred, and the other spirits appeared to nod in agreement, making me wonder if I had made a deal with the entire Oi delegation.

Turn away now, Kieren, Oi instructed, and I did as Oi's friends started floating toward the cylinders.

I couldn't see what was happening, but I swore I heard a burp and snippets of conversation, although it was more challenging to hear the other spirits and I had no idea who was talking to whom.

Would be better if glass, eh?

Yeah, glass. So much yeah.

Nom-nom. Glass crunchy. Fine glass best.

But metal fine too. Still crunchy.

I kept my expression blank as not to accidentally offend

anyone. Oi's friends' diet was the strangest thing I'd ever heard of.

The chewing and swallowing sounds continued until finally Oi allowed me to face them again.

"Are you okay?" I asked, eyeing the Oi crew and the empty spot where the cylinders used to be. They seemed less cheery after ingesting the magical explosives.

Okay, Oi replied. *No worry, Kieren. You go now.*

"Go where?" I asked, bewildered.

Oi eat dessert now, Oi said, and just like that, his shadowy shape started growing beyond the outline of the doll from Master Hanska's house, quickly reaching the height of my shoulders and growing larger still until he was towering over me.

My eyes widened as I realized what Oi meant by *dessert.* "You're going to eat the ship, aren't you?" I asked, astounded.

Yes, Oi said smugly. *Has glass. Nom-nom.*

I gazed at Oi in awe for a moment. What a strange spirit—and what a generous person. Despite the horrible things magicians had done to his home, Oi was here, willing to swallow the airship to save thousands of Bostonians and me from certain death while also preventing an international war and keeping the secret that could destroy our entire world.

"Thank you, Oi," I said wholeheartedly. "For everything."

No worry, Kieren, Oi purred again. *Remember deal. Okay? Come back later for pie. Now, go.*

I smiled. "Okay." With awful pain radiating through my busted rib cage, I forced myself to get up.

I took one more look at Oi and his courageous friends, whispered another thank-you, and hobbled into the magic stream.

CHAPTER 38
ESTEN

I rushed back to Ellis and Kieren at the first opportunity. Wyckett had to stay behind to send a message to Probos and deal with Nogg and the non-magicians he'd trapped in their cars, but I was free to go.

By the time I arrived back at the field, it was utterly destroyed. Chopped-down parts of trees, trenches in the ground, and pools of cooling metal were all part of the landscape now.

Kavender appeared injured but was still putting up a hell of a fight. There was a scythe swinging around, grounding Ellis's bolts of lightning and flinging whatever objects Kavender could find at her. Ellis seemed to have assumed a defensive stance, evading Kavender's attacks and counterattacking whenever she could.

I absorbed the scene with rapidly building terror until a realization hit me—Kieren was nowhere to be seen. Nearly tumbling over from exhaustion, I pushed myself into the magic stream and exited in a safe spot next to Ellis.

"Where is Kieren?" I gasped, dizzy from performing transport magic too many times.

"On the ship," Ellis said, deep in concentration; a small bead of sweat ran from her temple. "Trying to stop it from bombing Boston."

"What?" My mind reeled. I whipped my head around, looking for the Metal Giant, but it must have left the field a while ago. Panic shot through me. "Ellis, I need to get to him. Which way?"

But Ellis shook her head. "No, stay. I could use your help. I need you to trap that bothersome scythe so I can strike Kavender once and for all. Then we'll go to Kieren together, *if* he needs us."

"*If?* Ellis, he barely knows how to manage his rebound!" I was starting to hyperventilate. Maybe to a magician like Ellis, this wasn't a huge deal, but Kieren had already lost a hand. And I was responsible for it, for him.

"Esten," Ellis said strictly, sparing me a single glance before unleashing another bolt of lightning to explode a tree trunk flying at us. "You need to calm down. I wouldn't have sent him if I thought he would fail. Besides, I have a *feeling* Kieren isn't helpless and alone out there."

I stared at her blankly. What on earth was Ellis talking about? Meanwhile Kavender's scythe ran out of tree debris to throw. Instead it dug into the ground and sent a huge boulder flying at us.

Ellis blocked it, but she was undeniably frustrated. "This battle has gone on too long for my taste. Like every stubborn man in the history of the universe, Kavender won't quit until he's proven his point—or annihilated everything around him. I can't keep wastefully firing at him when I know his scythe can ground my lightning. My well is exceptionally managed, but it isn't unlimited. I need to get a clean shot. That's why I need your help *here*, Esten."

I bit my lip. I hated to admit it, but Ellis was right. Besides, the sooner this was handled, the sooner I could see Kieren.

"Okay," I said, and turned my attention to the scythe. If I could catch it near the ground, I could probably bury it. Not permanently—I wasn't delusional. I was too tired, and Kavender was still too strong, but I could keep it out of reach long enough for Ellis to strike a decisive blow. "I'll tell you when I'm ready," I said, and raised my arms.

Kavender's scythe dipped toward the ground once again in search of something to fling at us. My shoulders tensed, waiting for the right moment. Just then, a movement in my peripheral vision caught my attention. My breath stuttered as Kieren stumbled out of the stream some fifty yards from Ellis and me.

Such a wave of relief crashed over me that my knees nearly gave out. Kieren was here and all in one piece—a hand still missing, but *only one*. Never had I thought I'd be so happy to see only one limb missing on a person. Kieren's eyes found mine, and he smiled. I waved at him. Heavens, I wanted to run up and crush him in my arms.

Kieren turned to address Kavender. "Your ship is gone!" he shouted, and grimaced horribly, nearly doubling over. My breath caught in my lungs as Kieren clutched his ribs—he wasn't as well as I thought. But he straightened up and pushed himself to continue. "All your bombs are gone too. You have failed, Kavender."

That got Kavender's attention, and the scythe paused, hovering near the ground. "That can't be! You're bluffing!" he shouted back.

"It can, and I'm not," Kieren objected. "Didn't you feel your own magic disappear? There is nothing you can threaten us with anymore. Surrender now."

"No." Kavender laughed and shook his head, stumbling back a step. There was a manic look on his face, as though he couldn't fathom the possibility of such crushing defeat. "No. I won't give up trying to free our kind from oppression, from these *people* who limit our magic and keep us in chains. I will *never* stop. Never!" His one good arm started to rise again.

I seethed with rage. I didn't know what had happened with the airship, and I'd missed whatever conversation Ellis and Kavender had had while I was battling Nogg, but I'd heard plenty of similar garbage from Cynn's mouth. This time I had something to say.

"Cut the nonsense, Kavender," I yelled, fed up. "You're not doing this for some kind of justice or to help other magicians. You are not even doing it for magic, so stop with the lies. No one who's comfortable with killing innocent spirits or declaring fellow magicians necessary casualties should have the right to utter the word *magic*. No one willing to sacrifice others deserves power of any kind!"

Kavender's eyes filled with disdain. "Just what I'd expect from the puppy who can't see beyond his leash."

I gritted my teeth and was about to respond, but—

"Now," Ellis whispered beside me. "Do it now, Esten."

I remembered what my objective had been before I'd gotten distracted by Kavender's disgusting lies. I spotted the scythe. Simultaneously the strength of Ellis's magic warped the air around her, and a cloud appeared in the dark sky, hovering ominously above Kavender. Not wasting a second, I raised a wave of soil and buried Kavender's scythe.

"You're going to regret this!" Kavender yelled, and tried to command his weapon. The scythe pushed against the dirt, but I held it down, buying Ellis precious seconds to attack.

Kavender's gaze snapped to the spot where his scythe was held captive, and for the first time genuine fear flashed on his face. "There will be others who want this," he shouted desperately. "We are missing a huge opportunity—the war, we must—"

But before he could finish, Ellis struck.

A hundred purple ribbons of lightning descended from the cloud, illuminating the field with their electricity.

Kavender fell to his knees as the ribbons started to strike him one by one. He screamed, his body thrashing. It was a terrifying scene. I wanted to turn away, but I was afraid to break my concentration and release the scythe before it was over. Another strike sent Kavender's body into a violent twist, and he fell to the ground. He wasn't just screaming now—he was trying to say something. I frowned; I didn't want to hear his lies anymore.

By the time I noticed the wicked grin on Kavender's dying face and his right arm straining to rise and point, it was too late.

The trapped scythe wasn't the only sharp piece of metal that remained on the field. Some distance away lay the abandoned spear from earlier. Kavender barely had control over his movements, but he had enough strength to fling the spear at the person closest to it.

I wanted to run, wanted to drop the scythe and raise another wall to stop the spear, but there wasn't enough *time* to do any of those things. And Kieren—he looked so tired and injured, still new to magic. There were so many things I hadn't taught him, might never have a chance to teach him.

A look of panic flashed on his face as he too saw Kavender's weapon flying at him. It was going to pierce his chest, and there was nothing I could do to stop it.

I opened my mouth in terror and stumbled half a step

forward, nearly colliding with Ellis, as the spear came impossibly close to Kieren's body, and then—

Kieren *disappeared* a fraction of a second before the spear could hit him. It flew past the spot where he'd stood and tumbled, unchallenged, to the ground.

The scream died on my lips, replaced with shock. The lightning continued to buzz for another moment and then stopped abruptly as Kavender collapsed, motionless.

Ellis blew a lock of hair out of her face, turned to look at me, and put her hands on her hips.

"Ellis," I managed, my chest constricting and my eyes clouded with tears. My thoughts were in shreds, my words failing me. "Kieren, he ... what? ... I don't understand ... "

Ellis quirked an eyebrow and glanced at the spot where Kieren used to be. "Oh, he should reappear in about three seconds or so . . . *hopefully*," she added, with a slight note of uncertainty. Her eyes narrowed as though she was observing an experiment.

Before I could demand to know what on earth Ellis meant, something flickered in the air, and to my astonishment, Kieren's body reappeared in the same spot I'd last seen him. Except that now he was unconscious, so he promptly dropped to the ground like a sack of potatoes.

"Ooh, I guess it worked, then." Ellis grinned as I rushed past her to Kieren.

CHAPTER 39
KIEREN

I felt weightless and sort of bodiless. Like there were no edges to me, no border that separated me from the rest of the world. I was floating in an ocean of light that consisted of all colors of magic. If I looked closely, I could see the threads from all kinds of different beings rolling and tangling and mixing like waves with no beginning and no end . . . even my own.

Oh. That's right. That's what that was. A thread of rich burgundy was wrapped around me. It was a lively hue, lush and resonant, and I felt *at home* in it, just like Esten had said I would. My color. My magic. I smiled. I wanted to stay cocooned in it, float in this peaceful light and this boundless ocean that finally made me feel like I belonged.

But the thread around me was not the only place my color appeared. Somewhere—I felt it—there was more. It was calling out to me.

My eyeless gaze followed another tiny thread, a thin, continuous spill of burgundy that led farther into the ocean of light. Somehow I was certain that it was leading me to my right hand. If only I could follow it, find out where the thread went, then I would know where my missing limb had disappeared to...

But I didn't have a chance to investigate, because something unapologetically jerked me out of that place, and the world went black.

~

I woke up with a start. I was in my own room in Master Hanska's house. The morning light was streaming through the parted curtains. I blinked from the brightness of it, made to turn away, and felt excruciating pain shoot through my rib cage.

"Owww!" I howled, unable to stop myself. There were sparks in my vision. Well, at least if it hurt this much, it probably meant I wasn't dead yet, which was good news, all things considered.

I sighed. It was tempting to let the soft pillows claim me for at least the next month or so, but now that I was awake, I couldn't ignore the questions that were pounding on the back door of my mind. What had happened on the field after I'd blacked out? Was Esten okay? Was Oi? What about Ellis, Wyckett, and Cynn? The last thing I remembered was the horror of Kavender's screams and then the sight of a spear torpedoing at me. The piece of metal had already been too close, and I'd been too tired from destroying the explosives to summon any more magic to stop it. Someone else must have done it, though. They'd bandaged my ribs while I was asleep, too.

Wincing with pain, I rolled out of bed and stumbled dizzily into the hallway, trying not to breathe too deeply lest I disturb what felt like multiple cracked ribs poking my insides. I really had done it this time.

The house was strangely quiet. As I made my way downstairs, my anxiety started to churn. What if my friends were still fighting? Or worse, what if they hadn't made it? What if I was the only one left standing? I pushed the awful thoughts aside and carried on to the kitchen.

My heart jolted with relief when I smelled a waft of coffee in the air—someone other than me must have been home. Despite the shooting pain, I practically ran the rest of the way, then stopped at the dining room entrance. I certainly hadn't expected to find a familiar man in a plain brown suit reading the *Boston Times* and sipping coffee at the table all by himself.

"Probos?" I said, surprised. "Where is everybody? Is Esten okay?"

Probos lifted his eyes from the newspaper and smiled his politician smile. "He is quite all right, Kieren. Don't worry. Ellis has been making him run errands for her all morning while you were sleeping. Something along the lines of payment for saving your life. But they should be here shortly. In fact, the four of us are going to have a meeting."

"Oh," I said, relaxing a little, and stumbled to one of the empty chairs. A basket full of breakfast items was sitting on the table, but I was too nervous to eat anything.

Probos put down the newspaper politely, and I glimpsed the front-page headlines.

THE MIDNIGHT DISAPPEARANCE OF THE METAL GIANT: WAS THE SHIP EVER REAL? Also, STRANGE LIGHTNING STORM RAVAGES LANDS NORTHWEST OF BOSTON.

I tore my gaze away from the headlines. It seemed the general public still didn't know exactly what had happened last night. But neither did I, to be honest.

"Probos, what happened yesterday?" I asked. "Is Wyckett okay too? I didn't see him at all after we split up."

"Wyckett is safe as well," Probos replied, taking a sip of his coffee. "He is keeping busy dealing with the aftermath—transporting the prisoners and filing the evidence. But after that he has the rest of the week off. He wants to bury Cynn."

The ground dropped out from under the chair I was sitting on. Cynn was *dead*? Cynn...

"How?" I whispered, my throat suddenly tight.

The last I'd seen of her was back on the platform, standing beside Kavender and Nogg as though she belonged with them. What on earth had that meant? Cynn had refused to meet my eyes when I'd called her name, and now she was gone, and I would never have a chance to ask her for an explanation.

Probos sighed heavily. "Magician Cynn seems to have been"—he paused, looking for the right word—"*dissatisfied* with how magic worked in our society, so she secretly sided with Kavender, Spiht, and Nogg. She tried to lead you into a trap. That's how Kavender knew you were coming and ambushed you."

I shook my head. No. This couldn't be. Cynn, who was straightforward and always smiled—Cynn, the first magician friend I'd made, who had made me feel *welcome* here—that same Cynn had been trying to kill me? My fist clenched underneath the table. How was I ever supposed to reconcile those things in my mind?

There were many questions I needed to ask Probos, all the whys and hows of such a betrayal. But when I opened my mouth, what came out instead was this: "Was it wrong, Probos, what the Founders did?"

Probos's hand holding the coffee cup paused halfway to his mouth. He lowered it back down slowly without taking a sip. "You mean, lying to our entire world about its origins?"

I shifted uncomfortably. This was unusually blunt for him. "Yes. That. And everything that followed after."

Probos gave me a long, thoughtful look. "Of course it was

wrong, Kieren," he said simply, threading his fingers together in front of him. "Lying always is. Every child knows that. Furthermore, it rarely works out as intended in the long run. Truth has this stubborn tendency to come to light eventually. Sooner or later, someone always finds out and becomes disillusioned. There will in time be other Kavenders. Such is the nature of secrets."

My eyebrows knotted. "Then . . . why are we still doing this? Is it working? Is it even *worth* it?" The question Kavender had asked me back on the battlefield still hung heavy on my mind. Ellis might have saved me from having to answer, but that didn't mean I could deny what I'd been thinking.

Ever since I'd manifested, I hadn't encountered a single non-magical person who'd treated me like I was one of them. My family, friends, and my entire town had disowned me. I'd hurt them, yes, but it had been an accident. I never would have done such a thing on purpose. The protesters on the steps of the Assembly had screamed at me and tried to assault me when I'd done nothing to them. Even the airship crew last night had run from me in terror. I couldn't exactly *ignore* that. The mere fact that Kavender could sway someone like Cynn meant that something was wrong with the way magicians did things in this world.

When Probos finally answered, he sounded tired. It wasn't like the hope-infused speech he'd given Esten when he'd broken the truth about the world to us. Maybe back then, that was what Esten needed to hear. But here and now, *I* needed something different, something more honest, and Probos seemed willing to give it to me.

"It isn't a perfect system, Kieren . . . far from it," Probos said. "But it's the one we inherited. As such, it is a work in progress, and I truly mean that word—*progress*. Our ancestors made mistakes. Someday they will be judged for those mistakes. Maybe they already have been. But you can't deny that although things aren't perfect, they have definitely gotten better for all of us compared to the old world.

"These last couple of weeks are a bad example," he said, allowing himself to smile a little. "But usually no one tries to murder us or torture our loved ones simply because we have an affinity for magic. The protests aren't good for our relationship with the non-magical government, but they are nothing compared to what our ancestors had to endure.

"I don't know what the future holds, Kieren. It is a precarious balance this world is in, and many things can upset it, from disappointed magicians to power-hungry politicians and warmongers. The lie our Founders had to rely on can buy us time while we work through our differences toward a better society. We just have to stay alert and keep pushing forward as long as we can. Because that is the only shot at a future we have."

I nodded slowly, mulling over Probos's words. "But then, doesn't that mean that as long as we continue the way things are, we're going to *have* to keep the lie intact? You already said the truth is destined to get out someday. What happens then? If we don't prepare for that, it will be the end of everything."

Probos opened his mouth, but he didn't get a chance to answer because suddenly there was noise in the foyer. Ellis and Esten had finally arrived and were heading to the dining room.

Esten looked exhausted, as though Ellis had made him engage in actual manual labor, but his mouth stretched into an instant smile when he saw me. He tried to make a beeline for me, but Ellis beat him to it.

"Kieren! How are you feeling? Any noticeable side effects?" she asked with acute interest.

A deep sense of unease took hold of me. "What do you mean by side effects?" I asked cautiously.

Ellis answered without blinking an eye. "I performed time-shifting magic on you. That is, I sent you roughly ten seconds into the future. But I'd never done it on a human subject before, only on flowers. I'm very eager to hear your firsthand account of it."

My mind careened to the memory of Ellis and the crocuses in her garden—the way they had ominously wilted upon their arrival in the flower bed and Ellis's frustrated huff.

"You *experimented* on me?" I asked, feeling woozy.

"W-well . . ." Ellis looked briefly to the side. "Believe it or not, I *was* running short on my capacity to do thorned magic—it not being my specialty and all—and I had to think of something to stop you from being hit by that spear. I was also missing out on my precious experiment time, so I thought, why not *combine* the two?" She said that very matter-of-factly, as though experimental time travel in the middle of a battle was the only reasonable solution to the pickle I'd found myself in.

I was speechless for a moment.

Esten stepped closer, folding his arms. "Ellis did save your life, Kieren."

I blinked at him in disbelief. Was he actually endorsing this? "Thank you, Ellis," I said finally, trying to keep my voice from wobbling.

"So," Ellis ventured, "were there any side effects? Any pain? Are you perhaps feeling *out of it?*"

Well, I was, but not for that reason. "I think I ended up inside the magic stream," I said. "Or a place that felt like it. Except it wasn't a stream—it was more like an ocean."

Ellis's eyebrows rose, and she immediately produced a notebook from somewhere in the pocket of her gabardine jacket and pulled out one of the pencils that was holding her hair in place. "What did it feel like?" she asked, all studious and ready to scribble everything down.

I considered. "It was peaceful," I said, trying to make sense of the dreamlike state I'd been in while I'd time-traveled. "And I felt connected somehow. To all of magic, and other things... and, uh..."

Probos cleared his throat from the chair beside Ellis. "I am most interested in the progress of your experiments, Ellis, but I do have a meeting with the vice president in about half an hour. Seeing as we are short on time, I would like us to discuss what we have assembled here for. I am sure Kieren will be delighted to indulge your thirst for knowledge immediately afterward."

"All right," Ellis agreed all too easily, and stuffed the notebook back into her pocket. She and Esten promptly took the remaining seats at the table.

A wave of uncertainty hit me upon seeing the seriousness of Probos's expression. I glanced over at Esten but couldn't tell if he was as nervous to hear whatever Probos wanted to discuss.

"Let us talk about your futures," he finally said, addressing me and Esten both. "You have survived extraordinary circumstances and learned things most magicians will never have to encounter in their lifetimes. As such, you now bear a great responsibility for the future of this world, and you might very well find yourselves having to defend it and its *secrets* again." Probos's brown eyes lingered on mine for a second too long before he continued. "However, neither of you has formally completed an apprenticeship with a senior magician, and it's of great importance that we sort this matter out expeditiously. Knowledge is power, and you're going to need it. Kieren, considering what you know about the world and the strong nature of your magic, there are only a few magicians who are qualified to teach you. The good news is that Ellis has agreed to take you in for the time being."

Ellis tipped her head and smiled confidently at me.

My stomach flipped a bit.

"She is of course very busy, having two apprentices already," Probos continued, "but it is lucky for you, Kieren, that she is also interested in studying your kind of magic, so she will teach you."

I did my best not to show panic on my face. Ellis was amazing and incredibly strong. She was also highly educated and juggled many different types of magic with ease. If I could learn some of her skills, I probably wouldn't have to crack my ribs to disarm explosives the next time around. But then, Ellis had also casually *experimented* on me. And rumor had it that she turned people into frogs. Was that going to be a part of our arrangement?

Probos continued, "As for you, Esten, Councilwoman Ginko would very much like to have you as an apprentice." My memory immediately went back to the Council meeting, to the silver-clad magician who had delivered a eulogy for Master Hanska. "She was impressed with your performance throughout the investigation," Probos added, "and as an incredibly accomplished magician, she has much to teach you."

Something flickered briefly on Esten's face, an emotion that wasn't quite happiness. But he fixed it quickly. "Thank you, Probos," he replied politely. "It will be a great privilege to learn from the country's fourth-highest-ranking magician."

Probos smiled in return and unclasped his hands. "Well, if that's all settled, I'm afraid I must get going. It is quite unfortunate that we now find ourselves having to bargain with the non-magical government for what was left of Kavender's charged metal and Nogg's fuel stored at the airship factories.

Non-magicians should never have access to those dangerous things to begin with. But alas..."

With a courteous nod, Probos got up and transported directly out of the dining room.

～

Ellis eventually left too—but not before she asked me every imaginable and unimaginable question about the short ten seconds I'd traveled through time.

Finally Esten and I were alone again. Exhausted and hungry, we carried our breakfast plates to the parlor and settled on the cozy couch, which was a relief for my broken ribs. Although now that I knew the color of my magic, I wondered if it was also the burgundy shade of the couch's pillows that made me feel better.

For some reason, Esten had seemed quite moody since the talk with Probos, and I had yet to succeed at figuring out why.

"Are you upset that you're going to Ginko?" I asked, taking a bite of a deliciously crunchy croissant. It practically melted in my mouth. I would have to order those for breakfast from now on.

Esten blinked distractedly. "What? No... no, of course not. Ginko is an extraordinary magician. It will be my honor to apprentice with her. It's just that"—Esten paused, hands clutching his plate a little too hard—"she is based all the way on the West Coast..."

Oh. I read between the lines of what Esten was saying. "That's rather far from here, huh?"

"Yeah," he replied, looking away awkwardly.

A ball of anxiety curled in my stomach. Neither of us wanted to admit it out loud, but our time together in this house was nearly over.

"Well . . . we can both travel through the magic stream, you know," I said, trying to find some positives in the situation. "We're not like the non-magical people who have to take trains and airships."

Esten nodded bravely. "True. It's not a big deal distance-wise, but we're probably going to become very busy. Ginko is the head of the West Coast branch, and you've seen Ellis with her late-night experiments." Esten's gaze tilted skyward, and he huffed a soft laugh.

"Don't I know it!" I chuckled as well. In the near future, I would probably be the subject of many such experiments. "Well, at least we still have a few free days before then," I said, to cheer both of us up.

Esten's breathing stilled. For a moment he kept his gaze trained on the plate of food in his lap. Then, slowly, his eyes rose to meet mine. "How should we, um . . . best spend those days, then?" he whispered, a sudden blush rising to his cheeks.

My own heart fluttered, and warmth flooded my chest. I didn't give Esten a reply. Instead I leaned in, ignoring the protests of my rib cage, and kissed him.

It was soft and lovely and wanted. Esten was right; this was the best use of our time. He moved the plate out of the way, and it landed on the floor with a clatter. Careful not to aggravate my injuries, Esten wrapped his arms around me and pulled me down on top of him. I pinned him to the couch, tangling my hand in his hair, eagerly tracing the lines of his sharp mouth. I would have continued kissing him all day till the sun set and night fell . . . except that a noise caught my attention. I paused to listen: it sounded suspiciously like porcelain cracking.

Esten pulled away looking flushed, tousled, and slightly confused. "What was that?" he asked.

Reluctantly my eyes left Esten's face and found the source of the sound.

I grinned. "Oi! You're back!"

Hello, Kieren, Oi said from the spot on the floor where Esten's favorite teacup had been—it was likely on its way into Oi's stomach. Half of Esten's plate seemed to have met the same fate. Oi was unabashedly eyeing us both and still crunching on the porcelain. *Pay no mind to Oi. Do go on,* he added mischievously.

"Um, that's all right." I cleared my throat and untangled myself from Esten, making an awkward attempt to smooth out my rumpled shirt in the process. Esten did the same thing. "How are you feeling? Are your friends okay?"

All well, Oi purred, seemingly in good spirits. *Stomach healing. How Kieren? I see . . . good?* Oi asked with a note of amusement in his voice.

I flushed deeply but nodded. I had no idea how to explain that apparently, after I'd left Oi to deal with the ship, I'd been sent into the future to avoid being pierced by Kavender's spear. The whole experience still made my mind reel. This did remind me about my missing hand, though.

"I think I sensed my right hand through magic," I said. "I'd assumed it had vanished for good, but Ellis said maybe it simply went missing. I think she might be on to something."

Oi perked up with sudden interest. *That so?*

"Yes," I said, and explained what had happened.

Hmm, Oi purred, and thought for a minute. Then something seemed to change in his expression. *Divine witch lady right,* he concluded.

My eyes widened, both because of what Oi had said and the peculiar way he'd named Ellis. I'd never heard that word before—*witch.*

How about we make deal? Oi asked then, always ever-so-ready when it came to deal-making. *If Kieren bake pie, Oi teach find hand. Want deal?*

I could've sworn I saw the faint glow around Oi expand with the promise of adventure and pie. His painted eyebrows wiggled suggestively.

I found myself laughing.

"What?" Esten asked. In this world, he still couldn't hear Oi and had no idea what I was about to get myself into, which made me laugh even more. I grabbed my aching ribs and tried to calm myself, but it hardly helped.

Maybe we had only a few days left together in this magnificent house, and I would miss it so much. I didn't relish the thought of adjusting to a new life in a new place all over again.

But somehow, with Oi being his usual spirit self, making strange deals in exchange for pie, and Esten huffing indignantly by my side, for the moment everything felt right in the world.

"Deal," I said.

The end.

Also by Kit Vincent

US, ET CETERA

Spring 2023

For bonus content, including an *extra chapter* of **OF FEATHERS AND THORNS**, please visit

www.kitvincentbooks.com/extras

ACKNOWLEDGMENTS

I started writing Of Feathers and Thorns in the spring of 2020, during the pandemic quarantine, because I desperately needed a distraction from all the sadness and uncertainty and also because I wanted a magical adventure in my life. And what better adventure can there be than a book about two gay magicians and a mischievous spirit, who might or might not eat your fancy dinnerware? So I plunged myself into writing like there was no tomorrow, which at the time seemed like a very real possibility. Now it's 2022, and somehow, miraculously I'm still standing, and my book is ready to go out into the world. For this, I have many amazing individuals to thank:

Mom and Dad, without whose countless sacrifices I wouldn't have been able to move to America to pursue my dreams;

My dear friend James Bird for helping me shape this book into something I can be proud of, as well as Adriana and Sandra Mather for their encouragement and support;

Allison Cherry for being my copy editor extraordinaire;

Corey Brickley for designing the absolutely fantastic book cover (seriously, how gorgeous is it?!);

Nora Bellot for catching all the crazy mistakes and typos that escaped me with her keen proofreading eyes (seriously, copy editors and proofreaders are deities from other dimensions—nothing can convince me otherwise);

James Fouhey for narrating the spectacular audiobook for OF&T (everyone, go give it a listen!);

Chu-chu, Hoggins, Touda, Little Brother, Mormor, Banana, Von, Dunkin, and Princess for being their adorable, curious selves;

Oi, for not eating my laundry and my favorite pair of sweats that one time and generally keeping me on my toes;

Mr. Three Fish, Eke, Vincent I, and all the friends for saving me.

Love,
Kit

Ingram Content Group UK Ltd.
Milton Keynes UK
UKHW040625280623
424179UK00001B/81